By Jade Mere

The Architect and the Castle of Glass

Published by DREAMSPINNER PRESS
www.dreamspinnerpress.com

The Architect
and the Castle of Glass

Jade Mere

Published by
DREAMSPINNER PRESS

5032 Capital Circle SW, Suite 2, PMB# 279, Tallahassee, FL 32305-7886 USA
www.dreamspinnerpress.com

This is a work of fiction. Names, characters, places, and incidents either are the product of author imagination or are used fictitiously, and any resemblance to actual persons, living or dead, business establishments, events, or locales is entirely coincidental.

The Architect and the Castle of Glass
© 2018 Jade Mere.

Cover Art
© 2018 Jade Mere.
www.jademere.com
Cover content is for illustrative purposes only and any person depicted on the cover is a model.

All rights reserved. This book is licensed to the original purchaser only. Duplication or distribution via any means is illegal and a violation of international copyright law, subject to criminal prosecution and upon conviction, fines, and/or imprisonment. Any eBook format cannot be legally loaned or given to others. No part of this book may be reproduced or transmitted in any form or by any means, electronic or mechanical, including photocopying, recording, or by any information storage and retrieval system, without the written permission of the Publisher, except where permitted by law. To request permission and all other inquiries, contact Dreamspinner Press, 5032 Capital Circle SW, Suite 2, PMB# 279, Tallahassee, FL 32305-7886, USA, or www.dreamspinnerpress.com.

Trade Paperback ISBN: 978-1-64080-261-2
Digital ISBN: 978-1-64080-262-9
Library of Congress Control Number: 2017916618
Trade Paperback published March 2018
v. 1.0

Printed in the United States of America

This paper meets the requirements of
ANSI/NISO Z39.48-1992 (Permanence of Paper).

*Dedicated to my family.
Thanks for putting up with me and all my quirks.*

Chapter 1

THE WALLS had eyes.

It was something Tahki's brother often said. You couldn't do anything in the palace without someone seeing you. Even now, with the lamps long extinguished and the moon only a sliver in the desert sky, Tahki felt exposed. Objects that looked nothing like a person—potted aloe plants, an empty spice cart, silk tapestries—appeared suspicious.

He tried to keep focused on the sandstone path as he ran barefoot across the courtyard. Warm air filled his lungs. He left the palace and all its sleeping inhabitants behind. No one had seen him. Not tonight, not the previous night, and not the night before when this whole business of sneaking out had started, the night he'd made the decision to finally compete at the World Fair of Innovation and Invention.

Tahki tripped over a loose tile and stumbled, his tool belt crashing to the ground with a thunderous clank. He stood stock-still and waited, his eyes darting to the palace on the hill behind him. If anyone saw him like this, they might mistake him for a thief instead of the son of a renowned ambassador. He took a deep breath and rubbed his drawing wrist. If he rushed now, he might make a mistake. The fair was fourteen days away, which meant he had less than twenty-four hours to earn his father's permission to attend. All the greatest minds from around the world traveled to the fair every year to enter their inventions in competitions. Weapons experts, transportation designers, architects, they'd all be entering in their respective fields, and with any luck, Tahki would be submitting his architectural designs right beside them. Only his father stood between him and the fair. Between him and his freedom.

He scooped up his tools and continued down the path. Three years ago, Tahki had turned fifteen, and every year since, he'd asked to leave Dhaulen'aii and travel to the fair, but his father's answer had always been the same: too dangerous. Six months ago, when he'd turned eighteen, he realized that if he wanted to attend the fair, he'd need to prove to his father he was a capable architect.

And tonight he would prove just that.

Tahki stepped inside an ancient red-roofed temple and threw his tools atop a pile of paper and charcoal. The temple had stood over five hundred years. It smelled of tea tree oil, jasmine, and a musky odor he'd come to associate with unwashed monk robes. The temple was small, only one room that might fit a dozen people inside, an unused and neglected space after a sandstorm took out one of the eastern walls ten years ago. Almost every one of the twelve pillars looked chipped, and the tiles on the east roof sagged. The square room was empty, save for an altar against the far wall and a red rug below it. Monks still left food on the altar every few weeks to rot as homage to the gods. People starved on the streets, yet the monks wasted food every week to honor these deities who never came. He didn't understand how the monks leaving food for the gods was any different from children leaving baby teeth on their bed stand in exchange for a copper coin. Adults deceived children all the time, so why wouldn't they understand that they too were being deceived?

Flies buzzed around a pile of rotten mangoes. Tahki walked to the altar and threw the red rug over it to quiet the swarm. When you lived in the largest desert in the world, your greatest enemy was the heat. But the monks insisted on putting themselves in a deep meditative trance inside the sweltering temples. Sand fever had already claimed a dozen victims, and summer was still a month away. The monks were more at risk than anyone because they refused to leave the temple when it became too hot. It was stupid to suffer so much and get nothing in return but a sore ass, but then, he'd never understood meditation.

His father, however, did and joined the monks every afternoon for several hours of mindful practice. It was his father's love and dedication to the gods that had given Tahki the idea to repair the temple. Not just repair it, improve it. If he could make the temple more bearable to meditate in, his father would finally acknowledge his talent for architecture and allow him to enter the fair.

Before Tahki set to work, he checked his progress from the night before. He ran his hand along the unfinished support beams he'd paid a carpenter to craft from a Gojuri tree. He'd never constructed anything before, only designed on paper. But he wasn't building a new temple; he was fixing an old one. All you had to do was follow the schematics. Any simpleton could do it, if they had good designs to work from, and Tahki's designs were perfect.

He'd invented an in-home aqueduct system for the temple. The design was simple: a series of conduits ran through the walls. The conduits were fueled by a natural underground well that siphoned water upward into a series of bamboo pipes. Then he'd attached a line of gutters inside the roof. When activated by a pump lever, the siphon would draw water upward into the conduits that flowed to the gutters. The gutters would waterfall around the room, delivering cool water and mist for the monks.

Tahki smiled at the brilliance of his work. It would keep the monks cool when they meditated and keep the flies away. His father would love it.

He dragged a statue of one of the gods into a corner and went to work. He'd already installed the gutters. Now all he needed to do was connect them and the task would be done. He reached up and hammered a bamboo pipe into place carefully so it wouldn't splinter, and attached it to another he'd installed yesterday.

As he worked, his mind started to wander to grander places, places where people appreciated his talent. He pictured himself holding a large gold medal at the fair. People cheered and clapped, marveling at how someone so young could be so clever.

Tahki didn't hear the creak of the door until it banged shut and rattled the walls. His heart thumped against his chest. He dropped his hammer and pivoted on his heels. When he saw his twin brother, Sornjia, standing a few feet away, he relaxed.

"You did that on purpose," Tahki said.

"I couldn't sleep. I could hear the temple crying. I don't think it likes having its bones broken," Sornjia said. He gestured toward a pile of rubble.

In order to fit the pipes, Tahki had needed to cut away some of the support structure inside the walls. There were a dozen columns holding up the roof, so sacrificing a few wall beams wouldn't hurt.

Tahki picked up his hammer. "The temple should be so lucky to get an upgrade."

"Old things don't like change," Sornjia said.

Tahki ignored him. On the outside they might look identical—same white-blond hair, sun-bronzed skin, bamboo-green eyes—but on the inside, they were like fire and water. Tahki had been told once that twin boys shared a unique bond, that sometimes they knew what the other was thinking, but he'd never had the slightest idea of what went on inside his brother's head. He couldn't image anyone trying to make sense of Sornjia.

"Are you here to help or distract me?" Tahki said.

"I'm worried about the temple," Sornjia said. He reached his hand toward one of the walls but didn't touch it, just let it hover an inch away as though the contact might burn him. "It's unsettled. Like a crow dancing on a pinecone."

"You don't even know what a crow is." Tahki struggled to connect the pipes.

"A crow is shadows and mischief," Sornjia said.

"You've been reading too much Vatolokít folklore."

Sornjia shook his head. "I saw one in a dream once. I was in a dark cave, and the darkness turned into a bird. The bird told me it was a crow from the north, and then it plucked off my head like a grape and ate it."

Tahki's hand slipped and the hammer slammed into his thumb. He cursed and sucked on it. "Just go clean something, would you?"

Sornjia fluttered away into the temple.

For the next few hours they worked in silence. The temple didn't look as nice as Tahki had intended. He'd spent most nights working on the gutters and didn't have time to paint the walls. But he could fix the small things later. For now, he simply pushed bits of rubble loosely into the wall so it looked presentable, the way he used to shove all his toys under his bed when his father told him to clean his room.

The red sun peaked over the horizon at half past six. Tahki wiped sweat from his brow. His white and gold silk shirt was drenched. His fingers were blistered and sore, the skin on his palms callused. He gave his system one last check. It looked exactly like his drawings. All he needed to do now was turn on the water.

"Well?" Tahki said. "What do you think?"

Sornjia smiled. "It looks like a very fancy bath."

"Just go get Father. He should be having his morning tea."

Sornjia pranced away. He skipped lightly, like the ground was made of clouds instead of sandstone.

Tahki took a deep breath of hot air and glanced at the city. Outside the walls, sand dunes glowed bloodred. In the markets below, merchants set up shop. Silk carts spread colorful fabrics over wood tables, curry stands fired up stoves, fire camels and sandbulls tromped down the dirt streets, herded by skinny children and emaciated dogs.

Dhaulen'aii was a country of spirituality and tradition. People who lived inside the city walls were isolated from everything. Nothing terrified Tahki more than being stuck in this city, unable to experience new technologies, unable to be a part of something bigger, something grander. No one would ever know what Tahki was capable of if he stayed here.

He drummed his fingers against his side. Despite lack of sleep, his legs itched to move. He looked back toward the palace and rubbed his left wrist. It always ached, even when he wasn't drawing. On the slope leading up to the palace, he saw Sornjia trotting alongside their father, Lord Aumin. He released a breath and straightened his back. He should have changed into dry clothes, but there was no time. Besides, sweat showed hard work and dedication. That was what his father always preached.

His father approached with a look that read, *Please Gods, don't let him embarrass me again.* He hadn't changed out of his morning dhoti. Even in casual silks, his father could not be mistaken for a commoner. Broad shouldered, tall, chin always raised slightly high, he encompassed grace and dignity and pride. A true representative of their country. Everything Tahki was not and never could be and never wanted to be.

Tahki took a breath. He'd never felt nervous speaking before, but when his father stopped a few feet in front of him and folded his arms, Tahki's tongue felt too large for his mouth.

"I'm surprised to see you up before noon," his father said. His voice sounded calm and friendly. He'd always been good at hiding his nervousness. It was why he made such a good ambassador.

"I wanted to show you something," Tahki said. "A surprise."

His father hesitated and then smiled. "A surprise for me? I wonder what I've done to deserve such attention."

Tahki had an entire speech prepared about great advancements in the north, but he was too excited to remember half of it.

"The temple," Tahki said. "Don't take your eyes off it."

His father glanced at Sornjia, a *what is your brother up to* glance. He did that a lot, looked to Sornjia for help, because understanding Tahki was apparently too difficult to do on his own. Sornjia only smiled back.

"My eyes are yours," his father said to Tahki. Though his voice was warm, he watched the temple with cold suspicion, like it might suddenly grow feet and walk away.

Tahki cleared dead shrubs away from a wooden lever he'd installed the night before and put all his weight on the handle. The lever shook and groaned. He could feel the water pressure building and checked to see if his father was watching. He was.

At first, only a few drops fell. And then a few more. And then, in a sudden rush, water poured from the gutters. It streamed down, falling into a shallow ditch that circled around the temple. Tahki released his breath. The waterfalls looked magnificent, surreal. The temple was no longer an eyesore but a beautiful product of innovation.

He faced his father and grinned. His father stood still, an expression of surprise, but not distaste on his face.

"Well?" Tahki said. "Isn't it amazing? You have to think it's amazing. And the monks will love it. I know they will."

His father regarded him the same way he regarded a potential treaty deal, with honest and open respect. For the first time, Tahki felt his father finally understood that he had a skill to offer the world, and to deny him a chance to display his work at the fair would be irresponsible. This was the moment Tahki had worked for. The moment his father would say, "Yes, Tahki. You belong at the fair. I will no longer hold you back."

His father opened his mouth. "Tahki, this is—"

A loud crack broke the still air. Tahki faced the temple. The pipes on the pillars rattled up and down until a few of them broke loose. They swiveled out to the side like an unhinged door, one part still attached, the other spouting water in every direction. The waterfalls ceased, and a few final drops trickled from the splintered bamboo. The pipes swayed a little, tapping against one another, and then the temple was silent.

Tahki frowned and stepped forward.

"Tahki, no!" Sornjia yelled.

Tahki's brother grabbed him by the arm and yanked him back. They tumbled onto the sand. Tahki scrambled to his feet just in time to see the temple walls give in. The building didn't collapse quickly but eased itself into the sand, the way an old person with bad knees wobbles down into a chair. The columns broke apart like brittle bones. The walls crumbled. The tiled roof caved in and buried everything in a heap of red slate.

A cloud of dust blew over them, and after the final rumbles, the air turned silent. Even the animals and children in the markets below went quiet. Tahki's eyes widened despite the dust. The cloud stung and blurred his vision, but he hardly noticed. He ran up to the fallen temple and stared in disbelief.

This wasn't happening. His designs had been perfect. He'd done the math. Calculated everything. Checked and rechecked his work. It shouldn't have collapsed.

"Get away from there," his father yelled.

Tahki felt himself jerked away again.

His father spun him around, eyes wide. "Are you hurt?"

Tahki glanced back at the rubble.

"Tahki, are you hurt?"

Tahki shook his head.

"What in the name of the gods were you thinking?" His father held him by his shoulders.

"I didn't mean…," Tahki said. "I just wanted…." He felt a lump in his throat. He would not be allowed to attend the fair. All his efforts had been for nothing.

His father released a shaky breath. "Up to the palace. Both of you. Now. Tahki, meet me in the dining hall."

"But the monks—"

"Go. I will talk with them."

Tahki was tugged along by Sornjia. His mind felt hazy, like someone else inhabited his body while he floated above and watched. Dreams of the fair, of fame and applause, faded from his thoughts. All he could see now was scorched sands and endless walls.

He stumbled up the hill, leaving behind the fallen temple, his father, and his only chance of freedom.

AN HOUR and a half later, his father walked into the dining hall. Tahki knelt on a large red cushion in front of a low table. He didn't meet his father's eye. He knew they both dreaded the conversation to come. Neither liked confrontation when it came to family, a rare shared trait.

His father carried two cups of jasmine tea with perfect balance. He set one cup down in front of Tahki and then closed the doors. The windows bounced sunlight across the gold walls and red curtains. Statues of two rearing jade elephants sat on twin pedestals beside the doors. Tahki remembered he and Sornjia would steal the elephants to play with when they were children. He'd broken the trunk off one once and blamed Sornjia. To this day he still hadn't admitted it had been him, even though he knew his father knew the truth.

"I know I made a mistake," Tahki said. His father knelt across from him. "I know you won't allow me to attend the fair this year. I understand." He might as well be diplomatic about it. He already knew the outcome of this conversation, so it would be better to just take responsibility. Next year he would try again, and he didn't want to hurt his chances by arguing now.

His father raised an eyebrow and took a slow sip of tea.

"But you have to admit, the temple looked amazing," Tahki said. "For a moment, anyway."

His father set his cup down with a gentle clink. "You could have been badly hurt. Possibly killed."

Tahki shook his head. "I must have miscalculated something. Something in the support structure. It was a simple mistake anyone could have made."

"What if your brother had been hurt? Or one of the monks? Do you ever consider others before yourself?" His voice was calm but deep.

Tahki scowled. "I'm doing this for other people. I have a lot to offer the world. I can make it better. I can improve it."

"By destroying a five-hundred-year-old temple?"

"By making the world a better place to live in."

His father shook his head. "I don't understand."

Tahki folded his arms. "I don't need you to understand. I just need you to see that this is what I want to do with my life."

His father took another slow sip of tea. His patience was agonizing.

Tahki sighed. "I already know you won't let me attend the fair this year."

When his father looked at him, he didn't appear angry or frustrated but sad. Something about his expression said pity, not disappointment, which confused Tahki.

"I've spoken to the monks," his father said. "Gotem is deeply troubled by your actions, as am I."

Tahki bit his tongue. If he spoke badly about Abbot Gotem, it would only make things worse, even though Gotem was always out to make trouble for him, like when Gotem had told his father Tahki had stopped meditating, or when he'd caught him stealing a bottle of blessed rum.

"I'll help clean up the rubble," Tahki said. "I can even design a new temple. I won't do anything special to it. Just a plain, boring temple."

His father rubbed his eyes. "Tahki, you're very gifted. Your mother's blood runs strong in you. Even if you don't think I see it, I do. But this obsession you have with architecture, with technology, has fogged your judgment."

"My judgment is fine. I'm just not great at construction," Tahki said.

His father sat back. "I let you pursue architecture because I could see how much you loved it. You're imaginative and clever. But I can't overlook your actions today." His voice turned sharp and stern. "I'm sorry, Tahki. I can't allow you to continue this hobby any longer. You will turn over your tools, books, and drawings to me, and you will no longer pursue architecture."

Tahki opened his mouth, stunned. He stared at his father. "What do you mean?"

His father's face hardened with resolve. "Things might be different if you pursued normal architecture. But your designs... they are not architecture. They are dangerous. You are grasping for technology you don't understand. You need to find a more suitable career."

Tahki shook his head. "You can't. You can't." His father had never punished him before. He'd been sent to his room for mouthing off when he was a child, but nothing like this. The gods taught forgiveness, not punishment.

"You'll find something else to occupy your time," his father said.

"What if I promise not to build anything ever again? Just draw?"

"I'm sorry, Tahki. Gotem says I have to follow through on my punishments or you'll never learn."

"I'm an adult."

"I haven't seen any proof of that. You're still living under my roof. You have no apprenticeship to rely on, no form of career you can support yourself with. If you want to continue to live the lifestyle you're accustomed to, you'll abide by my wishes. And my wish is to have no thoughts of architecture or technology in our home."

"You can't do this to me." Tahki felt like a beetle on its back trying to pull itself upright. He'd come to terms with not entering the fair this year, but why did he have to give up what he'd spent the last ten years of his life learning?

"The servants will clear your room today. I think it will be easier if all temptation is removed," his father said.

Tahki's face burned. "You have no right." His father had always hated architecture, or more the idea of modernism and change, but he'd never restricted Tahki from doing what he loved. He knew he should walk away, cool his head, give his father a week to reconsider. Instead, he looked his father dead in the eye and said, "Mom would have never let you do this to me."

His father clenched his jaw but kept his voice steady. "It's because of your mother I'm doing this. Do you think she would want you buried alive by your own mistakes?"

Tears stung Tahki's eyes. "She understood me. She loved me."

"Tahki, everything I do I do because you are my son, and I love you and your brother more than anything."

"You love Sornjia. You tolerate me."

"You're being overly dramatic."

"Architecture is my life. You can't take my tools and books away!" Tahki hit his teacup with the back of his hand, and it shattered against the window. Pieces of glass slid across the marble floor, and tea dripped down the wall.

His father stood slowly. "My mind is set. We will speak no more of this."

Tahki didn't trust himself to speak again. He didn't want his voice to quiver or tears of frustration to start.

His father opened the door but didn't leave the room. "I truly am sorry, Tahki." And then he disappeared into the hall.

The Architect and the Castle of Glass

THEY TOOK everything.

Tahki sat motionless on the edge of his bed. None of the servants looked at him as they stripped his room. Gotem stood in the doorway, watching over the defilement. The servants put their grubby fingerprints all over Tahki's things, but it didn't matter. He'd never see his tools again.

The room felt hot and stuffy and exposed. Tahki couldn't remember the last time his curtains had been open. He squinted, watching as they moved out his rosewood drafting table, collected his schematics and designs, and shoved them into a box to be disposed of. How many hours of work had they tossed away? Five hundred? Two thousand? Ten thousand? He'd poured hours of his life into those designs.

They took his compass and all his books, even the ones that didn't have anything to do with architecture. When one of the servants picked up his favorite pencil, he leaped off his bed and snatched it from her hands.

"No," Tahki said. "Not this one." It had been his mother's pencil, crafted from black coral with a refillable graphite chamber. His mother had designed it herself.

The servant shot a hesitant look to Gotem. Gotem nodded, and the servant left Tahki alone.

Gotem sighed and walked over to Tahki's bed with his hands behind his back. His long yellow and red robes dragged across the floor, his bald head reflecting sunlight from the window.

"So, this is your revenge?" Tahki said. "I destroy your things so you destroy mine, and we're even?"

Gotem sat on the bed and straightened his robes. "That's not how I want things to be between us. Your father and I thought it best for your own safety that you give this up, before you hurt yourself or your brother."

"You need to mind your own damn business. You're not part of our family," Tahki said. Gotem was the abbot monk. His father sought his advice on every sort of matter after Tahki's mother had died. Personal. Political. Parental. Like sitting on your ass all day gave you the right to dictate how people should live.

"I know how badly you wanted to enter the fair," Gotem said. "Even though you're angry at me, you must believe me when I say Vatolokít is no place for you. It's no place for anyone from Dhaulen'aii. The people there are wicked and foul. They will hurt you."

Tahki scowled. "You don't know anything about them."

The World Fair of Innovation and Invention had been held annually in the northern country of Vatolokít for the last seventy years. Every country around the world was invited to share and discover new technology. Even Tahki's mother had attended one year when she was younger. Anyone who wanted to make a name for themselves entered their designs in competitions at the fair. It was where all the greatest architects and inventors of this century got their start. But ten years ago, borders between Dhaulen'aii and Vatolokít had been closed. Every Dhaulenian living in Vatolokít had been forced to move out. His father had said it was due to political and religious disagreements. But the reasons didn't matter. All Tahki knew was that if the borders had been open, he wouldn't have needed his father's permission to enter the fair.

Tahki was eighteen. He would have gone to the fair in a heartbeat, but he'd needed his father's diplomatic influence to gain him special access. Without his father's help, he'd be arrested if he tried to cross, possibly killed. Which meant this really was the end for him. Even if he moved out, winning at the fair was the only way he'd ever make a name for himself. And if he couldn't make a name for himself, if he couldn't be recognized by the world as great, he was nothing.

Gotem patted him on the back. Tahki pulled away.

"I know everything seems dire at your age," Gotem said. "But trust me, this is for your own good."

Tahki didn't reply, and Gotem took his leave. The servants completed the raid, then left as well. His empty room looked like every other part of the palace now. There was nothing of him left in it. It could be anybody's room.

He felt his mattress bounce. Sornjia scooted up beside him.

"The good thing about an empty room," Sornjia said, "is that it can always be refilled with something new. Something better."

Tahki held the coral pencil close to his chest. "There is nothing better to fill the room with. They took everything I care about."

Sornjia flopped back on the bed. "You shouldn't be angry with Gotem."

"Traitor. How could you defend him?"

"I'm not. But Gotem knows things. Normal people see the world in a fog, and Gotem is the wind that sucks in all the fog so people can see where they're going."

He didn't expect Sornjia to understand. Sornjia never had anything taken away. Everyone loved him. The servants, the monks, the merchants, and children. Even the animals liked him. Stray dogs would lick his hand. They only ever growled at Tahki. That had been another reason he so desperately wanted to travel. Here, Tahki wasn't Tahki. He was "one of the twins." He was "Sornj-Tahki." He had no outer identity, so he had to work extra hard to make an inner one. Not like his brother ever minded if they got mistaken for each other. Sometimes Sornjia would even pretend to be Tahki. If Tahki was rude to a merchant, Sornjia would go back and apologize. Sornjia was like a housemaid, following Tahki around, cleaning up his mistakes. He'd even tried to stop Tahki from fixing the temple.

"Leave me alone, Sornjia."

Sornjia sighed and sat up. "I have something for you."

"Whatever it is, I don't want it."

Sornjia pushed him off the bed and dug his hands under the mattress.

"What are you doing?" Tahki said. He watched his brother pull out a handful of oversized papers.

"I hid them before the servants took everything. I only saved a dozen or so, but I think they're some of your best work," Sornjia said.

Tahki took the papers. He looked down at his architectural schematics, floor plan designs he'd worked on over the last few years, both interiors and exteriors. Sornjia had been right. They were some of his best work. He wanted to tell his brother how thankful he was, but he'd never been good at expressing gratitude.

Sornjia smiled. "Your drawings are good. Sometimes I look at them when you're at the markets, and it's like watching a spider craft a web. Your study of the Timber Cathedral is my favorite. I thought it was the original. You know, if you wanted, you could make a career in forgery."

Tahki stared at his drawings. "Forgery?"

Sornjia sat back on the bed. "Well, forgery isn't honorable. I only meant that you're good at replicating work."

Tahki stared at the lines. He wasn't just good at replicating work. He was perfect at it. A perfect forger.

"Do you think I could forge a document?" Tahki said.

Sornjia's smiled drooped. He didn't frown. At least Tahki couldn't remember him ever frowning. Sornjia only had variations of his smile. This one wavered at the edges of his mouth. It was his "slightly troubled" smile.

"I don't think forging documents is safe," Sornjia said.

"It's only not safe if you get caught," Tahki said. He couldn't get across the borders, not with a Dhaulen'aii passport.

But he could with a passport from another country.

All he needed to do was create false travel documents. He could find some examples in his father's workshop. He could travel west before heading north, cross the borders into Vatolokít as a citizen of Lapanrill or Swikovand.

"You're thinking so hard I can hear the knobs in your brain click," Sornjia said.

Tahki looked up at his brother. "I don't need Father's permission to enter the fair." Hopeful excitement surged through him. "I can do this. I think I can really do this."

Sornjia shook his head. "Please, stay here."

"Don't you want me to be happy?"

"I want to see a bright sunny day when I look at you. But all I can see now is a thunderstorm."

Tahki folded his designs. He could enter them in a competition at the fair. He could win with them.

"I won't be gone long," Tahki said. "It's not like I'm staying in Vatolokít for any length of time. Two weeks over, three days attending the fair, and two weeks back. I'll be home before Dunesday." He would return home with a trophy and display it in the dining hall. Maybe he'd even find work in another country, no longer needing to live under his father's rule. He could buy more tools, make a new life for himself. He didn't need servants or a palace. Winning first place in the architectural competition at the World Fair would open up opportunities all over the world.

Sornjia put his hands over his ears. "Something bad will happen if you go. I can feel it strong as the tide feels the moon." His voice sounded hazy now. Sornjia said strange things every day, but once in a while, it was like his consciousness would go on holiday, and no one could make sense of him for a brief time, the way a day fever hits hard but heals fast.

"You could try to support me, you know," Tahki said.

Sornjia shut his eyes. "I'm drifting in a dark fog."

"And Father calls me dramatic."

"Black fangs and yellow eyes."

"I'm an adult. Adults leave home."

"There are walls of glass and faces looking back."

"This is my chance, Sornjia. If I don't win at the fair, I'll know architecture isn't my calling. I'll come home and work for Father. But I won't know until I try."

Sornjia's eyes popped open. "You and I have never been away from each other."

Tahki had thought hearing those words aloud would feel good. It meant he could finally live without a walking mirror behind him. But Sornjia's words felt weighted. Tahki tried not to show his apprehension. "It's not like I'm going away forever."

Sornjia's irises clouded over. "Promise me you'll watch for signs of danger."

Tahki sighed. "Of course I will. Now, are you going to help me pack, or are you going to sit there all day moping?"

Chapter 2

Escaping the palace had been easy. He'd written a note to his father explaining that he needed to be alone and had taken a carriage to their winter cottage in Phoritha. Sornjia said he'd deliver the letter to their father the next day. Then in the waning hours of night, Tahki had found a northbound carriage and left home.

The first week of travel had been excruciating. He had tried to ignore the other passengers, thinking he'd get in some good sketching time. But the carriage jostled about so violently that he couldn't get a single line down without running off the paper. Then he'd tried to make light conversation with the other passengers, something his father always excelled at, but no one seemed interested in architecture. For the next six days, he occupied his time by counting trees out the window and daydreaming about the fair.

He switched carriages when they arrived in Swikovand. The crossing from Dhaulen'aii into the mountainous territory had been easy. No one bothered to check documents. Snow-covered mountains towered over the small town that smelled like pine and rich chocolate. This was the farthest north he'd ever been. His father had brought him and his brother here once for a diplomatic meeting. Tahki remembered eating a chocolate bar the size of his arm and getting sick for most of the trip, but it had been the first time he'd seen snow. The sight of it, as well as the crisp and cool air, still delighted him.

He exchanged his Dhaulen'aii money for Vatolok coins at the travel shop, traded his silk clothing for leather garments, and then found another carriage. Instead of sandbulls, the carriages were pulled by gingoats, mountainous ramlike creatures with thick white coats and dark horns. Twelve out of the fifteen carriages were heading to the World Fair. He chose one with other foreigners who had even darker skin than him, thinking he'd blend in better, and they set off for another week of overwhelming body odor and hard wooden seats. He tried his hardest not to drink or eat anything. The carriage only stopped once every five hours for them to pee in the bushes or stretch their legs, and peeing in front of strangers was not something Tahki would do.

At dawn on the twelfth day of his journey, the border gate came into sight and excitement stirred in him. The carriages lined up to be examined. The gate was a large iron obstruction with no doors. It had been built for show, not function. There were no fences, but patrols rode in strict lines for miles where people might cross. When the borders first closed, some Dhaulenians tried to sneak across, because they offered better jobs in Vatolokít, but those who ran were arrested. Since then, security had become tighter and less forgiving.

As they neared, he caught sight of a pistol hanging at the side of a patrolwoman. She stood beside a man who examined everyone's documents.

Not examined, scrutinized.

Sweat broke out across Tahki's forehead. Did he look too Dhaulenian? Would his bronze skin give him away? He tried to remember if they still utilized the death penalty in Vatolokít and then wondered if he should run. He sat between an obese woman and a sleeping man. He might be able to push the man aside and get out the door, but how far could he go? Mountains surrounded them. He'd be lost or caught for sure.

When the carriage pulled up to the checkpoint, all the passengers handed over their documents. Tahki fumbled with his small blue paper, hesitated, then passed it over. He mouthed a silent mantra as the guard checked them. For the first time in ten years, Tahki prayed to the gods. He promised to never use foul language, to be kind to his brother and father, to meditate daily, to stop eating bull meat.

The man at the gate paused on his passport certificate. Tahki glanced at the door. Two patrol officers stood a few meters away. They could easily shoot him if he ran. He rubbed his wrist with shaky hands and made the gods more empty promises.

Finally, the man shoved the documents back inside the carriage and flagged them through. Tahki released a breath and let his head fall between his knees. The other passengers probably thought he was sick, but he didn't care. All he cared about was that his plan had worked. He'd made it into Vatolokít all on his own.

He wondered what his father would think of him now.

Two hours later, when volcanic rock turned to tundra and tundra turned into green hills, Tahki saw the blue gleam of the capitol building spire. It appeared suddenly on the horizon, dodging in and out of sight as they dipped down each hill, until the carriage came to a stop in a field just outside the city.

Tahki pushed out of the carriage and into the chill morning air. His nose filled with an earthy musk. The morning dew made his skin tingle. He took a deep breath and let the damp air fill his lungs. He didn't know greens could look so green. The mountainous hills, the aspen and maple trees, the fields of grass that came to his knees, all flourished before him. He felt like he'd drifted into a dream.

A woman bumped his arm as she lumbered by, and he remembered only a few hours remained to register for the competitions. All the passengers had gone. He waited for his bags to be fetched, but no one brought them. The carriage driver left the storage trunk open. Tahki hadn't ridden first class, so of course no one catered to him. He'd have to manage simple tasks on his own if he wanted to pass for a commoner.

He gathered his overstuffed leather bag, swung it over his shoulder, and then faced the street ahead. The citadel was the first thing his eyes settled on when he walked beneath the city gates. It looked exactly how he'd pictured in his mind, towering above everything. The blue spiral of the Innovation Hall glinted in the sun. Beyond the Innovation Hall lay the Calaridian Sea. Tahki could see the harbor to the left of the bazaar. Blue sails flecked the horizon, and white birds took flight. He didn't have any interest in seeing the ocean up close, but he couldn't wait to get a better look at the citadel. Other architects like him had stood in those halls and risen to greatness.

And now it was his turn.

The road mazed upward for a mile. Tahki had brought a map, but it was ten years out of date. He straightened his back and raised his head. He wanted to make himself look taller, more confident, like he knew where he was going. Everyone else seemed to know, and he didn't want to look like a confused foreigner. He meant to make a good impression on everyone who laid eyes on him.

He set off, jogging lightly behind a group of heavyset women and men with thick furs on their backs, and tried to ignore the cramps in his legs. He walked beneath an arcade built off to the side of the road. The design was genius. Pedestrians didn't have to negotiate the roads along with carts and carriages. They had their own separate walkway. Dhaulen'aii would never think to construct something like that.

Tahki felt dazed. He couldn't take in the sights fast enough. He passed an amphitheater that had been converted into a bazaar. He'd never seen so many different skin tones together in one place. He could identify eastern and northern clothing easy enough, but some travelers wore strange shawls over their shoulders, or pointy wooden shoes, or tall black hats as shiny as a beetle's back, and he wondered where they'd traveled from. The scent of damp leather and roasted pork washed over him, but he didn't want to stop and explore until he secured a place in the architectural challenges.

Domes and archways covered the horizon, fountains and bridges and white pillars tucked beneath them. He could almost feel the invisible perspective lines that ran through the city. He looked up at the horizon where some architect had carefully plotted the vanishing points on paper before the city had been built. Tahki walked along the roads where the architect had connected line after line in an aesthetic, functional way. The homes and shops he passed were made of wood, stone, brick, and another material he couldn't identify. Something hard and gray and seamless.

The city felt more like home than Dhaulen'aii ever had. He wished he could have grown up in a diverse, modern place like this. A city where the sewage system didn't flood and the ground didn't burn your feet. He wondered if his mother had felt the same spark of imagination when she'd visited.

He saw shops selling lightning rods and sextants, shops selling pistols and portable meat-smoking chambers. The chambers had only been invented two years ago. He'd read about the meat cooker in the paper and begged his father to import one, but his father hadn't seen the point of it. He hadn't seen the point of most technological advancements.

Tahki reached the entryway of the citadel, out of breath from the hike, shoulder rubbed raw where the leather strap cut into him. By this time of day, temperatures back home would have been unbearable. But here, the cool, salty breeze off the ocean brushed the hair from his eyes. He should have cut his hair before he left. It grew below his ears now and partway down his neck.

He stopped in front of a gold cat statue, the emblem of Vatolokít. It looked at least twenty feet tall, and he had to crane his neck to see the top. A powerful country like Vatolokít should have had something like a saber shark or a redclaw bear to represent it, not a silly house cat.

He caught his breath, and then his eyes settled on a sign below the statue. It had been painted with large red letters that read: Help Our Guards Keep The City Safe. Report Suspicious Figures.

Tahki stared.

Was he a suspicious figure? Was the sign meant to ward off illegal foreigners? People who walked by glanced at him. Had they been looking at him the entire time? He'd been too caught up in the city to notice. Surely he didn't stand out. People from all over the world attended the fair. He spoke perfect Vatolok, the world language. One good thing that came from his father's work as an ambassador: they spoke Vatolok more than they spoke his native tongue at home. He'd spoken it fluently since age seven.

"Tourists, walk on the left," a woman called over the crowd. "Vendors, you're on the first floor. Exhibitors, if you haven't registered, do so here. Already registered? Second floor!" She stood behind a bleached wood table and spoke in an authoritative voice to groups of burly women with greasy blonde hair. "No, sir," she said to a red-bearded man. "You want the medical advancement competitions. Second floor."

Tahki stood in line to register. A group of young people stood in front of him, three boys and two girls around his age. He thought he'd be the youngest person to enter. One of the girls in front of him hardly looked fifteen, which disappointed him for some reason. He considered asking them what area they'd be entering in, but something about the group appeared unfriendly. They stood close to one another, all of them ghostly pale. From the look of their tight leather clothing, he guessed they lived in the city.

One of the girls, a redhead with glossy pink lips and thin eyebrows, caught sight of him, but instead of giving him a friendly smile or saying hello, she stuck her neck forward and whispered something to her group. Two of the boys glanced back at him.

And then they all snickered.

Tahki frowned. The line moved up. The group eyed him again with amusement. He had no idea what they found so funny. He'd purchased new clothing in Swikovand: a boring gray coat, black pants, and boots. He hadn't bathed since he left home, but the smell from the animal exhibit would mask any off-putting scent.

The line moved up again. The group glanced back. Whisper, snicker.

Tahki pulled his designs from his bag and pretended to sort through them. Thankfully, the group registered quickly. As they walked away, however, the redhead brushed past him and said, "Nice earrings." And then she vanished into the crowd.

Tahki moved his hands to his ears. The higher class in Dhaulen'aii always wore small gold hoop earrings. It was tradition. A sign of wealth and authority. But here, there seemed to be something amusing about them. Some inside joke he didn't get.

"Next," the woman behind the table said.

Tahki snapped off his earrings and stepped forward.

"Conceptual or working?" the woman said.

"What?"

She spoke slower, louder. "What area are you entering?"

Tahki didn't know, so he held out his designs.

"Conceptual Architecture," she said without hesitation. She hadn't commented on the quality or skill of his designs. He thought they would have impressed her. Instead, she handed him a tag that read: Entry Level 5. Conceptual Architecture. Assn: 28. Then she told him where to go.

As he walked toward the atrium, he tossed his earrings into a waste bin.

Though the days of constant travel left him exhausted, he felt jittery. He'd made it across the border and secured a spot in the competitions. All he had to do now was win.

A row of royal guards stood outside the open doorway to the atrium. He tried not to look their way, but as he passed, one of the guards broke the line and walked a little ways behind him.

He ignored the guard.

He walked inside the atrium, a spacious courtyard enclosed entirely by glass. The Innovation Hall lay beyond. The structure stood five stories tall, a museum for sixteenth-, seventeenth-, and a new wing for eighteenth-century historical inventions. The curators had stored the permanent installments to make room for the temporary exhibits.

Fairgoers crowded around a stone pool to eat and rest. Carts selling goosechik legs and meat horns and grape cider filled the first floor. The exhibits were on the second floor. Tahki wanted to stop and admire the structure, but then he noticed the guard had turned up the same staircase.

And he'd gotten closer.

Once upstairs, Tahki followed the red carpets to a room with a sign out front that read Transportation Design. Though he was eager to get to his table, one exhibit caught his eyes. A man named Thomisan Corrine had built a prototype he called a steam locomotive. It smelled like oil and grease and looked like someone had taken every kind of scrap metal they could find and mashed it together. Using something as common as steam to make something so great fascinated him. The sign said they'd be powering up the locomotive for a demonstration later. He'd read about Thomisan Corrine's work and wanted to meet the man, maybe exchange design ideas.

He could have spent another hour examining the mechanism, but the guard entered the room, his eyes scanning the crowd until they found Tahki.

Tahki retreated. A sign for Conceptual Architecture pointed left, but he turned right instead, into the largest showroom labeled Weapon Advancement.

The guard followed.

Tahki stopped, pretended to lose his way, and then turned back the way he'd come.

The guard turned back too.

Tahki took a detour right.

The guard shadowed him.

He made a loop down the hallway.

So did the guard.

His heart pumped fast, and his palms started to sweat. Lightheadedness overtook him, and his stomach clenched. Finally, having nowhere else to go, he entered the room designated for architecture. In the center, a gold-and-teal globe the size of a carriage spun inside a fountain. He stopped at the fountain and pretended to sort out his papers.

The guard approached him.

Tahki felt heat rise to his face. His arms shook as he shuffled his papers.

"Pardon me," the guard said in a gruff voice. It wasn't a friendly greeting, more the kind of greeting someone says out of habit.

Tahki turned. "Me?"

"I need to see your documentation." The guard was a stout man with curly black hair peeking out beneath a silver helmet. His lower lip jutted out a little too far, and he breathed in heavy gasps. He reminded Tahki of the fat dumb oxen back home.

Tahki considered running. He might be able to make it out of the atrium, but where would he go? He'd come so far. No half-witted guard would ruin his chance at fame.

He rummaged through his bag and shoved his documents into the guard's thick hands. The guard scrutinized them, pulled out a pen, and made a few marks on a tablet he carried. For a brief moment, Tahki thought of the invasive way the servants had touched all his things when they cleaned out his room.

"Weather nice in Lapanrill?" the guard said.

"Nice enough."

The guard grunted. "How long do you plan to stay in the capital city?"

"Three days. The duration of the fair."

The guard squinted at him. "Your skin's a little dark to come from such a cloudy country."

"My parents are south islanders."

"Lapanrill's nicer than the islands, is it?"

"They pay better wages."

The guard rubbed his tongue against his teeth and then gave Tahki a slow look up and down. The way his eyes lingered made Tahki feel dirty, like he needed to wash himself. His gut pinched. No one back home would dare look at him so pointedly. But there was something else behind the critical look. Something dangerous. Something that made him want to bolt from the room and get far away.

But then the guard pushed the documents back at his chest. "Lots of unwelcome foreigners try to sneak into the fair every year. Filthy birds, they are. Some steal designs. Others have been known to sabotage displays. You see any funny behavior, you come to me straight away, you hear?"

Tahki clenched his jaw. He couldn't help but take the "filthy birds" comment personally. He felt the guard had singled him out because of his skin color.

Still, he managed a polite, tight-lipped smile. The guard gave him an indignant sniff and tromped away.

TAHKI'S LEGS stopped shaking from his encounter when he found an empty table to display his designs. The red-haired girl with too-glossy lips from registration took the table beside his. She didn't seem so intimidating without her friends around, but when she looked at him with a repressed smile, he felt embarrassed. He shouldn't have taken off the earrings. It only made things worse.

He tried to ignore her, but she inclined her head his way. For a moment she was quiet. Maybe seeing his designs would put her in her place. Tahki pretended not to watch. After a moment, she sat back in her chair.

"Nice designs," she said in the same sarcastic tone as before.

There was a specific word for people like her in the Vatolok dialect. Tahki had used it once on a clumsy servant years ago and had been grounded for two weeks when his father heard. But he wouldn't give in to her taunts again. He'd make her eat her words when he took first place.

Tahki arranged his designs on the table, being sure his signature was displayed proudly on each sheet. He'd used his first name but changed his last. Then he grabbed some kind of white bird meat from one of the vendors and gobbled it down. It was so bland he could barely taste it, like it had been boiled beyond recognition. He didn't see a single vendor with any kind of spice rack. He also purchased a jug of strawberry carbonated water. Normally he didn't like sweet things, but the fizz tickled his nose in a refreshing way. When he finished, he wanted to get another, but a gong chimed in the hallway.

Judging was about to begin.

Chapter 3

Tahki didn't care about the prizes. He only wanted recognition, so he didn't bother checking the prize list. He returned to his table and straightened his schematics. He placed the design for the temple in the front. It might have fallen apart, but that had been due to poor construction. The design was still one of his best. He really should have thanked Sornjia for saving it.

The architecture exhibit room fit thirty six-foot tables along its edges. Behind the fountain globe, in front of a panel of windows that gave a magnificent view of the cliffs, a stage had been built. In the center of the stage, an oil painting of a woman sat on a pedestal.

Tahki squinted.

A gold plaque below the painting read "Queen Genevi." He should have recognized her. He'd seen drawings of her in the papers. She was a pale woman with a fierce expression. Her hand rested on a slender gold cat with a blue face. She held herself straight and tall. Even in a painting, she had an air of command about her, an authoritative presence. She looked like she could take down a redclaw bear with a single blow. The last three rulers of Vatolokit had all been women, known as the Remarkable Three, but Queen Genevi had developed a ruthless reputation. She had been the one who'd closed the borders.

He wasn't sure if he felt relief or disappointment at her absence. He would have loved to meet the woman who so passionately encouraged industrial growth. But had he seen her fierce gaze in person, he might have thought twice about entering.

"Exhibitors, please return to your tables for judging," a thin woman with a squeaky voice announced. Spectators in fur coats shuffled in with pamphlets and smoking pipes in hand.

He sat up straight. The redhead's friends found her and wished her luck. Again, their eyes wandered to Tahki.

"I don't think he speaks Vatolok," the redhead said to her group.

He couldn't wait to see the look on her face when he won.

Judging started after the room settled. The judge was a short old woman, probably in her midseventies. She wore a blue sash over her shoulder and appeared to be of eastern ancestry. Everyone in the room gave her a wide birth, and though the top of her head only came up to Tahki's chest, something about her intimidated him. He wasn't the only one, either. Her narrow gaze sent children scurrying back to their parents, and parents back to their seats.

Tahki counted the seconds as she paused at each table. She spent exactly two minutes at every display.

His mouth itched, and his arms felt fluid and light. He tapped his foot rapidly against the marble floor.

The judge moved closer.

Her face remained impartial, no matter the quality of work displayed.

She shuffled nearer.

The hairs on his skin stood at attention. This was it. The moment he'd fantasized about while drawing in his room with the curtains pulled shut. The moment that had gotten him through the unbearable heat of a dozen summers. This could very well turn into the greatest moment of his life.

A shadow moved over his designs. Tahki's gaze broke away from the judge. A young man stood in front of him, arms crossed. At first, Tahki thought he was a part of the redhead's group, but something about him felt different. It was the way he looked at Tahki's designs. His cold gray eyes moved over them with deliberation. He didn't just look at the drawings. He examined them as though they were real, tangible things. Things to be considered and taken seriously. Tahki couldn't help but stare. Over three dozen people had visited his table, but none of them really *looked* at his work.

The stranger stood a few inches taller than Tahki, probably in his early twenties. His lean muscles flexed slightly as he straightened his back. He had hazel-colored hair trimmed short, except for on top, which stuck out a little longer. He wore a sleeveless dark leather shirt that fit tight against his body. He didn't fidget or sway or crack his fingers. He held himself perfectly still. The kind of unwavering discipline a soldier shows, like rigidity was his natural state.

He was also quite handsome.

Tahki's stomach did a little flip. The sensation surprised him. He could eat an entire demon pepper without so much as a stomach cramp, so he didn't know how a stranger could make him feel like he'd swallowed a bag of fluttering moths.

The stranger met his eyes, and Tahki's stomach lurched again. At first, the young man regarded Tahki with a curious expression. He looked at him as intently as he'd studied the drawings. Tahki should have looked away, avoided the awkward, silent eye contact, but he didn't. He stared right back.

But then the stranger's expression changed to one of slight frustration.

"These would never work," the stranger said.

Tahki blinked. "What?"

The stranger gestured to the temple design. "You need better support beams here and here. It wouldn't look as pretty, but without them, this design would cave in on itself in a second."

Tahki's stomach turned to iron again. "I think I know how to calculate load-bearing structures."

"Symmetry," the stranger went on, like he hadn't heard him. "You rotated the axis of this column to dissect it asymmetrically. You should have divided it in the middle. And tilted the pipes against it. And added at least three more columns to account for the extra weight. Here... and here. Maybe even one here for safety." His pale fingers brushed over Tahki's designs.

"I know how to support a roof," Tahki said. He usually hated when someone touched his work, but he couldn't bring himself to ask the stranger to stop.

"But you forgot to account for the added water weight of this... what is it, a gutter? The walls might have held it, but you hollowed out the northern facade and didn't add any additional support. In short, it's an interesting idea that looks pretty on paper, but it's not functional, which makes it no good."

No good.

Tahki glanced at his design and noticed that when he'd modified the temple, he hadn't recalculated the weight the water would add to the gutter, nor had he subtracted the support he'd lost from the reconstructed wall. That's why the temple had collapsed. It was such an amateur mistake.

When he looked up, the stranger had vanished. He searched the crowd but couldn't locate him.

"No prototype?" a voice said.

Tahki startled. The judge stood to his left, her eyes impatient.

"I'm sorry?" Tahki said. He sat up straighter, aware of how his nails dug into his arm.

"Do you have a prototype?" the judge repeated. Her voice was raspy, like she'd inhaled too much smoke. It surprised him when she spoke. She hadn't spoken to anyone else.

Tahki glanced around. Everyone had some kind of paper or wood model to accompany their drawings. "I didn't know I needed one." He hated the petulance of his own voice.

The judge pursed her thin lips. She moved on to the redhead's designs without looking back. She had spent thirty seconds at his table. One minute and thirty seconds shorter than she'd spent with anyone else. What did that mean? Did not having a prototype automatically disqualify him? Or had she only needed a quick glance to see the creativity of his designs?

Ten anxiety-filled minutes ticked by before the judge completed her rounds and submitted the results. Tahki tried to conjure the same excitement he'd felt before, but a cloud of doubt settled over him.

"Thank you all so much for your wonderful contributions." The squeaky-voiced lady again. She gave a short speech about how the entries would be used to advance the world. She said something about ingenuity. About courage. About intelligence. Tahki only half listened. He tasted metal in his mouth and realized he'd bitten his tongue.

"And now… the results!"

One of the panel judges, a stout man with a trimmed mustache, announced the winners.

"Third place goes to Esmin Tosla!"

Tahki held his breath.

"Second place, Og'Kor Vasten."

The room spun. He hadn't won third or second. But first? Had he won first? He must have. The judge had been looking at him since the man had started to announce the winners. He'd won. He'd taken the grand prize. It had to be him. Tahki shoved his hand in his pocket and grasped his mother's pencil for luck.

"First place...."

The man paused and pretended to shuffle his papers. Tourists laughed. The contestants did not.

"First place goes to.... Penki Toth!"

Women, men, and children clapped. The redhead next to him grabbed her cheeks, jumped up, and trotted to the stage to collect her first-place trophy. Tahki stared at the happy winners.

"Penki," the squeaky woman told them, "is the youngest contestant to ever win first place! And also the only contestant from the lower city to place! What a remarkable accomplishment!"

Not only had the girl won, but she'd been from the slums of Vatolokít. She was younger than Tahki and had grown up in far worse conditions than he had. He'd lost to a slum child.

Tears swelled in his eyes, but he didn't let them fall. Instead, he hastily gathered his bag. He didn't even feel like visiting the other exhibits. He wanted to leave. There was no place for him here. He was defeated. A fraud.

No good.

On the way out the door, he shoved all his designs into a trash box.

ONCE OUTSIDE, Tahki walked to the edge of the citadel. The scent of flowers from the rose garden below wafted up as a breeze swept off the sea. He stopped at the side of the pathway and put his hands on the stone rail. The ocean crashed on the rocks below. White birds screeched and swooped down to collect bits of dropped food. He took a deep breath.

Maybe losing was for the best. It made life easier. He would return home now, live a quiet life working alongside his father. He had enough inheritance money to live comfortably in the palace. Maybe he'd even take over his father's work as an ambassador.

The thought sickened him. If he went home, he would look like his brother on the outside and act like his father on the inside. What did that leave for him to call his own?

"You bolted fast enough," a raspy voice said.

Tahki swiveled. The judge stood behind him, sash removed, staring at him with a piercing gaze.

"I'm sorry," Tahki said. "I thought the competition was over. Was there something else I needed to do? Did I need to sign out or something?"

"You're a little high-strung, aren't you?" she said. "Trust me when I say that level of anxiety only makes you age faster."

Tahki had no idea how to reply.

The judge shuffled over to him and rolled her shoulders. A loud crack sounded, like one of her bones had broken. She sighed, "That's better." She looked at him. "Tell me something, Tahki—it is pronounced *Taw-kee*, isn't it? Why do you suppose I didn't choose your designs?"

It felt like a trick question, like she was digging for reasons to ridicule him. But he answered, "I didn't have a prototype."

"I didn't pick you," she said, "because your designs had no place in the city."

Tahki felt his mouth start to form a defensive reply, but he shut it quickly. What was the point in arguing?

"These competitions are all about practicality." She rested her arms against the rail. "A judge looks for functionality over creativity. Creativity is nice, but how many people really want a waterfall in their kitchen? Or a vertical, movable room that can take a person up or down on a rail system? Or a roof you can open and close with a lever?"

At least he knew she really had looked at his designs. He couldn't accuse her of not understanding them. He thought his vertical railway system would have impressed her. "I thought these competitions were about ingenuity," Tahki said.

The judge grunted. "These competitions are about making it seem like we're doing the public a great favor, when in reality, it's just a cheap way to steal ideas. We host these events and then offer the winner some flashy prize. It's more of a public attraction than anything. Like that girl who took first place. Can't remember her name, but I promise you she'll be forgotten in a week."

Tahki didn't know what to say. She made the great World Fair sound like some cheap roadside attraction. Something for unenthused parents to drag overactive children to. Something not worth risking your life for.

"Does that upset you?" she said.

Tahki shrugged. "Does it matter?"

The judge leaned over to him. When she spoke, her jaw shook, like she needed to open her mouth extra wide to get all the syllables out. "Your designs weren't right for the competition. But they are right for something better."

Tahki pinched his brow. "What do you mean?"

"I'd like to employ you, Tahki."

Tahki stared. "You want to give me a job?"

"That's what employ means."

"An architectural job?"

"What other kind of job do you think I'd be offering?"

He swallowed. Even if he had won, he knew the odds of being offered a job were thin. "But I thought you said my designs weren't practical." He didn't want to sound ungrateful, but he didn't want to get his hopes up, either. He'd experienced enough disappointment already.

"They aren't practical. They aren't functional, at least not yet. But they're... different."

"And different is good?"

"Different is good."

"Why is different good?"

"Sorry, but I can't tell you until you accept the position."

Tahki laughed. He knew it was rude, but he couldn't help it. This whole encounter felt so surreal. "How could I accept if I don't even know what I'll be doing? What if I'm not right for it? I could risk my entire career taking on a job I can't perform."

"You're a little on the dramatic side, aren't you? I say you're right for it, and my word is king. You want to be famous, don't you? You want your work known? That's why you came to the fair, isn't it?"

He looked down at his hands. "Doesn't everyone want that?"

"No, everyone does not. But those who do fight for it." The judge spat to the side. "If you accept this job, the entire world will know your name."

World famous. It seemed too good to be true. He bit his lip. "You can't tell me anything about this... project?"

"I can tell you who your employer will be. You'll be working for Queen Genevi. It's her project. I'm just a recruiter."

He gaped. This couldn't be a serious offer. Could she really want him to work for the ruler of the most powerful country in the world? His first impulse was to say yes, but then he felt goose bumps on his arm. The sun shone bright, but the air felt cool. He was used to a desert climate. To Dhaulen'aii's climate. The country whose people the queen went to great lengths to keep out of Vatolokít. He might have fooled the man at the checkpoint and even the ignorant guard, but there was no way he'd be able to fool Queen Genevi. If anyone found him out, he would be executed for sure.

"I can't," Tahki whispered.

"Come again?"

"I… can't accept your offer."

She clicked her tongue. "Is there a reason?"

"I don't think I'm the right person."

The judge stood a moment longer and studied him and then pushed away from the rail. "I leave in an hour. If you change your mind, you can find my carriage at the west harbor. Ask for Gale Utmutóta, or Judge Utmutóta. And if you don't change your mind, good luck with your future, Tahki." She strode down the path without a second glance back.

His head drooped. He leaned against the stone and rubbed his eyes. He couldn't believe his luck. Or that he'd let his dream job—every architect in the world's dream job—shuffle away. He had half a mind to throw himself into the ocean but shivered at the thought.

With a sigh, he stood and stuffed his hands in his pockets and turned to find a carriage home. His fingers brushed something smooth and hard. He pulled out his mother's pencil and stared at the sleek black coral. After his mother had died, he liked to hold the pencil against his chest at night, the way some children hold safety blankets. He wondered if things would have turned out differently for his mother had she been offered the same job. Would she have accepted the job?

Of course she would have.

His father was always going on about his mother's impulsive—borderline dangerous—adventures. She said yes to whatever life threw her way. That's what his father always told him, and she regretted nothing. Opportunities like this came once in a lifetime. If he didn't act on it, he might live to regret it for the rest of his life. One thing he knew for sure—his mother would have wanted him to go.

With his new resolve bursting like fireworks in his mind, he sprinted down the path, his bag bobbing against his back. He shoved through the throngs of people. Several curse words hit his ears as he pushed by. He took a wrong turn, bit down his pride, and asked a girl leading two gingoats where the east harbor was. She pointed right and he ran again.

Tahki arrived just as the judge—Gale, she'd said her name was—threw her bags in the back of a black and blue carriage.

He jogged up to her, panting. "I'll go."

Gale drew her lips thin. "You'll go where?"

"With you. The job you offered, I want it."

Gale smiled, or maybe it was a grimace. He couldn't tell with all the wrinkles. "Good." She looked him up and down. "This all you got?"

Tahki nodded.

"Then we can leave early," she said.

"Don't you have to judge the other contestants? I mean, isn't the fair another two days?" Tahki said.

"My job here is done," she said.

She walked to the side of the carriage and tugged the door open. Tahki went to get in but stopped dead. Sprawled across the back seat, with his head resting against the far door, was the stranger who'd stopped by his booth. The guy who'd said his designs were no good.

He glanced Tahki's way, his expression cold.

"This is Rye, my work associate," Gale said. "You two will be teamed together. He's your superior on the project."

Chapter 4

Over the next three hours, Tahki tried to make himself as small as possible inside the carriage. It only sat four, and Gale had stuffed one seat full of small crates she said were too delicate to travel in the back, which put Tahki beside Rye. On every bump, his arm would brush against Rye's arm. Or their knees would tap together. Or Tahki would fidget and hit his side. It was like when Tahki fell ill and his skin became overly sensitive. All these small contacts sent a spark through his body.

Rye didn't seem to notice. Though the carriage jostled at every turn, Rye held as still and straight as a baluster. He didn't stretch his arms or crack his neck, even after hours had passed. Maybe he hated sitting next to Tahki and loathed the idea of contact. Maybe Rye was afraid of catching a foreign illness. Maybe Tahki smelled bad. Or maybe Rye felt guilty about saying Tahki's designs were no good, or embarrassed because Gale chose to hire Tahki for this job. But Rye didn't strike him as the type who'd be embarrassed. Or feel guilty. Or have emotions.

Gale spoke a little at the start of the ride. Mostly, she talked about the secrecy of the project, how they wouldn't be allowed to speak with anyone about it. Not family or friends. Tahki's father always went on about privacy when he signed documents with allied countries. Sometimes Tahki would sneak in and read the documents, but they only contained contracts about housing restrictions or where livestock owners were allowed to drive cattle. Things no one needed to keep secret. Was this project like that? A secret not worth keeping?

At one point, Gale said something about the castle. Tahki's ears perked up. He inquired about what castle they'd be staying at—he knew all the castles and palaces and cathedrals of Vatolokít and could reproduce most of the exteriors from memory—but Gale didn't say and told him not to ask questions. She said she'd tell him more once they arrived and the carriage driver had gone.

They rode in silence for another two hours, which gave him lots of time to imagine what the project could be. Maybe at some point he'd meet the queen. He still hadn't decided if he feared or yearned for a face-to-face encounter with the most powerful ruler in the world.

Tahki rubbed his wrist, wiggled his shoulders from side to side, rolled his head until the bones in his neck cracked a little.

"Stop fidgeting," Rye mumbled. It was the first thing he'd said since the fair. He hadn't even said hello when he saw him in the carriage, or apologized for his behavior, or explained what being a superior meant on a project like this. Tahki also noticed Gale had introduced him only as Rye, no last name. Then again, she hadn't told Rye the fake last name Tahki had entered the competition under. Maybe last names weren't as important here as they were back home. In Dhaulen'aii, your last name held your status, your heritage. It told everyone everything they needed to know about you. But there was no sense in worrying about it, because for the first time in his life, he actually had someone he could talk to about architecture.

"What did you think about the results?" Tahki said.

Rye opened one eye. "What?"

"At the fair. What did you think of the winners?"

Rye gave a stiff shrug. "I trust Gale's judgment."

"But did you take a good look at first place? The girl wasn't exactly top of her game. I mean, all she did was take an existing cathedral and add a few hallways and balconies."

"Huhn," Rye mumbled and shut his eye.

Tahki didn't want to let the conversation die. "I think Gale gave her first out of pity."

"Pity?"

"She was from the slums. It's not her fault she was born in a lower class, but those kinds of people just don't receive a proper education. You don't hear about any famous architects ever growing up in the lower cities." Tahki remembered the way the redhead had laughed at him. "Those kinds of people don't ever make it far in life."

Rye opened both eyes and stared at him. "You're a moron."

Tahki blinked. "What?"

"Gale," Rye said. "Switch places with me."

Gale peeked at him from under a wrinkled eyelid and then stuck her head out the window and told the carriage driver to stop. They stretched their legs and swapped places.

"What did I do?" Tahki asked Gale when they started on their way again.

Gale smirked. "Guess where Rye grew up."

"Where he grew up?" Tahki glanced at Rye. He had his eyes shut again, his head resting against the window. "The lower cities."

Gale nodded. "Maybe next time, tuck that entitled attitude away when you're trying to make friends."

He hadn't meant to offend anyone and knew he should apologize. But every time the words edged to the tip of his tongue, he pushed them back. They sounded needy and desperate in his mind, but mostly, they sounded insincere.

Instead of making peace, Tahki pressed his forehead against the glass window and watched the hills speed by.

THE EMERALD hills turned into golden wheat fields, and the fields turned into mountains. The mountains shrank, the ground leveled, and pale boulders the size of houses appeared beside the dark dirt road. Tahki didn't remember when the fog moved in, but soon after, he could see nothing but a bleak white mist out his window. The fog made the world seem smaller, more condensed. Like nothing lay beyond. Like no seasons touched this place. Not sun or snow, just an endless fog.

The wooden wheels popped over small rocks in the road as the carriage tipped down a hill. Tahki planted his feet firm on the floor to keep himself from falling forward.

Rye and Gale spoke about fishing, a subject Tahki knew nothing about. Not that he'd try to join if he did. Rye hadn't looked at him since he woke up thirty minutes ago. Gale said something about a boat she'd found for sale, and this made Rye smile. Tahki thought a smile wouldn't fit Rye's face, but he looked even more attractive when he smiled.

Tahki wished he knew what to say to make things right. These people worked for Queen Genevi. He wanted them to like him, to accept him. He didn't want Rye to think he was a snob, but maybe he was. Back home, had he mentioned the slum girl to the empress's daughter or to the son of a visiting duke, they would have laughed and agreed with him. But now he felt foolish and petty. Outside of what he'd read in the papers and gossip from merchants, he really knew nothing about the lower cities of Vatolokít.

The carriage leveled out and slowed.

Gale sat forward in her seat. "Finally. Any longer and my bladder would have popped like a gutted fish."

Tahki cringed and peered out the window. The fog had turned into a low layer of clouds. He couldn't see any town on the horizon. Unlike the capital city, which had burst with energy and life, this place looked desolate. Tufts of brown grass grew in pale dirt. They hadn't passed a single town or farm or stray house for miles. Cliffs towered on one side, and on the other, nothing but a flat horizon. If he died out here, would anyone know? The overwhelming sense of isolation drew a shudder from him.

The carriage stopped. Tahki heard rushing water—a river, maybe. Rye swung the door open and jumped down. Gale followed, and then Tahki. His feet sunk a little into the ground. What he thought was pale dirt turned out to be sand. Not like the red sands back home but wet white beach sand. He peered toward the horizon. They stood below bleached cliffs. The sand field stretched as far as Tahki could see until it dissolved into the gray sky. Rain hovered on the horizon, but none fell.

Someone threw his bag at his feet. He turned and saw Rye striding away. The carriage driver shut the doors and drove off, leaving them stranded.

"Let's go," Rye said.

Tahki scooped up his bag. "Go where? There's nothing here."

Rye didn't answer. He walked toward the cliffs.

"Security measure," Gale told him. "We can't have the carriage driver knowing our location. From here, we hike."

"How far is it?" Tahki said.

"Five miles."

Gale said five miles like it was nothing more than a light morning walk. Tahki's legs nearly collapsed at the thought. He hadn't gotten good sleep in weeks or eaten a proper meal. He must have looked dismayed because Gale said, "You'll survive."

Gale led the way up a winding path, and when they reached the top of the cliff, they headed east. Tahki panted and tried to catch his breath, but a few minutes after reaching the top, he started to fall behind. Gale and Rye grew smaller on the horizon. Tahki tried to jog to catch up, but his legs refused. He was too tired. All his limbs begged him to rest, to lie down on the doughy ground, cover himself in a blanket of cool sand, and sleep.

Then he heard Rye's voice and saw they had stopped. When he caught up, Rye was hunched in the dirt, fiddling with his bag.

"What's the holdup?" Gale said to Rye as Tahki approached.

"Nothing," Rye said. "I thought I left my compass in the carriage. But I found it here." He threw his bag over his shoulder. Gale gave him a strange look. Rye's compass was hanging on the side of his bag. The clunky silver disk was the size of a large man's fist. Tahki could see it a mile away. He wondered if Rye had stopped intentionally to allow him to catch up.

He brushed the thought away. Rye clearly didn't like him. They'd probably gossiped about him after he'd fallen behind, or made fun of him. Someone his age unable to keep up with a seventy-year-old? What a laugh.

When they set off again, he noticed Rye had lost a little of his rigid exterior. He slouched, which slowed the pace, and Tahki was able to stay in step with them this time.

TAHKI HAD seen castles before. Swikovand was full of them. They were as common a sight as temples were in Dhaulen'aii. He knew what to expect from a castle: massive gray stone structures with drawbridges, towers, and moats. Some had chapels and stockades, pinnacles and keeps. Most countries didn't build castles anymore because they just weren't practical.

He'd drawn at least a hundred castle designs out of books and from imagination, for learning purposes. They weren't his favorite to draw, but they were easy, predictable, malleable. Nothing about a castle ever surprised him.

So it was a great shock to him when he first saw the black spires crest the horizon, and he realized he couldn't identify them. None of his books contained anything similar. Even from a distance, there was something about the black exterior that struck him as odd.

Not odd. Foreboding.

The sky and sand and pale rocks were so white the castle felt like a dark stain on the land. Looking at it made his skin itch, though no amount of scratching seemed to satisfy the urge. Tahki felt ridiculous for thinking it. It was just another castle. He'd never disliked a castle before. After he'd rested and eaten and washed, he'd feel better about it. The interior probably wasn't as dreary.

It was another twenty minutes before they came close enough for him to get a good look. Unlike the clunky rock castles of Swikovand, this castle looked slender. More vertical than horizontal, like if you sat at the highest point of the highest spire, you could touch the moon.

The light in the sky faded, and as it grew dim, Tahki saw the faintest bit of red sun reflect through the low clouds and bounce off the walls. He'd never seen a castle shine before. It frustrated him that he couldn't identify the material. The black spires looked thin and sharp enough to prick open the sky. He counted seven spires in total. The castle, perched on a cliff's edge, looked as though it had been built over a waterfall. He hoped it hadn't.

Something about the stark silhouette held him. His eyes couldn't break away. Suddenly, he felt his body jerk back, and he saw Rye holding on to his arm so tight it pinched his skin.

"Let go," Tahki said.

Rye appeared annoyed. "Watch where you're going."

Tahki pinched his brow and then glanced to his left. His toes almost touched the edge of the cliff. Another step and he would have gone over. He stumbled backward into Rye. Rye steadied him and then pushed him away.

"You won't last long here if you're daydreaming all the time," Rye said.

Tahki should have said thanks, but Rye would probably roll his eyes and call him a moron again.

He steered away from the cliff and made sure to focus on where his feet landed.

GALE MADE to part ways with them before they reached the castle.

"You don't live in the castle?" Tahki asked.

"No, I don't live in the castle."

"Why not?"

She jabbed one bony finger into his chest. "Explaining myself to you is not something I need to do."

Before she shuffled away, Rye snatched her sleeve. "Are you sure about this?" he asked her.

"You have to trust me," she said.

Rye let her go. "If you say so." And then she was gone.

Tahki followed as Rye led the way. "Is she going to be all right?"

"Gale is the last person in Vatolokít you need to worry about."

"But where will she go?"

"She lives below the cliff in a small home she built herself," Rye said. "She says the castle gets too drafty. And she needs her own space."

"What did she mean when she said, 'You have to trust me'?"

"We'd get there faster if you didn't ask so many questions." Then after a moment, he said, "She and I had a disagreement."

"Over what?"

"You."

Tahki let out an indignant huff. "Gods, what did I do?"

Rye turned toward him. He gave him the same kind of pointed look as before, and Tahki wondered if he'd said something wrong.

"She thought you'd be good for this job." Rye faced the path ahead. "I didn't."

At that, Tahki realized nothing he could say or do would get Rye to like him, so there was no point in trying.

When they reached the castle, he noticed a river flowing beside and beneath it. If he knew his geography right, that river was called the Misty River. It ran all the way from the Calaridian Sea to the other side of the continent, and it looked like the castle had been built overtop of it. Water fell over the edge of the cliff. A waterwheel had been built beside the castle over the river. Why anyone would want their home on top of a river, on top of a waterfall, was beyond him.

He took a deep breath and tried not to let his anxiety show. Rye already seemed to think so little of him. He didn't need to know how terrified Tahki was of drowning.

The entryway arched fifteen feet above his head. Two solid doors made of dark wood rose before him. The light had nearly gone now, and no candles burned inside. Outside, someone had crumpled lightning roots into a ball and stuck them in a lantern. They flickered blue and sputtered as a breeze rattled the lantern.

Motion inside caught Tahki's eye. He craned his head so far back the skin on his neck pinched. Something moved behind one of the high windows. Tahki squinted, and that's when he saw her. The palest woman he'd ever laid eyes on. The people of Vatolokit were fair-skinned, but he still hadn't seen anyone who compared to her. She looked drained of blood, her face gaunt. Though he couldn't see her eyes, he swore she looked directly at him.

He shuddered as Rye yanked the door opened. They stepped inside. He could smell a fire burning somewhere, but cool drafts slid along the white marble floor, keeping the inside chilly. Rye stretched his arms, the first attempt at relaxation Tahki'd seen.

Stepping inside the castle felt like stepping inside the belly of a whale. Though spacious, the walls somehow seemed to press in around him, the high windows watching through half-lidded eyes, as though the castle might try to digest him if he stood in one place too long. A sharp scent hit his nose, like someone had burned coffee. The air, too, tasted thick, like it had sat too long undisturbed.

He shook the feelings away and slid his hand along one glassy wall, his fingers massaging the hard surface.

"Obsidian?" Tahki said. "That's a strange choice." The volcanic glasslike stone was used in many northern countries for jewelry and statues, but never for buildings.

"It's mixed with other minerals," Rye said.

"You can't mix obsidian. It's too fragile."

Rye raised an eyebrow. "You know best."

Tahki felt like rolling his eyes. Instead, he studied the room they'd entered. He couldn't see the ceiling but imagined it came to a point where the spires rose. Black columns held up the second floor. A row of doors stood to the left. In the center, a wide staircase led to the next floor. The walls were black, the floors white. Not so much as a colored vase to brighten the entryway.

Tahki looked up and noticed a circular room hung on the third floor, over the center of the castle. An odd design choice, but not as odd as the lack of castle paraphernalia. Tahki didn't see a single painting on the walls. There were no rugs or chairs or tables. No draperies over the windows, no flowers to liven the place. There was nothing to show that anyone lived here, and again, a feeling of isolation seized him. He felt out of place, not welcomed.

A list of questions ran through Tahki's mind, but before he could ask them, he heard footsteps tapping on the stairs.

"You're late," said a young man. "I was beginning to think you'd finally had enough of me and ran away to the capital."

Tahki watched the man glide toward them. His movements were precise, like he planned every step before he took it. He looked about the same age as Rye. His golden hair hung in wispy locks, parted to the left side, a close cut on the back and sides. He wore white and royal blue clothing trimmed in gold and strode over to them with fluid motions. He studied Tahki the same way a horse breeder might assess the worth of a broodmare, and suddenly Tahki realized how shabby he must look in comparison to this well-dressed and, if he was being honest with himself, alarmingly handsome stranger.

When the young man approached, he swung his right arm over Rye's neck and drew him in for a hug. Tahki thought Rye would resist. The intimate greeting seemed in such contrast with his stoic demeanor. But to Tahki's surprise, Rye embraced him.

"This is Dyraien," Rye said when they broke apart. "Dyraien, this is Gale's solution, Tahki."

Tahki had never been introduced as a solution. The way Rye said it, though, made him sound less like a solution and more like a problem.

"Nice to meet you," Tahki said. He extended a hand, because it was the formal Vatolok greeting.

Rye cleared his throat. "I mean, this is Prince Dyraien Királye."

Tahki retracted his hand. Prince Dyraien. He should have recognized the name, and suddenly forgot how to show respect to a Vatolok prince. Should he bow? Touch foreheads? Offer him some kind of gift?

Dyraien gave him a gorgeous, princely smile. Tahki wanted to smile back, but he didn't trust himself. He was too tired. A smile might come off like a scowl, and he'd probably already insulted him.

"I'm sorry, Your... Highness. I didn't recognize you," Tahki said. When princes and princesses would visit the palace, he'd always stood as their equal, thanks to his father's reputation. He never had to worry about being disrespectful. Now he would have to tread with caution.

"Don't let Rye fool you," Dyraien said. "He's only jealous he won't get all my attention now."

Rye clicked his tongue and shook his head.

"And don't apologize," Dyraien went on. "You may address me as Dyraien. Titles are reserved for those who lack self-assurance."

His words sounded so fluid, so lyrical. Vatolok was a language of harsh syllables, but Dyraien wove his words like fine silk. And then Tahki remembered bowing was the correct edict. He started the motion, but Dyraien reached out, grabbed his wrist, and tugged him closer. He held him by the arm, smelling of rosewater and pine.

"You are my guest," Dyraien said. "Don't think of me as a prince, think of me as a host. If there is anything you need, ask."

Relief washed over Tahki. It had been the first kind words spoken to him since he'd arrived. Finally he'd found someone who didn't treat him like a burden. This was the kind of welcome he'd been accustomed to back home. Tahki tried to pull away, but Dyraien drew him a little closer. The gesture felt almost intimate.

"I do mean it," Dyraien said. "The seclusion will get to you. But I will do everything in my power to make this feel like a home away from home for you." His thumb lightly brushed Tahki's palm.

"Thank you," Tahki said. "I think I'll feel better after some sleep, and after I know what I'm getting myself into. I mean, the details of the project. That's all. I didn't mean to say that I'm getting myself into anything... sorry. I just...." Dyraien's finger lingered in his palm. The touch felt so faint it might not have even been intentional.

"Dyraien," Rye said. "It's late, and he looks tired."

Dyraien's smile wavered slightly. "You really shouldn't apologize so much, Tahki. If you ever do something that truly demands an apology, it won't feel as sincere." He released Tahki's arm. "I'll go over the project details with you in the morning. It's only us three in the castle tonight, so you shouldn't have anyone disturbing you. Now, you look in desperate need of a bath and supper."

Tahki released a shaky breath. "That sounds wonderful." His eyes drooped a little at the thought of warm water and a comfortable mattress.

Dyraien motioned for him to follow. Rye moved silently behind him. Dyraien made grand gestures with his hands when he spoke, his body constantly moving along with his mouth. Rye kept his back straight and said as little as possible.

As they walked up the stairs, Tahki remembered the woman in the window. His father would say it was rude to question your host on the first night, but Dyraien seemed open to questions. "It's only us in the castle you said?"

"Is that so odd?" Dyraien replied. "I've become accustomed to life without servants."

Tahki hadn't even considered how strange it was for royalty to be without anyone to cook and clean and saddle mounts for them. "Forgive me for saying so, but I saw someone in the window. A woman. She looked at me. At least, I think." He realized then he might have imagined it.

Dyraien and Rye stopped. They exchanged a cryptic glance, and Tahki felt like an imposition.

"I see," Dyraien said at last. "I was hoping this could wait for morning, but we might as well get this out of the way. Up here, step quickly, please."

They reached the end of the hall on the second floor and stopped outside a door with red-tinged wood.

"You look quite exhausted," Dyraien said. "It's my turn to apologize for keeping you so late, but there is something I need to show you before you consent to work here."

Tahki swallowed as he imagined what horrors might lay behind the door. "Sounds very secretive." He tried to make light of the situation, but Dyraien turned serious.

"A secret is a beautiful, dreadful thing," Dyraien said. "It is of the utmost importance you know how to keep secrets, Tahki."

If they only knew. "I was raised to respect confidentiality," Tahki said.

Dyraien smiled. "That's very comforting to hear." He removed a key from his pocket. Whatever hid behind those doors, it needed to be locked in. "I need you to understand that this entire project depends on discretion. If anyone were to find out about this place, about what's behind this door, it would ruin everything. I've worked ten years on this project and handpicked everyone who has set foot inside this castle. Except you. For the first time, I charged Gale with the task of selecting someone to help us. So I must ask: Can I trust you, Tahki?"

"Yes. You can trust me." Tahki tried to sound like his father when he signed a new decree or treaty. Authoritative. Honorable. Dependable. But his voice peaked a little at the end.

Dyraien didn't open the door. "I don't want to frighten you, but please understand that if you do happen to slip, if you tell anyone about this, even if it's only a hint or a whisper, and I feel you might endanger this project...." He paused. "No. No, I don't think it will come to that. I have a good feeling about you, Tahki. I know you won't do anything to displease me."

Tahki stared. Had Dyraien just threatened to kill him if he told anyone? He hadn't said the words outright, but the air around them felt thick with implication.

As Dyraien unlocked the door, a small lump of fear rose in Tahki's throat. They stepped inside. An old oak bed in the center took up most of the space. The pale woman from the window sat in front of the bed, hunched over, mumbling a string of nonsensical words. Her hair was a tangled blonde mess. It looked as though someone had attempted to cut it with dull blades. She chewed on her fingertips and looked up at them as they entered. When she smiled, Tahki knew she was dumb in the head. He'd seen a few simple men back home. The servants called it mind-melt. They lived on the streets without a concept of who they were. They smiled when they bled. They laughed and pointed when animals walked by. They spoke with thick words, as though their gums were swollen. Back home, people like this were considered a nuisance. A thing to avoid. Merchants claimed stepping on their shadows would bring drought and famine.

Dyraien smiled at the woman, but it was a sad smile. "Tahki, I'd like you to meet my mother, Queen Genevi."

Chapter 5

Tahki woke for the second time that night. He had never been so tired he couldn't sleep before. The room Dyraien had given him was on the second floor, but he could still hear the river tremble below the castle.

He drew a scratchy blanket up around his neck. His fingers and toes felt numb from cold, but at least he was clean. He'd found a heated bath waiting in one of the rooms. He wasn't sure if it was meant for him, but Dyraien had insisted. There were no servants, which meant Dyraien had drawn the bath himself. It seemed strange for a prince to perform such a task.

Tahki flipped on his side. A window above his head let in dim light. The walls cracked a bit every time the wind blew. He couldn't see the moon, but fog outside glowed with silver light.

He put his lumpy pillow over his ears and closed his eyes.

When he couldn't sleep at home, he'd try to picture what his mother looked like. Not his mother from the portrait his father had commissioned after she'd died, but her face when she was alive. Smooth bronze skin. Moonlight-silver hair. Eyes that shone greener than a rainforest. He'd tried to draw her many times before, but he wasn't good at drawing people. Sornjia had told him once that she had been reborn as a beautiful golden elephant, but the idea his mother was alive somewhere, and in the body of a dirty animal, only upset him. He didn't care if Sornjia thought it was a great honor to be reincarnated as a golden elephant, or that his father always seemed pleased when Sornjia talked about it.

His mother was dead. He couldn't write to her and ask what she thought about Rye. About Dyraien. About accepting this job. About lying about who he was. About the secret Dyraien made him keep.

The queen was out of her mind. But why keep it a secret? The most powerful woman in the world had been reduced to a mumbling heap of crazed woman. That would put Dyraien in command. Wasn't that what every royal child wanted? To rule in place of their parent? Dyraien had said she'd fallen ill ten years ago and never recovered and that her condition worsened each year, so there was no hope of recovery.

Maybe Tahki had been hired to build the queen a home, where she could be hidden away and kept safe until… what? It was strange and a little unorthodox to keep her illness from the citizens. Someone would find out sooner or later. He wondered how they'd gotten away with it for so long. He'd tried to ask more questions, but Dyraien had smiled and told him, "In the morning, Tahki. All your questions will be answered in the morning."

A small part of him delighted at knowing such a tremendous secret. It made him feel special. But another part of him recoiled at the danger. If Dyraien, or any of them, found out he was from Dhaulen'aii, what would they do? They would kill him for sure. Yet Dyraien had been so kind to him. And Rye… he didn't know what to think about Rye.

Tahki started to drift off again when the table across the room rattled. His eyelids parted. The room appeared darker than it had a moment ago. He sat up, groggy.

On the other end of the room, a dark shape hunched in the shadows. For a moment he thought it was just part of the small desk, but then it twitched ever so slightly.

"Sornjia?" he said instinctively. It took him a moment to remember he wasn't in his own room, and his brother slept miles away.

The dark shape swayed.

"Who's there?"

The darkness stilled.

And then the most unusual sensation struck Tahki. He felt as though he was looking at nothing. Like the dark shape was not a shape but the lack of something, of everything.

His heart pumped and anxiety stirred his brain. He put his feet on the chilly floor, ready to hop out of bed, when the shape jerked upward.

Tahki froze.

A set of dim eyes blinked open across the room and stared at him. A face in the dark wall. Human or animal or something else, he couldn't tell.

The shape looked slender now, but he could distinguish no features. Maybe an animal had crawled in through a window. He knew nothing about the wildlife around here.

And then the dark shape took a step toward him.

Tahki spun around and fell off the other side of his bed. The blanket wrapped around his feet and he struggled to free himself. He heard a gentle *pat pat pat*. Footsteps. The thing walked toward him. He unraveled the blanket and hurled himself forward in the dark. His face hit the wall and he let out an involuntary cry. He could feel something warm on the nape of his neck, but when he spun around, the room was empty.

His pillow and blanket lay on the floor. He panted and stared a long moment before he considered finding Rye. But what good would that do, and why had he thought of Rye before Dyraien or Gale? Rye would laugh at him.

Night hallucinations were not uncommon. Lack of sleep and anxiety could play a nasty tune in your mind. Obviously he'd had some kind of lucid nightmare.

Tahki returned to his bed. He sat up for a long time, but the room stayed undisturbed. He stared up at the dark ceiling until a dreamless sleep relieved his thoughts, and he dozed uninterrupted until morning.

HE FELT more himself when he woke. His muscles ached and his stomach growled, but his mind worked like a well-oiled clock. His first thoughts were of the dark thing in his room, but he dismissed them as a nightmare. If it had been an animal, it would have left smudge marks or hair or something on the floor.

He slid out of bed, hoping he hadn't slept in too late. Someone had laid clothes outside his door. He slipped them on, a tight sleeveless white shirt with dark leather sides, and boots and pants to match. There was a coat, too, white and short and made of fine leather, but he didn't think he needed it. He wanted his skin to acclimate to the cold climate as fast as possible.

He'd never cared about fashion, but as he walked down the stairway and caught a glimpse of himself in a window reflection, he couldn't help but think he looked decent in Vatolok clothing. They were so different from the baggy, colorful silks back home. So sleek. So modern. So not like anything he'd worn before.

In the foggy light of day, the castle didn't seem so ominous. He heard metal clinking and followed the sound. The scent of fried ham and garlic washed over him. He reached what he assumed was the kitchen and poked his head inside.

Rye sat hunched in a chair, mulling over a paper in his hand. He sipped a cup of black coffee. "Bread's in the wooden box on the counter," he said without looking up. "Meat's hanging in the pantry. Cheese is here. You'll have to brew more coffee if you want some."

"Not really a coffee drinker," Tahki said. "Tea would be nice."

"There isn't any."

Tahki lingered by the door. The kitchen had a stove and exactly one pot, one pan, and one spatula in sight. There were a few eggs in an egg tray and some garlic. An island took up most of the room. Long windows let in light beside the table where Rye sat. Outside the window, he could see the dark wooden waterwheel, motionless in the fog.

He had never seen such a small kitchen. Castles were supposed to be grand estates, and kitchens should be large enough so the servants could make feasts. But Dyraien had said they didn't have servants. Did that mean the castle was built intentionally like this?

Tahki's stomach growled again. He stepped up to the counter. Eggs sounded good, but he didn't know how to make them. He could probably crack one open, but how long did they cook for? Back home, he ate curry omelets almost every morning but never saw them made. He decided to make fried bread instead. If he undercooked it, it wouldn't make him sick.

He found a knife and sliced off a piece of bread. The first time, he sliced too thin. It crumbled into tiny bits. He tried again. This one came out jagged but thick enough to fry. He put the pan on the stove and found a match in a jar. The stove was a great black clunky contraption built into the counter space. It looked nothing like he'd ever seen, probably a newer design. The ones back home utilized an open flame, but even those were only used by the servants. They did the cooking and cleaning and all the other simple tasks that suddenly didn't seem so simple. But he was only frying bread. It couldn't be that hard.

He found a chamber below the stovetop with kindling inside. He lit it, and it blazed fast, growing too large. When he tried to fan it away, the flame burned his hand. He yanked away.

"Something wrong?" Rye said. Tahki looked up. Rye was watching him.

"No," Tahki said. He grabbed the iron pan and set it on the hot plate and then tossed his bread in.

The bread wasn't doing anything. He remembered watching merchants fry food. It usually sizzled. Why wasn't it sizzling?

He glanced up. Rye stared at the pan.

"What?" Tahki said.

Rye shook his head. "Just wondering what you're doing."

"Frying bread."

Rye raised an eyebrow. He waited a moment and then walked over to Tahki and looked in the pan.

"What did you coat it with?" he said.

"Coat it?" Tahki looked down. "Oh." He grabbed butter from one of the shelves, cut off half the stick, and plopped it in.

"Is this how you normally cook?" Rye said. "It's a wonder you aren't five hundred pounds. I've never seen anyone make fried bread like that before."

"Well, this is how we make it back home." Tahki moved the bread around until it started to smoke. "Shit." He grabbed the pan. The hot iron burned the same hand the fire had before and he released the handle. It clanked back onto the stove. The smoke grew thicker. Tahki swept the room for some water, but by the time he found a jug, Rye had removed the pan from the stove and thrown the bread in the sink. It was completely black on one side, white on the other.

Rye placed the pan back on the stove. "Don't think I've ever met anyone who couldn't fry bread."

"I'm used to my kitchen back home," Tahki snapped. His hand hurt. He blew on the burn.

"Did your family have money?" Rye said.

"What?"

"You can't cook. You acted like meeting a prince wasn't anything special. You think very highly of your architectural work, so you're educated. You think people who grew up in the lower cities have no chance in the world. So I assume you come from money."

Tahki scowled. "So what if I do?"

"You should know this isn't a normal castle. There isn't anyone to serve you or hunt for you or make your bed."

"I can do all those things just fine," Tahki said. Was he supposed to have made his bed? He'd just left his pillow and blanket on the floor. Had someone made his bed back home? He'd never noticed.

His hand stung. He held it close to his body. Rye watched him a moment before reaching for the bread. He cut a new slice with no jagged edges. With his free hand, he cracked an egg in a bowl and beat it with a fork, then coated the bread in egg and dropped it in the pan.

Tahki started to protest, but Rye moved so fluently he couldn't ask him to stop. He stood behind Rye, close enough to smell coffee and linseed oil and salt.

After a minute, Rye jerked the pan forward and back, arm muscles flexing as he flipped the bread. It sizzled. The cooked side glistened with golden fried egg. Tahki stared. With every small motion, Rye's muscles tensed, then relaxed, then flexed. His bare shoulders rolled, the bones in his right wrist rotating smoothly when he flicked the pan.

Tahki had never paid attention to anyone's arms before. Maybe he hadn't gotten enough sleep. Sometimes when he was groggy, he would fixate on small things, like how dark his pencil marks were or how textured his paper was. He tried to shake off the fixation. He felt like some swooning twelve-year-old who'd found their first crush. Maybe entering a new country triggered some hidden urges.

His father would have been delighted. He'd done everything in his power to try to get Tahki to take interest in someone—anyone— because it would be healthy. It would be normal. But Tahki had always been more interested in the homes they visited than the inhabitants. Even when his father discovered Tahki preferred men—and he would be denied grandchildren—he still pushed him to date. There were services, his father told him, that offered a surrogate mother or man, if two men or two women were married and wanted children. The entire conversation had been uncomfortable. Dating seemed like such a chore. He had architecture, and that was enough.

"Can I ask you something?" Rye said.

Tahki focused his eyes on the bread. "Nothing's stopped you so far."

Rye glanced up at him. "Yesterday, on the way to the castle, you said 'gods.'"

Tahki shrugged. "So?"

Rye was silent. When he opened his mouth again, he spoke carefully. "As in multiple gods. As in southern religion."

It took a moment to register what Rye implied. Most countries around the world believed in what they called the Mother Goddess. A single female deity who created and watched over the world. The only country who still believed in the old gods was Dhaulen'aii.

Panic swept over him. Rye watched the bread. In his mind, Tahki listed all the countries he could remember and tried to think if any still followed the older religions.

"Pa'kakin," Tahki said.

"What?"

"My father was an orphan. He grew up in a Pa'kakin household." They believed two gods created all life. It was a smaller religion, and very cruel, full of sin and punishment, but oftentimes the people of Pa'kakin would take in orphans and raise them to spread the word of their gods. "Wealth was from my mother's side," Tahki went on. "When my father married her, he stopped practicing, but he still said 'gods' all the time. Habit. Guess I picked it up."

Rye flipped the bread onto a plate and handed it to Tahki. It smelled delicious and looked perfectly golden.

"I see," Rye said. He walked to the cabinets and took out a jar of what looked like mashed leaves in gravy and handed it to Tahki. "For your burn." And then he walked out of the room before Tahki could say thank you.

He ate alone, scrutinizing the story he'd just told Rye, hoping it hadn't contradicted something he'd already said. It was getting difficult to keep his story straight.

TAHKI FOUND Rye at the bottom of the wide steps as Dyraien made his way toward them from upstairs.

"You clean up nicely," Dyraien said, looking as princely as he had the night before. It was amazing to think he took care of himself, of the entire country, all without servants to dress him or cook for him.

"Thank you again for the bath," Tahki said.

"Did you sleep well?"

Tahki thought of the dark thing in his room. "Perfectly. And I'm very eager to learn more about this castle."

Dyraien raised an arm and threw it over his shoulder, like they'd known each other a long time. "Of course you are. We're all terribly excited to have you join our team." Tahki should have felt flattered, but there was something about Dyraien's doting that felt purposeful.

Tahki had met a merchant once who'd convinced him to buy a dress for a girlfriend he didn't have. He had no idea how he'd gotten talked into it, and all he remembered was a man who spoke very fast and fluently, and the next thing Tahki knew, he was handing the man a silver coin in exchange for a hideous dress. His father had found it quite amusing and explained to Tahki about manipulation. That's what it felt like with Dyraien. Like Tahki was being pushed toward something, though he didn't know what.

"I'd like to personally show you around the castle," Dyraien said. "And then we'll talk about the project."

Tahki found himself being swept away up the stairs. Rye followed.

"Rye doesn't seem to think you're a good fit here," Dyraien said. "I think it will be fun proving him wrong, don't you?"

Tahki glanced at Rye. Rye had made it clear he didn't think Tahki was right for the job but never said why. He couldn't just hold a grudge against him for what he'd said about the lower cities. How was he supposed to know Rye had grown up in the slums?

Tahki pulled away from Dyraien. "Actually, I'd like to know why he doesn't think I'm any good."

"I told you before," Rye said, his eyes never wavering. "Your designs aren't practical. They're more like something you'd read about in a Juliani Vornask novel. Interesting in concept, but not functional for the real world."

"What gives you authority to judge my work? You only saw a few concept sketches at the fair. You have no idea what I'm capable of," Tahki said. He knew he was being rude, but Rye wasn't a prince. He wasn't sure what Rye was.

"Careful, Rye," Dyraien said. "When a cat gets its back in the air, claws are soon to follow."

Rye shook his head. "He doesn't have claws. He has entitlement issues and no idea what's expected of him here." Rye scuffed his feet and walked back down the stairway, leaving Tahki and Dyraien alone.

"I've never seen anyone get under Rye's skin like that," Dyraien said. "Well done." He clapped Tahki on the back.

Tahki composed himself. "I was out of line."

"Please, I found it entertaining." Dyraien continued up the stairs. "Rye said more words to you in the last few minutes than he said to me in the first few months we met."

Tahki rubbed his left wrist. He hadn't meant to get under anyone's skin. "I just don't understand where he gets off telling me I'm no good."

Dyraien ran a hand through his hair. "Tahki, I typically take Rye's word on everything. Though I'm happy to have you here, and I know you'll make us all proud, I am cautious about you."

Tahki frowned. "Is Rye your advisor or something?" Noble advisors were old women or men who knew how the system worked. But maybe, in this modern world, Dyraien wanted someone younger. He still had no idea what Dyraien and Rye's relationship was, or how someone from the lower cities managed to land a position in a prince's court.

"No," Dyraien said, amused. "He's nothing like that, but don't dismiss his skepticism. He's the one who built this castle, so he has some credibility when it comes to architecture. That's why I asked him to attend the fair with Gale."

Tahki gaped.

"He didn't build the castle by himself, mind," Dyraien said. "And not from scratch, but he's made all the modifications. This castle looked quite different just a few years ago. He oversaw the renovations and worked as lead constructor. He has a real gift. He can build anything and build it well."

Tahki's stomach tightened. Rye knew what he was talking about after all. It would take someone with great skill and vision to build a castle like this, even if he hadn't designed it himself.

"Don't think too hard on it." Dyraien winked. "I'm sure you'll be impressing us all in no time. From what Gale told me earlier this morning, you have a very unique eye. Now, I'd like you to pay very close attention. You'll need to know the castle's structure as well as you know your favorite pencil."

Dyraien led him from room to room. Most of the rooms were empty, save for a scattering of loose obsidian or pile of marble dust. There wasn't anything of great interest about how it had been built, but the way Dyraien spoke captivated him. Dyraien talked about the castle like it was a person. Not just a person, a loved one. It touched Tahki to think someone else had such a deep respect for architecture. Or maybe it wasn't even architecture. Maybe the castle held some sentimental meaning to him.

He asked about why most of the rooms were empty, and Dyraien replied that there was no need for furniture. He asked why they used obsidian as a foundation. Dyraien hesitated and then said because it looked nice. The answer didn't satisfy Tahki, but he didn't press.

Seeming to sense Tahki's eagerness, Dyraien talked about his life before the castle. He said he and his mother lived in the capital city, that they moved to the castle because of its seclusion. Now, Dyraien traveled back to the capital on his mother's behalf to attend to political business. The city was run by a council of six women, who seemed happy with the queen's absence. But lately, people had started to ask questions. Suspicion was, Dyraien said, the most dangerous weapon in a kingdom.

Tahki tried to remember the layout of the castle as they moved along. It wasn't large, but everything looked the same: black walls, white floors, empty rooms.

None of the rooms caught his interest until they entered one of the larger wings on the second floor.

Tahki froze just inside the door. Every inch of wall was covered with animal heads or animal parts. Antlers, horns, feathers, teeth, claws—all he could think about was how much Sornjia would hate it here. How disgusted he would be that all these animals were killed for no other purpose than to decorate a room.

Even Tahki felt a little unnerved by all the dead eyes staring at him, but it also amazed him. He'd never seen so many unique species. The predators had been displayed on pedestals or wooden boxes around the room. Some had been posed walking, others in a fierce fighting position. He recognized striped bear-wolves and tusked gators, red-clawed eagles and horned stoats. In the very center, a large black wildcat sat. Her specular coat shined in the pale light from a northern window, a hint of red woven into her fur. She was as big as a horse. He'd never seen an animal quite like her. The only predators back home were emaciated wild dogs. Sornjia had rescued a young pup with a broken leg one summer. He raised the dog for a few years, until it got run over by a cart. Sornjia had cried for days. Tahki had bought him another dog as a replacement, a proper, well-bred dog, but Sornjia had said it wasn't the same. To this day, Tahki didn't understand why.

"You look disturbed," Dyraien said. "Don't tell me you're one of those bleeding hearts who thinks it's cruel to hunt. They're only animals." Dyraien flicked the nose of the black cat. "This one here? She reminds me of you."

"I remind you of a dead cat?"

"You remind me of one of those eastern jungle cats. The big ones like this. You slink when you walk, eyes wide, skittish when you come across something unexpected. They're clever, these cats. Hard to hunt. But their pelts make beautiful rugs."

"So you think I'd make a good rug?"

Dyraien gave him another handsome smile. "I think you'd look nice draped across my bed."

Tahki fought to keep his cheeks from reddening. No one had ever spoken to him like this. People of Vatolokít weren't as reserved as people from Dhaulen'aii, and a small part of him liked the attention.

Tahki coughed and tried to change the subject. "The castle is so empty, it makes this room seem a little… extravagant."

Dyraien nodded. "Before my mother fell ill, she was a great hunter. She often traveled overseas on safari and brought back magnificent animals from her hunts. When I moved her here ten years ago, I brought her animals with us. It comforts her to be around them. For a long time she loved to sit in this room and stroke their fur and talk to them. But now… now I don't think she recognizes them."

Tahki bowed his head. "I'm sorry. It must be very hard on you to see her that way." Not only did Dyraien take care of himself, but he tended to his mentally ill mother. Tahki couldn't even make bread.

Dyraien shrugged. "We're all dealt a different hand in life. We choose either to play that hand or to fold."

"Still, it's sad what happened to your mother."

Dyraien plucked a feather from the eagle on a pedestal. "She knew what she was doing."

Tahki frowned. "What do you mean?"

Dyraien smiled, but it was cold. "I only meant, had she taken better care of herself, maybe she wouldn't have fallen ill."

A tense moment passed between them, and Tahki hated himself for asking so many questions. Dyraien was the only person who had shown him any kind of good faith.

"Gale says she's never seen anything like your work," Dyraien said.

Tahki swallowed. He had never felt both pride and fear at the same time when someone talked about his work.

"I would love to say I'm the right man for your project," Tahki said. "But I don't know anything about it."

"Then it's only fair I tell you, isn't it?" Dyraien nodded, more to himself than to Tahki. "My mother and I lived in the capital city. I moved her here when she fell ill. It's been a struggle, to say the least, keeping something like this a secret. If it weren't for Rye, I think I would have gone quite mad myself." He brushed a stray blond hair from his face. His eyes filled with something—bitterness or hatred or resentment. "In normal situations, if my mother were to pass away or become unfit, I would take over as ruler of Vatolokít. But our country, bless my dear country, is changing. Did you know the queen no longer acts as prosecutor if a woman or man is guilty of a crime? No, the council chooses five citizens and presents them with facts. The citizens then vote on if the accused is guilty. Fascinating, isn't it? Such power in the hands of the people. What a remarkable time we live in."

"It is remarkable," Tahki said. "I think it's the reason so many foreigners try to find work here."

Dyraien licked his lips. "But it's not perfect. No country is, I suppose. See, I received a rather nasty shock just before my mother fell ill. It seems the people like the idea of having a say in their country's law. So much, they feel they should also have a say in who rules their country. I was warned by the council that when the queen leaves the throne, be it for failing health or death, there will be a vote to decide who rules next."

Tahki stepped forward. "But your bloodline has ruled for centuries."

Dyraien smiled. "It was my mother's idea."

It seemed cruel for a mother to deny her only child a chance at the throne. "But your family has done so much for this country by introducing modernism into their lives. I'm sure they'll want you to rule them."

Dyraien rested a hand on Tahki's shoulder. "You're very kind. Unfortunately, I've not been around the capital much. All my time has been spent tending to mother and running the country in secret. I'm not a familiar face among my people. Even you didn't recognize me."

Tahki bowed his head.

"It's all right," Dyraien said. "I've come to terms with it. I only care about my country's future. So long as it's safe and in good hands, I can rest easy. Which is where you and this castle come into play."

Tahki looked up at him, into his blue eyes. The drumming of his heart quickened.

"Tahki, this castle is a gift to my country. I need you to change it."

"Change it?"

Dyraien drew him close. "I need you to turn this castle into a weapon."

Tahki waited for further explanation. When none came, he said, "Do you mean I should order and install cannons or something?"

Dyraien shook his head. "I don't want you to buy weapons and equip them. I want this castle to *be* a weapon. Not like a warship, not like an armory. A complete weapon."

Tahki tried to understand. "The entire castle. A weapon."

"I need you to think of this castle as a living, breathing thing. A great and powerful force. Something the world has never seen. A machine that could destroy an army in a single assault."

A machine. Tahki had read about a surge of mechanical inventions. Newspapers were calling this an age of enlightenment. From machines that spun cotton to engines that pumped water from mines. But he'd never heard of anyone turning an entire castle into a machine. It didn't seem possible. He said, "What kind of energy could power something this large?"

Dyraien let his hand fall away. "There is a river below this castle that produces tremendous energy. Use the water, and turn my castle into a war machine. I want this to be a prototype. When my family is relieved from its duty, I'd like to give this castle to the council as a gift."

Too many thoughts weaved through Tahki's mind. He couldn't wrap his head around what was expected of him. He'd never drawn a complete blank before when it came to architecture. Was this even architecture? Or was it invention? But wasn't all architecture invention? Hadn't his mother always pushed the functions of existing objects to make something new and exciting? Something surprising and innovative?

"I want to help. I really do. But I'm no weapons expert," Tahki said. He didn't want to lose this job, his first job. But getting in over his head wouldn't benefit him, either.

"I've already tried a weapons expert. He proved inadequate. But it made me realize that I need a creative mind for this special project."

Tahki scratched his left wrist. "Why can't you just return to the capital city and gain the people's favor? I'm sure there's someone who will watch over your mother." It seemed like an easier solution.

Dyraien's face darkened. "I didn't bring you here to give me advice on how to rule my country."

Tahki's hands dropped to his side. "Of course not. I'm sorry. I didn't mean to...."

"I like people to owe me things. I like control. This castle is to assure I still have some standing in the eyes of the council. I need them to need me, and I need you to do this for me, Tahki. Everyone else has been a disappointment, to say the least. You are my last chance to leave behind a legacy. Please, tell me you'll try?"

His eyes looked so intense, so pleading.

"All right," Tahki said. "If the castle can be made into a machine, I'll find a way."

Dyraien broke into a handsome grin. "If you do this for me, I promise you'll be the most famous architect ever known. Every country around the world will know your name."

They were the words he'd always wanted to hear, yet excitement eluded him. Not only did he feel unqualified for this, but something about Dyraien's explanation didn't add up. Dyraien didn't strike him as the kind of person to simply give up his rule without a fight. Also, if the castle was to be a gift, why build it out in the middle of nowhere? Maybe Dyraien planned on threatening the council, but that didn't explain why he built it all the way out here.

Still, Tahki had been hired to do a job, and he planned to do it well. He couldn't pass up the opportunity to become the most famous architect. Everything he'd ever wanted had just been handed to him. He'd be a fool to abandon it.

Dyraien finished the tour in a larger room on the second floor close to his bedchamber. "This will be your workroom. I'll pick up a drafting table when I go to Edgewater. That's the town nearest to here where I conduct my business when I'm away from the capital. Until then, try to make the room your own. You'll be working here for the next few months. I want you to be comfortable." And then he said his goodbyes and headed off.

Tahki stood alone in the room. He could feel the weight of the castle walls pressing in around him. A part of him felt the need to stand close to the door so he could run, like the walls somehow wanted to trap him. But that was only nerves from his bad dream last night. He could easily fit several tables in here. Though the castle walls absorbed light, the windows gave him more than enough to work by. If he purchased some furniture, maybe some lightning root lanterns, a rug to take the chill off the floor, it could actually be a nice workspace.

His own workspace. His own job. Suddenly, Dyraien's reasons for building the castle didn't seem important. This was the start of a new life. A life he'd made on his own without his father's influence.

As he started to plan where he'd place his table and tools, Gale stomped in. Her gray hair had been pulled into a tight bun, and her eyes narrowed in on him.

"Good morning, Gale," Tahki said.

"Good morning, my ass. You and I need to talk. Now."

Tahki frowned. Gale grabbed his wrist and yanked him down the steps with frightening strength.

"What's going on?" Tahki asked.

She didn't answer. They left the castle, traveling at an urgent pace. Low clouds hung in the sky. They started down the path off the cliff. In the distance, a mile or so away, he could see the gray ocean. The cliffside was covered in clumps of long brown grass. He nearly jogged as she strode on. How a woman old enough to be his grandmother could walk so fast he didn't know. Her short legs were covered in blue veins that popped as she sped into the mist. He tripped over a few rocks in the dirt before reaching the wet sand fields. Gale's house had been built at the base of the cliff and looked less like a house and more like a shoddy wooden shack. Two, maybe three rooms wide.

He yanked his arm away when they reached her porch. "Gale, I really insist you tell me what this is about." Tahki panted. "I should be working, and—" Tahki cut short when she shoved open the door.

There, sitting at a small wooden table with a teacup in his hands, was Sornjia.

Chapter 6

Tahki stared at his brother's face. Sornjia should have been far away, in another world. But here he was, sitting in Gale's kitchen, clutching a cup of tea like it was just another lazy afternoon in the palace lounge.

"I don't understand," Tahki said aloud. It wasn't to Gale or Sornjia, but to himself.

"I found him wandering around Edgewater," Gale said. The wrinkles on her face twisted as she scowled. She looked a little scary. "He was walking around asking if anyone had seen someone who looked exactly like him. Thought it was you and you'd lost your mind."

"She hit me over the head with a limp fish," Sornjia said.

"What?" Tahki said.

Sornjia shrugged. "She slapped me across the back of the head with a trout."

"You didn't tell me you had a twin," Gale said.

Tahki's mouth felt dry. "I didn't think I'd have to."

"You're angry," Sornjia said. He spoke so matter-of-factly. Tahki wished he had a trout to smack him across the back of the head with too. Sornjia acted so casual, so innocent.

"Sornjia, why are you here?"

Sornjia set his cup down. "I was worried about you."

"Worried? I'm an adult. I can take care of myself."

Sornjia hugged himself and leaned forward in his chair. "After you left, my body felt like dust caught in a shadow. A bell rang in my head, the sound the sky makes right before it rains." He looked at Tahki. "When I closed my eyes at night, I could see dark spiders skittering across my brain, and I knew I had to save you."

"Is he ill?" Gale's eyes narrowed. "Brain fever? Damaged nerves? You'd better be straight with me, Tahki. I put my neck on the line for you." Her tone sounded dangerous, and despite her age, Tahki realized Gale wasn't someone he wanted to cross.

"He isn't ill," Tahki said. "He just talks strange. But he's harmless, I promise."

"Harmless?" Gale scooped up a wooden spoon and shook it threateningly at Tahki. "Do you have any idea what would happen to both of you if Dyraien found out you brought your brother, who clearly isn't right in the head, to a place that he has sacrificed so much to keep secret?"

"I'm perfectly fine in the head," Sornjia said. "But sometimes, places and people and things visit me inside my mind. They show me things. They don't stay long, and when they leave, everything goes back to normal."

Gale stared at Sornjia.

"I didn't bring him here," Tahki said. "I don't even know how he got here."

"I traveled east and hid on a boat," Sornjia said. He spoke like it was simple, like he wouldn't have been imprisoned or put to death had someone seen him. "Much easier than forging documents. If you weren't so afraid of water, you wouldn't have had to go through the effort of creating a fake passport."

Tahki thought Gale looked frightening before, but now, he thought for sure she'd ram that wooden spoon down his throat.

Instead, she eased herself into a chair across from Sornjia. "You're going to tell me everything, or I swear, I'll drag both your bodies out to sea and drown you."

Tahki shuddered. He could think of no lie to cover up the mess Sornjia had made. So, over the next twenty minutes, he explained everything to her. He expected some kind of outburst from Gale, but she remained still, her hands folded together, contemplating.

"So you're from Dhaulen'aii." She shook her head. "I should have known. Your skin isn't dark enough to be from the south islands, and it's a little too golden."

"I'll send Sornjia home," Tahki said. "No one will know he was here. Please, don't tell Dyraien where I'm from. Let me keep this job."

Gale's head snapped up. "Of course you'll keep your job. Telling Dyraien would only cause me trouble. I don't exactly have a clean reputation." Though Tahki didn't ask, Gale went on. "I was once a renowned architect, you know. Unfortunately, my love for the bottle was greater than my desire to hold down a job. I've been fired eight times for working drunk. When I couldn't land architectural work, I became a judge. Things went fine for a while, but I couldn't redeem myself."

"That sounds like an awful situation," Sornjia said.

She licked her thin lips, a little saliva dripping down her chin. "It was, but it was my own fault. I was a washed-up old hag on the streets when Dyraien found me. He gave me a chance to work on this castle, gave me a chance to get sober again. Well, Rye helped with the sobering part.

"But I wasn't right for the job. Even though I couldn't turn the castle into a machine, he kept me on, put me in charge of finding someone to replace me. He said I would manage the new architect. Do you understand what that means? I'm responsible for you."

Tahki swallowed. "Dyraien won't find out. I promise."

"Do you understand the risk of staying here?" Gale said. "If he discovers you're from Dhaulen'aii, he'll think you're a spy. That means you're dead. I'm dead. Your brother is dead."

"But you don't think I'm a spy, do you?"

Gale laughed. "A dead fish would make a better spy than you. You're too hotheaded for that line of work."

Tahki let the insult slide. "Dyraien won't find out. Sornjia will leave right away."

Sornjia shook his head. "I'm not leaving."

"Gods, Sornjia, you already almost ruined me once. Don't do it again."

"That's another thing," Gale said. "You haven't said 'gods' to anyone, have you? Only southern religions use that term."

Tahki thought of Rye. "No. I haven't."

"Good. Now." She turned to Sornjia. "Why do you feel the need to put my life in danger, young man?"

"I'm sorry, Ms. Utmutóta. I don't mean to put your life in danger, but there's something wrong with that castle. Something oppressive. Suffocating. It makes the marrow in my bones itch."

Tahki rubbed his wrist. "Sornjia, whatever crazy dream you had about the castle, it's not real. I've been in every single room. There's nothing wrong with it. You're going home, today."

"I can't," Sornjia said.

"Yes, you can."

"No," Sornjia said. "I mean, the ship I came over on doesn't depart until end of summer."

"Then I'll forge documents for you."

"You'll need special paper for that," Gale said.

"How long will it take to import?"

"A week, maybe."

Tahki covered his face with his hands. This was too much for him. Turning the castle into a machine challenged him enough. He didn't need Sornjia here to endanger him.

"All right," Gale said. "Here's what we'll do: your brother will stay with me. I'll keep him out of sight. We'll order the paper, wait for it to arrive. Then you can forge his documents and he'll be on his way. Dyraien has never visited here. Not once since I built it. And I can tell Rye I don't want to be disturbed. He's too respectful to ask why." She cracked her knotted fingers. "You had better be worth the risk I'm taking."

Tahki swallowed, feeling more pressured than before. It wasn't much of a plan, but he could see no other option. He didn't trust his brother to stay alone. His odd way of speaking drew too much attention.

"I'll be a grain of rice in a sand dune," Sornjia said. "No one will see me. I promise."

"What about Father?"

"He thinks I'm at the winter cottage with you."

Tahki felt a lump in his stomach. It had been growing larger ever since Dyraien had told him about the project.

"I'll tell Dyraien I'd like to see your work every morning," Gale said. "That will give you an excuse to come here and check on him. Until then, you better make progress on the castle, or this deal is off. Understand?"

Tahki nodded and took his leave. As he walked back to the castle, he told himself it would only be for a week. Just a week and things would be back to normal.

HIS THOUGHTS moved in a circular pattern: the castle, Rye, mad queen, Dyraien, a weapon, Sornjia. He stared up at the ceiling with his head against his lumpy pillow. The wind outside thrust across the windowpane.

His best ideas came to him right before he fell asleep, so he always had a piece of paper and a pencil beside his bed, ready to jot down ideas.

None came.

He tried to sketch the castle in his mind, but the lines wouldn't connect. After everything that had happened today, he found himself picturing his brother, remembering how Sornjia would often pop into his room when they were kids with some harebrained idea.

"I think we should drain the courtyard pool," Sornjia said. "And turn it into a pen for injured animals."

"They'd all eat each other," Tahki said.

"We'll make pens and separate each species."

"The pool isn't big enough."

"Then we'll dig a bigger pool. We'll tunnel right to the other end of the world, and all the sands in the desert will drain into the ocean, just like they did thousands of years ago."

And they'd continue on like that, Sornjia's words growing stranger, Tahki's frustration mounting, until their father, in his kind but stern way, told Sornjia he couldn't save all the animals, and that only helping a few wouldn't be fair, so it was best to let nature be.

Twins were supposed to have a special connection, but Tahki had no idea what his brother spoke about half the time. No one did, not even their father. Gotem said Sornjia was blessed. All his life, Tahki had felt like the peculiar one, the outcast, while Sornjia sat there prattling on about how plants grew better when you sang to them. In any other part of the world, Sornjia would be locked away for insanity. As children, Tahki hadn't minded so much. Sometimes it would even benefit him, like if they were playing somewhere they weren't allowed, Sornjia would know someone was coming before they were found. But this time was different. This time, Tahki's life was at risk.

A loud thump sounded in the hall. Footsteps tapped outside his closed door. He sat up. Someone stopped in front of his room. He squinted through the dark and saw a shadow beneath the gap. Then the door handle rattled. It wasn't locked. Anyone could simply turn it and walk inside.

"Rye?" Tahki said.

The rattling stopped.

He hopped out of bed and put his face close to the crack. "Sornjia?"

A low throaty noise resonated against the wood. Tahki's heart drummed faster. The handle shook again. He grabbed it and held on.

Silence.

Tahki swallowed. Dyraien had said the castle toyed with your mind. It was probably just the wind banging against his door. Someone must have left a window open.

He tiptoed back to his bed, grabbed his mother's pencil, and held it like a knife. He put his hand on the doorknob and counted to three, then yanked it open. The hallway was empty. Silence lingered, as if he stood in the wake of a storm, so quiet his ears rang. He stepped outside and walked to the railing where he could see the entryway. He searched the ground until he caught movement on the staircase.

Someone stood on the steps. A dark shape against a dark wall.

Sweat broke out across his neck. His first impulse was to flee to his room and barricade the door, but he didn't move. What if Sornjia had decided to come to the castle? If anyone saw him, if anyone spoke to him, he was dead.

Tahki moved quickly to the stairs. By the time he reached the top, the figure had vanished. He descended, one careful step at a time. Before he reached the bottom, he noticed something odd about the floor.

It moved.

He stopped on the last step. The floor looked black as the obsidian walls, only it shimmered and rippled, and he could see his reflection.

The entire first floor was filled with dark water.

Tahki took a step backward. He didn't understand what he was looking at. Had the river flooded? Why was the water so dark when it couldn't be more than two feet deep?

He retreated up the stairs to alert Dyraien. As he climbed, a sudden furious roar sounded above his head. The cry stung his ears and left his head throbbing.

Tahki looked up.

A river rushed toward him, uncontrolled, through the hallway. Water thrashed over the banister and rolled down the staircase.

Panic seized him. "What?" he breathed aloud. "What?" This was a dream. It had to be. It felt too horrible to be life. He tried to wake up, but he couldn't.

Tahki stumbled backward and made a break for the bottom floor, every muscle rigid with fear. He splashed through the knee-high water in the entryway. He could hear the river crashing toward him as it devoured pillars and forced open doors on all sides, flooding rooms. Before he reached the front doors, the water surged left, forcing him to the right. He opened the first door he came to and discovered another stairway leading down to a lower level of the castle. Dyraien hadn't shown him this place, but it looked to be his only escape.

He pushed through and slammed the door behind him. His feet caught on the stairway and he tripped, tumbling a moment before his body smacked into a dirt floor.

Tahki panted into the ground and didn't move for a moment. The chaos left his body trembling, and the fall had twisted his right arm. He sat up. His pulse beat hard. Breath caught in his throat, and he huddled against the stairway and listened.

No sound came from the floor above.

His stomach convulsed, and he dry hacked. Clear dribble fell from his chin. He wiped it away and rose to his feet. Though his legs should have been soaked, they felt dry. His white cotton shirt was also dry. There was no sign of water anywhere, except sweat under his arms. He couldn't even begin to make sense of his current state. Instead, he turned his attention to the room.

It smelled musty. Light trickled in from around the corner. He stepped back, trying to get a sense of the area, when his back hit something hard.

Two black gates towered over him. They stood at least fifteen feet tall, which meant the castle was much larger than he originally thought. He must be in the basement, and those doors probably led outside. Something about the gates felt wrong, out of place. He remembered Sornjia had once seen a dead sandbull in the road, and he'd said, "It was like trying to look at something with needles in your eyes." Looking at the gate didn't just feel uncomfortable. It felt painful. The back of his eyes throbbed, and warmth trickle down his lip. He wiped his nose. Blood.

Tahki rubbed his face with his shirt and took a deep breath.

He didn't know what this place was or why Dyraien had neglected to show him. What concerned him more were his dry clothing and the blood. The only explanation he could think of was that he'd dream walked, and the fall had woken him. He didn't have a history of nightwalking, and the idea his body and mind had separated for a moment frightened him.

Tahki grabbed his head. Maybe he'd eaten something toxic, or the anxiety of seeing Sornjia had pushed him over the edge. He felt lucid now. If he walked back upstairs, he was sure the water would be gone.

Still, he hesitated and took a shaky breath. He focused on the gate. Something in the back of his mind whispered *pull, pull, pull*. Looking at the gates was like looking at a lever someone told you not to touch, so you naturally wanted to touch it.

Tahki reached out a hand and rested it on one of the circular iron handles. There were two, each as thick as his arm and big as his torso. He pulled, but it was locked. It was odd to lock yourself inside the castle, unless the gate didn't lead outside. He couldn't remember seeing the gates from the exterior and let the handle fall with a loud clunk.

After one last look, he made his way back up the stairs. He found his mother's pencil on the top step where he must have dropped it. With his left hand, he scooped it up and held it close to his chest. He didn't look back to the gates again. When he reached the top, he opened the door to the main floor. Like he'd expected, only moonlight flooded the entryway. The white floors glowed, shiny and dry. There was no dark thing on the stairway. There was no water.

He returned to his room exhausted. Before getting into bed, he slid his small table in front of the door. That way, if he dream walked again, the screech of the table against the floor would wake him if he tried to leave.

He crawled into bed and yanked up the sheets, his mother's pencil still pressed firmly against him. His fingers curled tightly around it as he forced his eyes shut. Shivers and shakes ran through his body, but the blood had stopped, and his mind felt heavy with sleep.

Chapter 7

A WEEK went by, and Tahki did not dream walk again. His recollection of that night dimmed, and after a few days he'd convinced himself the whole incident had been fabricated due to stress.

Dyraien had brought him a present from town every day of the week: a new drafting table, reels of paper, a new kind of chair that swiveled from side to side—he really, really loved the chair—a set of pens, a new compass, several rulers, and lots of books. Most of the books were on architecture and inventions, but once he'd brought him a book of poems. Tahki had been surprised, but Dyraien said poetry allowed the mind to escape, and a brain at rest often produced the best ideas. Tahki tried to thank him, but Dyraien only smiled and said it was his pleasure, which made Tahki feel a little guilty he hadn't come up with any ideas yet.

Tahki visited Sornjia early on the seventh day. "Did the paper come?"

"Not yet," Sornjia said.

Tahki frowned. "It should be here by now."

Sornjia stirred a pot of fish stew. "Tomorrow it will come, I'm sure."

Gale sat at the table sipping tea and said, "If you're not a prince, people don't usually rush your order."

"I'm sorry, Gale," Tahki said. He thought she'd be furious.

"It has been nice," she said, "having a helper. Don't think my pistol collection ever looked so shiny."

Sornjia smiled. He lifted a bowl of fish stew and handed it to Gale.

"You two are very different," she said to Tahki, and shoveled in a mouthful of creamy stew. "Your brother is calm, compassionate, agreeable. You just complain a lot."

"I don't complain that much," Tahki mumbled.

"Tahki is like a catapult," Sornjia said. "He's calm when left on his own, but if someone winds him up, that's when he starts throwing stones."

Sornjia's comment made Tahki sound like an upset child, but something sparked in his mind when his brother spoke. He cradled the thought all the way back to the castle, mulling it over, drawing the lines in his head.

When he got to his room, he pulled out a book Dyraien had brought him titled *The Woman Behind the Machine*, an illustrated book about Adrinia Kov'kai, the current expert machinist who'd been responsible for the last seven great machine inventions. He forgot about dream walking, about the dark thing in his room, and for the first time in weeks, Tahki lost himself between thin black lines and carefully plotted points of perspective.

HE COMPLETED his floor plan around noon. Back home, he would have tucked his design out of sight for a week. It gave his brain a chance to reset and see the flaws. But he had a good feeling about this one. He'd created a twenty-foot launching mechanism that could be attached to the side of the castle and controlled from inside. It swiveled around the walls, so no matter what side someone attacked, the invention could be moved on a rail system.

With a smile, he gathered up his design and searched for Rye. It annoyed him he had to gain Rye's approval before showing Dyraien, but a small part of him delighted at proving himself.

He found Rye in the stables mucking out gingoat stalls. The animals snorted when Tahki approached. Rye placed his hand on their snouts to calm them. He was covered in mud, and a thick earthy scent attached itself to him.

"That doesn't look very fun," Tahki said.

Rye shrugged. "Needs to be done."

"Don't you mind that Dyraien makes you clean up animal crap?"

"Dyraien doesn't make me do anything," he said. "And no, I don't mind."

Tahki approached one of the stalls. The gingoat nearest to him, a bulky beast with long white fur and black horns, snapped its flat teeth at him. He jerked back.

"If you show fear," Rye said, "they won't accept you."

"I don't need an animal's approval."

Rye petted its muzzle. "You sound like Dyraien."

Tahki shifted his weight. "I have a completed floor plan. I'd like to show Dyraien before he leaves for town."

Rye stepped out of the pen and frowned, like he'd already made up his mind not to like what he saw. Tahki bit his tongue to keep his temper down. Rye washed his arms in a trough and reached for the paper. His hands still looked filthy, and Tahki hesitated handing over the design.

Rye took it from him anyway. He looked over the plan in the same careful way he had at the fair. Then something lit up on his face. A kind of understanding or approval. Tahki could see it in his eyes: he liked the design.

Tahki repressed a smile and rubbed his left wrist. He focused on one of the gingoats. She stared back, big black eyes watching him like he planned on making dinner out of her. She snorted and turned her rear in his direction. Tahki scowled.

"This won't work," Rye said.

Tahki jerked his head up. "What?"

"It won't work." He handed the paper back.

"I'm positive it will," Tahki said. "You can't just take five seconds and decide it won't."

Rye picked up his shovel. "Even if it could work, this isn't what Dyraien is looking for."

"How would you know?"

"You created an external weapon, a weapon that looks like something Adrinia Kov'kai already designed, and attached it to the castle. Dyraien wants this entire castle turned into a machine. An oversized catapult won't cut it."

Tahki swatted at a fly. Rye had liked the design. He'd looked at it with such surprise, such open admiration. Why had he said it wouldn't work?

"Maybe you're what's not working," Tahki said.

Rye raised an eyebrow at him. "This should be interesting."

"You're so quick to dismiss an idea. I bet Dyraien found lots of solutions, but you keep rejecting them, so the project remains at a standstill." Tahki didn't really believe the words that left his mouth, but they kept coming. "Maybe you're not as good a constructor as Dyraien thinks you are, and you know it, so you're afraid to try my designs."

Rye stared at him. Tahki thought he might take a swing at him, but Rye remained composed.

"You're not used to people telling you you're wrong," Rye said in level tones. "So this is going to be hard for you to hear. When a goat acts up, Dyraien gives it three chances to correct its behavior. Good goats get to stay, and bad ones are sent to slaughter."

Tahki swallowed. "You're threatening me?"

"I'm saying that I train the goats myself to keep them out of the butcher shop. I'm the buffer between you and Dyraien, so listen when I tell you that if you don't drop the entitled attitude, you're going to find yourself out of a job."

"Don't talk to me like I'm some ignorant child."

"Then don't act like one." Rye ran a hand through his hair. "Your design is sloppy. Rushed. I know you're under a lot of pressure, but take your time. Dyraien is set on using the river as a power source. Maybe try incorporating that into your next design."

Tahki turned from the stables and stomped back inside the castle. He didn't need Rye's advice, and he didn't need to use the river as a power source. Water power had been used for centuries, but now, with all the new-age machines and inventions, it had become obsolete. He didn't know why Dyraien was so set on using the river as part of the design. Maybe he didn't think there was any other way. Maybe it was up to Tahki to show him a better solution.

He walked up the stairway and heard Dyraien's voice down the hall. Before he knew what he was doing, he turned right instead of left at the top and headed toward the queen's room. He stopped outside her door. Voices hummed beyond. He knew better than to go inside. Dyraien had said none of them were to ever disturb the queen.

He glanced down at his work. The catapult was a good, practical design. It would make a fantastic weapon. Maybe it had been inspired by something already done, but Tahki's modifications fit all the criteria, except for the part about using the river as a power source, but that seemed a minor thing.

Tahki reached for the door. It opened easy.

Dyraien sat beside his mother on the bed, whispering to her. His head whipped up as Tahki stepped inside.

"What the hell are you doing in here?" Dyraien said. "Get out!"

Tahki froze. He'd never heard Dyraien speak with such harshness. This wasn't the same gift-bearing, flirtatious prince as before.

"I'm sorry," Tahki said. "I found a drawing. I mean I drew a drawing. I drawn… I have drawn… here." He stepped toward him and reached his design over, as if it were a shield that would protect him from the man's sudden temper.

Dyraien snatched the drawing out of his hand.

The queen swayed back and forth. She reached for Dyraien's arm and pulled him back down to her. "Such a beautiful child," the queen muttered. "My only baby boy."

Dyraien ignored her and kept his eyes on Tahki. "You found a solution? You've designed a machine?" A little softness crept back into his voice.

Tahki nodded.

"And Rye thinks it's a good idea?"

"Y-Yes."

"Yes?"

"Yes."

Dyraien unfolded the paper and scanned it. Tahki held his breath. The queen gazed wide-eyed over his shoulder, like a child looking at a picture book.

And then Dyraien frowned. "Rye approved this?"

Tahki swallowed. "He… he said…."

"Toxic!" the queen yelled. Her voice sounded deeper than before. Harsher. The voice of a woman who'd brought down kingdoms. "Toxic, foul, wrong!"

Dyraien let Tahki's design fall to the ground. "Mother, please, we can't have you worked up. You'll hurt yourself again."

Queen Genevi stood and smashed her foot against the paper. "Evil. Wrong. The sky is singing tears, the ground grows teeth to peel my skin." She hissed and grabbed her head, and for one disorienting moment, Tahki was reminded of Sornjia.

Dyraien pushed her firmly onto her bed where she curled up and started to cry. He plucked the floor plan off the marble, grabbed Tahki by the arm, and dragged him into the hall.

"What the hell is this?" Dyraien said, the paper balled in his fist.

Tahki didn't know what to say. His design had been clever, creative. "I thought it's what you wanted."

"What I wanted?" Dyraien said between clenched teeth. "Even my crazed, sick mother can see that this is all wrong, and she doesn't even recognize me most days."

Tahki felt his throat close up. The cruelness in Dyraien's voice resonated through him. Before he could reply, apologize, beg for his job, he heard footsteps.

Rye ran up beside them, still covered in mud. "What's going on? Why is the queen screaming?"

Dyraien let Tahki go and shoved the design in Rye's face. "Did you really approve this? Did you tell him to come find me and show me this... this joke?"

This joke. Tahki's work was a joke. He'd been so worried about Sornjia ruining his chances here he hadn't seen the self-destructive nature of his own designs. Rye had been right all along: he was no good. And now, Rye would tell Dyraien the truth, and Tahki's career would be over. None of them would ever trust him again.

Rye looked only at Dyraien and pulled the design gently from his grasp. Dyraien's white knuckles eased a little.

"Yes," Rye said. "I approved it."

Tahki wasn't sure he heard right. He stared at Rye, at his calm expression, not daring to speak, not daring to wonder why he lied.

"Nothing has worked so far," Rye said. "I thought maybe we'd take a chance."

Dyraien's face relaxed a little. He studied Rye, and the longer he looked at him, the more composed he became. There was trust in his eyes, and something else Tahki couldn't place. Hurt, maybe, like he wanted to be angry but something about Rye prevented him.

"I see," Dyraien said. He turned to Tahki. "I didn't expect Rye's judgment to be so poor. I apologize for taking my anger out on you. Please, try harder next time. Things are not going well in the capital, and time is running out." He faced Rye. "Be sure this doesn't happen again."

Dyraien strode back into the queen's room and shut the door behind him.

Tahki tensed, bracing for the inevitable patronization.

Instead, Rye said, "I'd like to show you something." He motioned toward the front door.

Tahki rubbed his wrist, listed a dozen horrible things Rye would do to him as punishment for disobeying a senior order, but followed anyway.

He moved an arm's length behind Rye. They walked northeast on the dirt road, and Tahki noticed the faintest bit of green blooming on the brown grass. The cool air chilled him, but it was better than the intense heat back home. One summer, he'd run outside without shoes on and burned his feet so badly an entire layer of skin had peeled off. He had thought he'd never walk again. How foolish he'd been, overreacting to a little burn, now that he had real troubles to worry about, like where Rye was taking him, if he'd lost Dyraien's trust, if he'd be asked to resign.

After an hour, when his legs grew tired and the silence grew unbearable, Tahki said, "Are you taking me to the middle of nowhere to shoot me or something?" He meant it as a joke, but it came out a little too serious.

Rye slowed so they walked beside one another. "Has anyone ever told you you're overly dramatic sometimes?"

"I like to think of it more as logical pessimism."

"You really think highly of yourself, don't you?"

Tahki shrugged. "There's nothing wrong with confidence. I know my flaws as well as my strengths."

"And what do you think your flaws are?"

"Apparently, I'm overly dramatic sometimes."

This won him a smile from Rye, and despite the recent failure of his design looming over him, Tahki smiled back.

And then he pictured himself kissing Rye. The sudden thought was both ridiculous and surprising, since Rye had never given any indication he was interested in him. And why should Tahki want him to be? He and Rye seemed worlds apart. Still, Rye had been right about the design. Maybe he really was looking out for him. Why else lie to Dyraien?

Tahki scolded himself for letting his mind wander to such a place. Now more than ever, he needed to find a solution. For the second time since arriving in Vatolokít, his architecture hadn't stood up to expectations. If he didn't get this next design right, he'd be finished.

They walked another ten minutes before Tahki saw a pile of stones in the distance. As they grew on the horizon, he noticed they weren't rocks but ruins. They followed the Misty River up to the stones. Rye stopped inside a broken rock wall and folded his arms, waiting for Tahki to look around.

Tahki examined the rubble. The dark red and brown stones lay strewn across the pale dirt in an orderly fashion, like they marked graves. Broken pillars had fallen across the cracked ground. Bits of marble lay here and there. Part of the roof that hadn't been demolished came to a point at the top in a non-Vatolok style. Vines of brown ivy climbed the walls. He found traces of dark oak tables and some shattered blue pots. Then he came across one column still intact, and noticed small golden elephants painted on the side. On another wall, a half sun had been carved in relief.

He stared at Dhaulen'aii's emblem, not quite registering it, like when a stranger calls your name but you don't recognize them, and there's an awkward moment where your brain tries to remember something that's not there.

The Dhaulenian temple was out of place here. It didn't appear destroyed from age or weathering elements. It looked ransacked. Tahki stopped in front of the altar. Back home, it would be covered in gifts for the gods to take back to their home, a place called the Dim. He remembered he and Sornjia would help their father craft colorful gifts out of paper to leave on the altar. Their father would tell them stories of the Dim, how when people died the gods brought their spirits back with them to this afterlife, where they were given a new body and new life. Tahki had asked his father why the gods did this, what they hoped to gain from the process, but his father's answer was always frustratingly vague.

"It's a Dhaulen'aii temple," Rye said. He didn't pronounce the name exact, but it was a difficult name to pronounce without speaking the language. Tahki almost corrected him but then thought better of it. "They used to have a lot of temples like these around the capital, but after the borders closed, they were demolished."

Tahki's thoughts turned dark. Did Rye know where he was from? Was he going to ask Tahki to leave, to turn himself in? Was this a courtesy? A warning? He'd read a book once where a man adopted a wild black-winged fox, but when the fox grew up, the man realized the animal didn't belong in civilization, so he took the fox into the jungle and released it before someone killed it. Was that what Rye was doing? Releasing Tahki from his duties because he knew he didn't belong? Maybe his plan all along was to get rid of him.

"It's sad that the borders were closed," Rye said. "Dyraien says it's for the best, but I think it will only cause more tension between the countries."

Tahki took a breath. Rye didn't know where he was from, or he would have said something.

They sat down next to each other on a stone wall. "It was well-built. I can tell by the condition of the roof," Tahki said.

Rye didn't look at him. "Do you know why I brought you here?"

"Since you don't have a pistol, I assume my 'shoot me' guess was wrong."

Rye didn't roll his eyes, but his mouth twitched upward in a slightly exasperated way. "I wanted to show you this place because I know how overwhelming the castle can be. When I first came here, I felt like the castle was watching me. But that's just the isolation playing games with you." He glanced at Tahki. "The first day I started renovations on the castle, I knocked out the wrong wall. One of the inner supports collapsed. I'd never made a mistake like that before in my life. Lucky for me, Dyraien found it amusing." Tahki sat still, shocked at Rye's sudden openness. "The castle is not a home."

"And this place is?" Tahki said.

"No, but it feels real here. A reminder that there's a world out there. Coming here helps me clear my head."

"So you brought me here because you want me to clear my head?"

Rye nodded. "You've shut yourself in your room for the last week. That kind of seclusion fogs your judgment." They sat so close their hands almost touched.

"Why did you lie to Dyraien?" Tahki said. "I went against your word. I thought you'd love the opportunity to humiliate me."

Rye signed. "Your designs are good, Tahki."

"Then why did you say they weren't?"

Rye slouched a little. "You have talent. Your designs, I can't really put a name to what they are. At first, I thought they were ridiculous, but after seeing your design today, I realize you might be the only person who can give Dyraien what he wants."

"But you rejected that design."

"Of course. It looked too influenced by something already done. But it had potential. A kind of intuitiveness this project needs." Rye ran a hand through his hair. When Tahki messed up his hair, it looked like a rat's nest, but Rye managed to make his look intentionally good-messy. "I want you to come here, to this temple. I want you to walk here or take a gingoat the next time you think up a design. Get away from the castle. Get it out of your head. Sit here, think about the design."

Tahki massaged his wrist. "I'm sorry Dyraien blamed you for my mistake."

"He won't stay mad long."

"He seems to really trust you," Tahki said.

Rye shrugged. "Dyraien saved me from a bad situation. I came to live with him when I was fourteen, just after the queen fell ill. He gave me a home, an education."

Tahki didn't know what to say. He knew Rye came from the lower cities but couldn't imagine a prince inviting someone from the slums to live with him. Maybe their relationship was romantic. But he'd never seen them kiss or go to bed together.

"We lived in the capital a few years after the sickness took hold. The queen was still able to make appearances for a time. She acted normal enough, only she'd say odd things that just didn't make sense. I mean, they sort of made sense, it was just an odd way to say something, like she saw the world different. You probably have no idea what I'm talking about."

Tahki did know and worried Sornjia might suffer from a similar illness. But Sornjia had spoken that way all his life.

"Her health continued to deteriorate slowly, and then rapidly, until she couldn't remember who she was. We moved to this castle for privacy, traveling back and forth as needed. A few years after living here, the queen forgot her own son, and it was then Dyraien dredged up this plan to turn the castle into a weapon. Dyraien hired a weapons expert before Gale, but he wasn't right for the job. We tried for years, different plans, different designs. But nothing ever satisfied Dyraien."

Tahki inched closer. "But the castle seems like so much effort for not a lot of gain."

Rye shrugged a stiff shoulder. "Dyraien is the kind of person who needs to be needed. Who needs people to owe him things. I think this castle will prove him to be a capable leader, show he can defend his country while advancing it technologically."

Tahki bit his lip. Too many questions dodged in and out of his mind. "You said he saved you from a bad situation. What kind of bad situation?"

"You don't have many boundaries when it comes to asking personal questions, do you?"

"Sorry." Tahki found a stick and drew circles in the dirt.

"Everyone has something about them they'd prefer to keep private. I bet even you have some secrets you don't want me to know about."

Tahki glanced at Rye, and for the briefest moment he considered telling him who he was and where he was from. But it didn't seem worth the risk. Rye had finally opened up a little. Confessing might ruin the moment.

"Rye, do you know what's behind the black gates?"

"The black gates?"

"I was wandering around the castle and found two large gates, but they were locked."

Rye frowned. "You mean the gates in the basement?"

"Yes."

"I don't know."

"You've never been down there?"

"Once, when the river flooded. But I never saw what's behind them." Rye thought a moment. "Dyraien said it was something his ancestors built and that I was to leave it alone in my renovations. I think he used to take his mother there sometimes. He said she liked it down there."

Tahki threw the stick. "It still seems strange he'd keep the queen a secret."

"Dyraien loves his people," Rye said. "He wants them to feel safe and protected, and if they saw their ruler in such a state, they might panic. I think Dyraien just wants to prove to them he has both the intelligence and means to protect them."

Rye sounded so certain, but Tahki was still missing some vital piece of information about the castle. Whatever it was, he felt sure Rye didn't know. Bringing Tahki here, motivating him and opening up, all felt so genuine. So raw. Like nothing anyone had ever done for him. No one had ever been on his side, had ever wanted him to succeed. Not since his mother died.

He remembered how he used to sit on her lap when he was a child and watch her draw. How pleased she was when he'd sketch next to her. How patient she was when he'd try to draw a cube, but it didn't come out perfect, and she'd tell him, "Keep practicing. There is no perfection in art, just improvement."

"I'll find a solution," Tahki said. "Just give me a little more time."

Rye stood. "I'm happy to hear that. Dyraien will be too."

Chapter 8

"I can't remember the last time you took an interest in someone," Sornjia said. "I can't remember you *ever* taking an interest in someone. For a time I thought you were like the sand worms. The ones who don't mate, they just cut off their own tails to make offspring."

Tahki peeled an orange for his breakfast over Gale's sink. "I don't have an interest in Rye. I just think he's interesting."

Sornjia washed a dish beside him. "You've been here an hour, and he's all you've talked about."

"I respect him is all."

"Your ears are turning red."

Tahki walked to the old gray couch across from the kitchen table and sucked on a tangy slice. He wiggled and sunk down into the lumpy cushions. The couch smelled like smoke and fish. Shelves to his left displayed an impressive collection of pistols. "So what do you and Gale do all day?"

"You're changing the subject." Sornjia smiled and joined him. "I help her with chores, and she brought me a lot of books to read. She tried to teach me how to shoot yesterday, but guns aren't for me. Too loud. They rattle my brain, and I don't think I'd ever have any use for one."

"Are you speaking normal to her like I told you?"

"Normal as the trees speak to the stars."

Tahki paused on an orange slice and glared at him.

"Yes, Tahki. I try to keep my words like yours. Contained."

"Good," Tahki said. "She's been very patient with us."

"I know."

Tahki had been frustrated that the paper still hadn't arrived, but a small—oh so small—part of him was happy to have his brother there. Tahki had given up everything he'd known, the good and the bad. His home, the heat, his lifestyle, servants, good food, his comfortable silk sheets. It had been exciting at first. But after a few days, Tahki had started to crave the routine he'd become accustomed to for the last eighteen years. Having Sornjia there was like a buffer, though he'd never admit it out loud.

"Sornjia," Tahki said. "Why did you say there was something wrong with the castle?"

Sornjia sat back. He picked at his bottom lip with his teeth. "Do you remember that year we were obsessed with the book series Alabaraiin and the Magic Sandbull, and we spent all summer reenacting his adventures?"

"I remember stealing all the curtains and building a giant fort in the dining room." The servants had complained, but their father just laughed and let them keep it up.

Sornjia nodded. "Well, remember what happened in the Gojuri tree?"

Tahki frowned. He remembered climbing the tree, thinking he could swing from branch to branch. Only the trees in the palace were thin and brittle. Most of the trees in Dhaulen'aii were. He'd climbed high, and a branch gave way. Sornjia had been standing beneath him and broke his fall. He'd ended up with a twisted ankle, Sornjia a broken arm. If his brother hadn't been there, in that exact place at that exact moment, Tahki's head would have split open.

"I know you don't like the way I speak," Sornjia said. "But sometimes I get these feelings, and I don't think words are meant to describe them. Sometimes… sometimes it's like I'm standing on the face of the sun looking down at everyone, and I can see the whole world all at once, so it's easy to understand what's about to happen."

"And you think something bad's going to happen at the castle?" Tahki said.

Sornjia shook his head. "No. I think something bad has already happened."

Tahki sighed. "Are you ever going to be normal?"

Sornjia shrugged. "Will the moon ever give light to the sun?"

Tahki pushed off the couch. "I need to borrow some socks. After all the walking yesterday, I wore a hole in mine." He entered a small room to the right of the kitchen as Sornjia returned to the dishes. The space was only large enough for a small bed and a dresser, but Sornjia hadn't complained.

As he rooted through the drawers, he heard the front door open and close with a bang. Gale must have returned early from Edgewater. After collecting a pair of white wool socks, Tahki went to greet her. He reached the doorway and stopped dead.

There, in the center of Gale's home, Dyraien stood, his eyes locked on Sornjia.

Every nerve in Tahki's body flared up. The hair follicles on his arms rose, and his heart pumped waves of anxiety through him.

He darted back inside the room, praying he hadn't been seen, and peeked around the edge.

Sornjia turned, a dish in one hand, rag in the other, and stared back at the prince.

"Tahki," Dyraien said. His voice sounded cautious, concerned. "Why, might I ask, are you down here cleaning Gale's dishes while she's away?"

Sornjia studied him. Dyraien wore fine white clothing, his hair and skin washed clean. He stood with such elegant posture, Sornjia had to know who he was.

"Dyraien," Sornjia said slowly, as though testing the water before jumping in. "Prince Dyraien."

"I thought we were beyond formalities."

Sornjia set the plate in the sink. "I had to get away from the castle a moment. Helping the elderly clears my mind."

Dyraien squinted at him. They looked identical. Even their father had trouble telling them apart by appearance only. But Dyraien was so observant. A few days ago, he'd asked why Tahki had changed the thickness of graphite in his pencil, when even Tahki hadn't noticed he'd accidentally switched to a lighter tone. The prince's perceptiveness had impressed him then. Now it terrified him.

Tahki held his breath.

"I see," Dyraien said at last. He seemed to relax a little. "I'm happy I ran into you here. I'd like a word, if you have a moment between scrubbing fish guts off the counter."

Sornjia stood still. "We could talk back at the castle." Tahki could hear the strain in his voice, how he tried hard to speak the way Tahki spoke.

Dyraien fluttered his hand dismissively. "Here is fine." He took a step closer. "I owe you an apology. My behavior the other day was uncalled for."

Tahki hadn't told Sornjia about his design error.

Sornjia didn't break eye contact with Dyraien. "Everyone has moments when they feel mice skittering across their mind. Sometimes it's like they chew through the wrinkles of your brain and make you say and do things you don't mean to."

Dyraien stared. His lips parted slightly, brow furrowed.

Tahki was doomed.

"Well," Dyraien said. "I suppose that's one way to put it."

Sornjia smiled. "No storm can rage on forever."

Dyraien studied Sornjia more intently than Tahki would have liked. "Are you quite all right? You're acting... strange. And did you change your clothing from this morning?"

"I fell in the mud and had to change." Sornjia rubbed his left wrist the way Tahki did. "I guess the stress has made my mind foggy."

Dyraien nodded. "Of course." He reached out and rested his hand on Sornjia's shoulder. "And I'm partly to blame for that, I know. How frightened you must have been by my little outburst. Try to understand, Mother has been particularly bad as of late. Her tantrums are growing more violent. It hurts my heart to see her in such a state."

"Mothers are delicate things. As children it's hard to understand, but they break just like the rest of us."

"Yes. They do." Dyraien reached up and traced his thumb across Sornjia's cheek. It was the kind of flirtatious gesture he'd performed a dozen times, when he'd bring Tahki gifts or visit him throughout the day. A small hug. A kind caress. A crooked smile. Tahki had never minded. He'd enjoyed the attention, the kind of affection that didn't require anything in return, just small moments of feeling important.

"What are you doing?" Sornjia said.

"What do you mean?"

Tahki silently begged Sornjia to just leave. Walk out of the house, say he had to get back to work.

"You're petting me like I'm a dog," Sornjia said.

Dyraien's smile faltered. "I'm only being friendly." He removed his hand and ran it through his hair, pink coloring his cheeks. It was the first time Tahki had seen Dyraien blush.

"You should be careful, being friendly like that," Sornjia said. "Some people might take it the wrong way."

"What if I intended it to be taken the wrong way?" Dyraien said. Some certainty seeped back into his voice.

Sornjia gave him a patient smile. "If the moon only rose on intentions, the tides would never flow."

Again, Dyraien could only stare, probably caught between confusion and slight disbelief. It had taken years for Tahki to decipher Sornjia, and even now he had difficulty. Maybe, if they got out of this situation without being discovered, he could convince Dyraien he'd been drunk, or accidentally eaten a mushroom he'd found under a rock, or been dream walking. He'd read some people could carry on entire conversations in their sleep.

Thankfully, Dyraien pulled out a piece of paper from his coat pocket and said, "You seem busy, so I won't keep you. I came here to drop off order details. I need some very specific minerals ordered."

"And you need me to order them?"

Dyraien laughed a little. "No, no. Better leave this task to someone a little more experienced."

Tahki frowned. How would Dyraien know if he was experienced or not? Had his encounter the day before shown that he couldn't be trusted with a simple task?

Sornjia nodded, and Tahki felt annoyed. He wished Sornjia would have told Dyraien he was capable, or that he had lots of experience filling orders. How difficult could it be to drop off a piece of paper?

"I'm leaving these for Gale," Dyraien said. "Our supplier, Zinc, can be a little rough around the edges. He runs a gambling house in Edgewater, and not in the best part of town. I only want Gale doing business dealings with him."

Sornjia shivered, no doubt having one of his bad feelings. Luckily, he said in a straightforward tone, "Will Gale be safe?"

Dyraien grinned. "Your compassion is noble, but don't look so grim. Though we must go through less-than-reputable channels to attain some of our supplies in a timely manner, Gale has worked with far more unstable people. She can handle herself quite well."

Dyraien walked to the table and placed the order details beside a wooden fruit bowl. Then he stuck his hand back in his pocket and retrieved a handful of blue rectangular paper. It took Tahki a moment to realize they were Vatolok notes. The country had recently integrated paper money into their markets to save their copper, silver, and gold supplies.

Dyraien faced Sornjia. "I trust I'll see you back at the castle once you've cleared your mind."

Sornjia gave him a startlingly kind smile. "You can trust me as a fish trusts a stream to carry it to sea."

A final look of doubt crossed Dyraien's face, but he said nothing and left Gale's home without a glance back.

Tahki lunged out of the room. "Are you crazy? Why, why couldn't you have just insisted you talk back at the castle? He probably think's I've lost my mind."

Sornjia sat at the table. "There's something not right about him."

"Don't," Tahki warned. "Don't even start with me." His eyes traveled to the order details. He picked up the paper and read it over. The contents of the list surprised him: Graphite, pyrite, magnetite, olivine, dundasite, bornite, augite, celsian, epidote, calcite, kaolinite, quartz, zippeite, vauxite, abernathyite, brookite, gummite, and at least a hundred more had been scrawled across several pieces of paper.

"I think you should leave it alone," Sornjia said.

"Gale won't be back until late. She won't be able to deliver this until tomorrow."

"Tahki, don't."

"Don't what?"

"Don't deliver the order yourself."

"What makes you think I'd do that?"

"You have that look in your eye." Sornjia leaned forward. "I know you want the people here to like you. You want to prove yourself."

"We owe it to Gale for all she's done for us," Tahki said. "And yes, I'd like Dyraien to come to me for important tasks too. Is that so wrong? Gale said Dyraien never visits her. Ever. These order details must be crucial to our success." He remembered how Dyraien had laughed at the idea Tahki might deliver the details himself. He wanted both Dyraien and Rye to trust him.

"Dyraien said he wanted Gale to deliver them. He seemed adamant about it," Sornjia said.

"Because he trusts her. He doesn't trust me."

Sornjia sighed. "Why do you have to do everything yourself all the time?"

"That's what being an adult is. It's independence. It's being able to do things on your own without help." Tahki scooped up the money and stuffed the order details into his pocket. Before Sornjia had a chance to protest, or to foresee some dark thing in his future, Tahki was out the door, heading back to the castle.

TAHKI STRUGGLED to saddle a gingoat. Rye had shown him how, but it was still difficult. He rode fire camels back home, but the servants always prepared the animals for travel. It didn't help that the creature fought with him now. Every time he walked around her front, she snapped at him. After twenty minutes of curses and struggling with leather, he managed to get on the animal and set off. A light drizzle fell, the fog bank in the distance a familiar sight. He hadn't realized how vibrant the sands back home had looked. The castle here seemed to be caught in a perpetual drear. The road crept along the beach's edge for miles. He would have gone faster, but even at a slow pace, the saddle bruised his rear and his hands blistered from holding the leather reins.

Three hours after he'd left the castle, Tahki rode into town, sore and thirsty. Boats bobbed up and down on the gray sea. The scent of fish attached itself to everything, so thick and pungent Tahki gagged. He didn't understand how anyone could live in a town that reeked like this. Wooden buildings, most weathered by the salty air, closed in tight around him. They all looked scraped together with things that had washed up on shore or parts of other buildings that had been demolished. A series of wooden walkways and planks connected the buildings, as though the inhabitants expected the streets to flood. Steam rose from the cracked cobblestone street. Damp heads glanced up as he rode by. The townsfolk walked at an oppressively slow pace. They all looked so pale or red-faced. He hadn't felt out of place at the capital, but here, he felt exposed. Men and women pulled their dark coats around them, like they wanted to blend into one another, like buying potatoes at the market was a crime. It felt odd to be among so many people again. So many dark eyes darting his way. Was it because he looked like a foreigner, or an easy target, or both?

He tried to avoid eye contact. The market looked so different from the one back home. There were no bright silks hung or merchants competing for his attention or cups of curry shoved in his face. Most of the stalls sold colorless fish. The largest shop sold shiny pistols, the only new-looking things in town. He rode close to one shop with wood planks over the windows. The sign outside read Jaraloine's Brothel. The doors opened for a woman with a hood pulled close around her neck, and the rich scent of perfume stuck thick in his nose. He coaxed his gingoat to move faster.

He wasn't sure where to go but saw a white arrow painted on the side of a building with the words Gambling House below it. It pointed down an alleyway. Dyraien had said Zinc owned a gambling house, and in a small town like this, how many of them could there be?

After dismounting, he found a place to hitch his gingoat. A few other mounts had been tethered to the pole. Then he made his way down the alley, the drizzle soaking him, his heart pounding a little faster than he would have liked. The gambling house wasn't a shop, he discovered, but a series of underground tunnels that ran below the town like a mouse's maze. He found the entrance near a sewage outlet by the beach. He smelled smoke and ale and another warm, salty scent he couldn't place. The tunnel was made of stone and dirt. He swallowed and walked down the throat of the cave. It was lit by a series of green-glowing lightning roots that flickered with every gust of wind that swept behind him.

The first door he came to appeared on his right. He took a deep breath, felt in his pocket for the money and order details, and then knocked. The sensation to run overtook him. Maybe he could find Gale in town, give her the orders, but the door flew open before he could change his mind.

The man's face looked ominous under the dim light. He wasn't old, early thirties maybe, but he had a roughness about him that gave Tahki pause. His hair was shaved close on his head. The corners of his mouth pulled a little too far up his face. A series of white scars ran down his left arm. His tongue dodged in and out of his mouth as he spoke.

"You one of Jaraloine's?" He spoke in a drawl, the kind of accent Tahki identified as southern Vatolok. "Because I asked for a girl."

Tahki frowned. "Dyraien sent me. I have order details. I'm looking for Zinc."

The man clicked his tongue and gave Tahki a slow look up and down. "D said he'd be sending Gale. You don't look like a Gale." The top buttons on his shirt were undone, and sweat gleamed off the black hairs along his chest. His neck looked thick and out of proportion with his body, and his jaw pointed a little too steeply.

"My name is Tahki. I've come in Gale's place."

"Tahki," Zinc said. Tahki wished he hadn't told him his name. He didn't like the way it slithered through Zinc's lips. "Sounds southern. Very southern, when you say it twice. Didn't know D employed so far below the border."

Tahki clenched his jaw. "Are you Zinc?"

"At your service." His words sounded cold, unwelcoming.

Tahki shoved the paper toward him.

Zinc didn't take them. "Snippy, ain't you? Order's in here." He walked backward with a slight limp. Tahki hesitated and then followed. Once in the room, his insides clenched. He plunged his left hand into his pocket and touched his mother's pencil for reassurance. He hadn't felt this much apprehension since he'd crossed the border.

The room was as large as a tavern. No windows, just dirt and rock walls and a bar with dying lightning roots on the counter. Men and women in leather coats drank and smoked at circular tables, playing dice games and shuffling cards. Some of the tenants looked dazed, like they'd just woken from a long nap. They swayed in their seats or held their arms up to the ceiling. A woman sprawled her body across the floor. Another woman sat beside her and stroked her hair.

A child sat under one table, picking at a bowl of almonds. She couldn't have been more than ten years old. Seeing her among the sweaty, drunk inhabitants gave him the sudden urge to grab her and run. Neither of them belonged here.

"This way," Zinc said. He pulled back a dark curtain and Tahki stepped inside a smaller room. The walls were lined with material samples and minerals, some of which he knew were rare and illegal to mine. An old woman in ragged gray clothing shuffled over to them. She held out her hand.

"Order list," Zinc said. He took a tin from his pocket and stuck a piece of what looked like brown tar in his mouth.

Tahki handed over the list. The old woman took it without a word, read it over, and then gathered samples from the wall. She handed them to Tahki along with a small chisel and hammer. He assumed she meant for him to check the quality. He tapped every sample, held one to his ear, smelled a few. He had no idea what he was doing, and for the first time since reading the order list, questioned why Dyraien would need these minerals.

"Nice, ain't it?" Zinc said between chews. He gave Tahki a toothy brown grin.

"Yes, this is fine," Tahki said. He tried to sound authoritative as he handed Zinc the money.

"Right, right," Zinc said. "So you have two hundred notes here. That will get you about half your order."

Tahki frowned. "Two hundred notes should cover everything."

"Say again?"

"Dyraien gave me two hundred notes for the entire list, not half."

Zinc cracked his neck from side to side. "You tryin' to play me, kid?"

"What? No. No playing." Tahki wished he hadn't given him the money. Maybe Dyraien had made a mistake in his calculations.

Zinc spat a black glob on the floor. Some of it splattered on the old woman's bare feet, but she didn't seem to care. "You think I don't know how to do math? D and I go way back. I know what he wants and how much he pays. I'm not the kind of man you want to ex-asberate."

Tahki raised a brow. "Do you mean exasperate?"

"I know what I said."

"Look, I'm not leaving until you honor my order," Tahki said. Zinc clearly wasn't very intelligent. He must have made some calculation error.

Zinc studied him and then threw his head back and smacked himself on the forehead in a dramatic fashion. "I get it. D didn't tell you how this works."

"How what works?"

Zinc moved close to him. Too close. His breath smelled like rotten fish as he exhaled in wet, hot waves. "D comes here all the time, buys some supplies and wins the rest."

"Wins the rest?"

"Sure, sure. Everyone who comes here plays the game. It's the only way we do business. D didn't tell you? See, you take your two hundred notes, bet the money in the rings, win more. It's the only way D can afford it. You know those slimy council bitches back at the capital actually limit his funds? If he withdraws too much, they become suspicious. And we don't want them finding out about D's poor mad mother, do we?" He cooed with a kind of forced patience, the veins on his neck sticking out a little as he spoke.

Tahki stared, stunned. Dyraien had said only Rye and Gale knew about the queen's madness, no one else. Did that mean Zinc also knew about the project? He didn't seem like the type of man Dyraien would trust.

"You look confused," Zinc said with forced sympathy. "Here, let me show you."

Zinc pushed Tahki through the curtain. He maneuvered him around the room, stepping over several people until they found a large table with a group of men and women tossing dice. Tahki wanted to protest, but he didn't know what to say. This was all too much for him. He thought Dyraien's reputation would protect him, but clearly he'd missed some vital piece of information about Zinc and Dyraien's business dealings.

Zinc pushed him down into a hard chair.

"New player?" a woman said. She wore an extravagant red dress that sparkled in the dim light.

"D sent him." Zinc said the words the same way two friends sharing an inside joke might speak.

The woman pursed her lips.

Another woman approached Zinc. She threw her arms around him and whispered something in his ear.

"In a minute. I'm working," Zinc said.

Tahki's legs were shaking. Everything about this felt wrong. He wanted to run. To be far away from Zinc and his smoke-filled den.

"You seem nervous," Zinc said. "Don't worry, kid. You'll do fine. This is a game of intelligence, and you seem very, very smart. Now you just watch those dice. Don't take your eyes off them, you hear?"

Tahki watched. Each player had a gold ring about the width of an apple in front of them. Two larger silver rings were set in the center of the table. A man with a beard placed a paper note in the gold ring and then picked up two of the four dice in front of him. He tossed the dice into one of the silver rings.

"Gain one hundred," the woman in red said. "And earn another throw."

One die was marked with numbers, the other with symbols. He saw a few of the symbols on the sides: two doves, the letter V, a skull. The man picked up the other pair of dice in front of him and threw them in the empty silver ring.

"Gain one hundred. Earn double. Two hundred total gained," the red woman said.

The man smiled and raised his cup of ale.

"See?" Zinc said. "Happy winners. My humble establishment is full of them."

Zinc pushed new dice in front of Tahki. Tahki looked down at them like Zinc had placed a vial of poison in front of him instead.

"Dyraien will be very pleased you've won him something," Zinc said. "And he always rewards those who please him."

A woman with a thin pipe in her mouth reached over and placed the dice in Tahki's hand. They felt heavier than the dice back home, smooth to the touch, made of bone or ivory.

"You said this was a game of intelligence," Tahki said. "But it just seems like dumb luck."

"Just roll the dice, kid."

Suddenly, Tahki didn't want to be holding them. He didn't understand the game, the situation, these people. He wished Rye were here to tell him what to do.

He threw the dice into one silver ring. One landed on a three, the other a skull. Zinc let out a low whistle and popped his lips.

"Down fifty," the red woman said.

"What does that mean?" Tahki said.

"It means," Zinc said, "you'll have better luck next roll. No one wins the first roll."

"I lost?" Panic swept through him. His palms felt sweaty. He rubbed his wrist. The same set of dice appeared in his hands.

"You're only down fifty notes. You still have a hundred and fifty more. Roll again. Trust me."

Tahki shook his head. "I don't think I should." Zinc rested his hand on his hip. Tahki glanced over and saw a pistol strapped to his side. The man's fingers traced over the leather grip.

"I think it would be best for you to roll," Zinc said.

Tahki swallowed. He didn't understand how Zinc had the nerve to threaten him. When Dyraien found out about this, Zinc would be thrown in prison. But then, Tahki realized the only way he'd be able to tell

Dyraien is if he returned victorious. He couldn't lose and go back with nothing or he'd be the one arrested.

Tahki flicked the dice onto the table.

"Down fifty," the woman said.

Zinc handed him the dice. Tahki stared at them.

"I know you'll win this next one," Zinc said.

Tahki rolled the dice around his fingers. The symbol die felt heavy, but only on one side. Instead of rolling, he dropped the dice straight down.

They fell on a five and a skull.

He dropped them again.

Six and a skull.

Again.

Two and a skull.

"These dice are weighted," Tahki said. He announced it loud, so the whole room would hear and know Zinc had cheated them.

The men and women around the table remained silent. No one stood up and shouted with outrage or disgust. They all drank their ale and shuffled their decks. Because they hadn't been playing with weighted dice. Only Tahki had, and they'd all known.

Zinc sucked in a deep breath. "You have about two seconds to clean that dirty mouth of yours, or I'll do it for you."

Tahki stood. His whole body resonated with righteousness. He'd been clever enough to see through Zinc's games. "You're a cheat. When Dyraien finds out, he'll be furious."

"Kid, just accept your losses and leave," Zinc said. Again, his fingers brushed his pistol.

"Best do what he says." The red woman wiggled her fingers at him, and he noticed she was missing her ring finger. "He's got a nasty little temper."

Tahki hesitated and then said, "Just fill part of the order. What I have money for."

Zinc looked at the woman in red. He smiled at her, and she smiled back. Zinc sighed and leaned toward Tahki. "All right, kid. Since D is a good friend of mine, I'll fill the order and you can be on your way."

"Really?" Tahki said, surprised. "I mean, thank you." He felt a surge of adrenaline at his victory. He followed Zinc to the materials room.

"Out," Zinc told the old woman. She left in a hurry.

"Doesn't she need to fill the order?" Tahki said.

A burst of stars appeared in his vision before he tasted the iron in his mouth. His hands slapped the floor when his body fell, and he spat out red. The only sound he heard for a moment was a ringing in his ears. His teeth rattled, and he spat again. Warmth trickled down the side of his head. Everything above his shoulders throbbed in agony.

"Real sorry about this," Zinc said. "But I did warn you. Gave you a chance to leave. Don't say I didn't." He grabbed a fistful of Tahki's hair and yanked him up. Tahki tried to free himself, but Zinc thrust him to the ground, hunched over him, and brought his fist barreling into his throat.

Tahki couldn't swallow any air. He wanted to cry. To scream. To beg someone for help, but his throat burned and constricted and nothing came out. He grasped the black curtain and pulled himself up. Zinc waited patiently, until Tahki finally gulped in ragged, panicky gasps of air. When he could breathe again, he called as loud as he could for help.

Zinc smiled. "That won't work, kid." He lifted Tahki by his shirt and threw him across the room onto a table. Then with slow deliberation, he walked to the table and picked up a saw. "What do you think?" Zinc said. He flicked the blade. "A broken jaw, or maybe a few ribs. Or maybe I cut off that left wrist of yours. You seem so fond of it. 'Course, I could just throw you back out there, let my people do what they want with you. Enria, she's got a taste for young dark-skinned boys."

Tahki heard Zinc's boots click forward. His saliva tasted heavy, and his nose filled with the scent of sweat and blood. The room spun as his hand flailed around for something, anything, that might deflect Zinc. His fingers touched something hard and smooth: a hammer. It didn't have much weight to it, but the end came to a sharp tip. Zinc closed in and grabbed Tahki's shoulder. Before the man could attack again, Tahki heaved the hammer with all his force. He wanted to hit Zinc's face, but his aim was low, and the hammer stuck into Zinc's shoulder instead.

Zinc let out a surprised yelp and stumbled back. "Fucking little shit!"

Tahki kicked him in the stomach. Zinc tumbled back into a pile of crates, and Tahki ran through the curtain. He sprinted beyond the tables, past the men and women at the counter. He ran out the door, down the dark tunnel. His legs cried, and his head felt like a dull weight on his shoulders. It was only after he made it outside, down the cobblestone road, fetched his gingoat—or someone's gingoat, they all looked alike—and was galloping down the dirt road toward the castle, that he started to cry.

Chapter 9

The humiliation burned worse than his jaw. He felt like a fool. A failure. A child. Nothing had gone right since coming here. He wiped his face with his coat sleeve. He'd cried for a while, replayed the incident that had occurred, tried to figure out where it had all gone wrong. He had no idea how to explain himself to Dyraien. He remembered the conversation he'd had with his father before he'd run away, when he'd claimed to be an adult and his father had said he'd seen no proof of that. Going to Zinc's alone hadn't been an adult decision. It had been a childish one.

He needed help.

His first impulse was to find Gale, but she'd already risked so much for him. If she found out he'd lost all Dyraien's money and the order details, she'd do more than hit him over the head with a dead fish.

He arrived back at the castle around midday, untacked his gingoat—who he was pretty sure was male and not the female he'd ridden over—and put it in the stables. When he entered the castle, he touched his face and winced. Blood crusted the edge of his mouth, and the scabs tore painfully when he moved his jaw. He wanted to go to his room to clean it off, but he heard a scraping noise coming from his left. He followed the noise; wood sanding, it sounded like. The sound led him to one of the larger rooms. When he stepped inside, wood dust filled his nose.

Rye worked with his back to him, sanding what appeared to be the underside of a boat. Schematics of boat designs were scattered across the floor. Tahki recognized a few models. They had been displayed in one of the rooms at the fair. He didn't know a lot about boats, but these designs, with their narrow hulls, looked fast.

For a moment, all he wanted to do was watch Rye work. He looked so content.

A flake of wood dust caught in Tahki's throat and he coughed.

Rye glanced up. "Where have you—" He did a double take and dropped his sanding block. "What in the hells happened to you?" Rye was beside him. He looked Tahki up and down, his mouth parted slightly, brow furrowed.

Tahki swallowed the knot in his throat. He felt his legs go weak right above the knee, but he refused to collapse. He wouldn't give Zinc the satisfaction.

"I did something wrong," Tahki whispered.

Rye rubbed his mouth and looked around. "Let's stop the bleeding, and then you can tell me." He led him to a room at the left of the staircase. Dyraien hadn't shown Tahki this place before. The room tucked beneath the staircase and the second floor, giving the area a spacious feel on one end and a cozy feel on the other where the ceiling slanted. The walls were lined with bookcases and brass nautical instruments. Maps of the Calaridian Sea hung on the walls. Dust floated across a pale ray of light let in through an east-facing window.

Tahki felt his body gently pushed onto a wide bed. The sheets had been tucked with precision. Likewise, the entire room looked neat and orderly, aside from the dust. He filled his mouth with air tasting of linseed oil, brass polish, and coffee.

He was in Rye's room.

Rye opened a cabinet and took out what looked like medical supplies: bandages, rags, vials of various green plants, a clear substance in a jar. He laid them beside Tahki on the bed and hunched down in front of him. "Are you in pain?"

Tahki composed himself. He didn't want to break down in front of Rye. He'd cried long enough.

"I'm fine." His jaw throbbed, his legs cried with every movement, the cuts on his body pulsated as blood clotted.

"Tahki." Rye held Tahki's chin up. "Are you in pain?"

Tahki nodded.

Rye fetched two green pills from a cabinet above his bed and handed them to Tahki. "These might make you a little drowsy and light-headed." Then he fetched a glass of water. Tahki swallowed the entire glass in three gulps, then let out a long breath. He picked up the bandages and tried to wrap his arm. His fingers felt swollen from gripping the gingoat's reins.

"Are you going to tell me why it looks like someone tried to make dog food out of my lead architect?" Rye said.

Tahki fumbled with the bandages. They wouldn't stay in place.

Rye took them gently from his hands and unwound them. "Take off your shirt," Rye said. He said it so casually, but Tahki felt too tired to blush. He slid his shirt over his head and cringed as it scraped open the cuts on his stomach. He rested his head against Rye's pillow. It felt firm and smelled like him. Rye took a rag and started to clean the blood from his body. "Talk to me. Tell me what happened."

Tahki stared at the ceiling. "I don't know where to start." He should have been embarrassed, excited, terrified to be in Rye's bed with his shirt off, but his mind didn't seem to want to acknowledge the fact. It didn't seem to want to acknowledge anything. A pleasant haze settled over him, like the fog outside had drifted into the room.

"You weren't at breakfast this morning," Rye said as he dabbed a rag against Tahki's stomach. His hands were rough from working with stone and wood, but also careful, methodical. "Where were you?"

Tahki blinked and took a deep breath. "I was at Gale's."

"Why?"

"I wanted to borrow some tea."

"Did anything happen at Gale's?"

"No. Yes. Dyraien stopped by. He dropped off order details."

"Order details?"

"He needed minerals ordered in Edgewater."

"And?"

"And he asked Gale to order them." His eyes found Rye's face. Concern pressed into the crook of Rye's brow, into the slight downward slant of his mouth. "I went to Edgewater to fill the order for her." He told Rye about his encounter with Zinc, how he lost the money, how Zinc hurt him.

Rye sat beside him after tucking the supplies back in the cabinet. Tahki looked down at the white, bloodstained bandages around his body. He pressed one finger down on his stomach and watched as a bloom of blood appeared around the indent.

Rye pulled his hand away and held on to it. "Are you sure it was Zinc?"

"You don't believe me?"

"I believe you, but Zinc would never cross Dyraien. He's a bastard with sick tastes, and I wish Dyraien wouldn't do business with him, but Zinc's known him longer than I have. It just doesn't make sense he'd scam you. It doesn't make sense Dyraien would send Gale, either. Dyraien insists on ordering the materials himself."

Tahki watched Rye's mouth. His lips formed each syllable with such perfection. Everything about Rye was so exact, so measured. If Rye had gone to Edgewater, Zinc wouldn't have dared cross him.

"Dyraien's going to kill me," Tahki whispered.

"We're not telling Dyraien anything. Not yet."

Tahki rocked his body back and forth until he managed to pull himself upright. The pain numbed, but he still felt tired. "What are you going to do?"

"I'm going to pay Zinc a visit." Rye dropped Tahki's hand and stood. There was anger in his voice. A kind of restrained rage Tahki had never heard in him before. It sounded like Rye took it personally, as though he had been the one who'd been scammed.

Tahki grabbed Rye's arm. His skin felt smooth and firm. The muscles beneath tensed. "I'm going with you."

Rye carefully pushed him away. "You need to rest. Just tell me where the gambling house is."

Tahki stood, wobbled, steadied himself. "This is my mistake, Rye. I want to fix it." He couldn't let him go alone. If anything happened to Rye, he didn't think he'd be able to live with himself. Not that he'd be much help, but the idea of waiting here for the next six hours for Rye to travel there and back seemed unbearable.

Rye studied him. His eyes moved over his injuries. "You're bleeding from all ends and you still won't listen to me."

Tahki straightened his back, the painkillers giving him false strength. "But this is different. I'm not being stubborn because of pride. I want to go because I want to help make things right. I know I can't do it on my own, but I can't let you go alone, either. If anything happened to you, I'd—" Tahki stopped himself. The drugs had loosened his tongue, and he was afraid of what he'd almost confessed. "I'd... I'd feel very bad. Besides, you need me to show you where the gambling house is."

Irritation settled in Rye's eyes, but after a moment, he relaxed a little. "Fine, you can come. But promise me you'll leave at the first sign of trouble."

TAHKI LEANED his head against Rye's back as they rode. He felt Rye's shoulder blades roll in and out as he steered the gingoat. Tahki must have dozed, because they'd only just left when the smell of fish woke him. His damp hair fell against Rye's back. He watched it swish across the dark leather a moment and then jerked his head up. His hands were wrapped around Rye's waist. He loosened his grip.

"You awake?" Rye said.

"I think." His mind still felt a little hazy. "Where are we?"

"We're almost to Edgewater. You're sure you can find the gambling house again?"

Tahki craned his head forward. "Yes, I can find it again. So, you've never been there?"

"No. Like I said, Dyraien always handles that stuff. He's very particular about it, and I avoid Edgewater when I can."

"Why?"

"It's just a bad town."

Tahki rubbed sleep from his eyes. He bumped one of the bandages on his face, but the cut beneath didn't bleed. Rye had wrapped and cleaned it well. "Why do you think Dyraien wanted Gale to deliver the order this time?"

Rye shrugged. "I'm more interested in why you went in her place."

Tahki shifted in the saddle. "After what happened the other day, I thought Dyraien thought I was incompetent. Like one mistake and he couldn't trust me. Ordering the minerals seemed like a good way to prove to him I wasn't worthless."

Rye slowed the gingoat. "Everyone makes mistakes. That doesn't mean you're worthless." He hesitated and then said, "You don't have to try so hard. You've got a gift. Don't spoil it by overthinking and rushing ahead."

Before Tahki could reply, Rye tugged the animal to a halt. The town didn't appear as unfriendly as it had before. They'd entered a different area, avoiding the brothel and fish market. Shop owners sold stands of buttered bread; a woman who owned a smaller pistol shop helped a young man shoot a gun; a red dog ran beside a boy in the street.

Rye dismounted and then helped Tahki down. Tahki held his breath as Rye gripped him.

"How's the pain?" Rye said.

Tahki almost said fine but stopped. Rye was right. He didn't need to try so hard to prove himself. "The pain isn't crippling, but it isn't comfortable, either."

Rye nodded, reached into his bag, and gave him two more pills. Tahki popped them in his mouth as Rye tethered the gingoat. Once the animal was tied, Rye pulled a sheathed hunting knife from the saddlebag and secured it to his hip. The sight of the knife sobered Tahki. He'd never seen Rye with a weapon before.

"You don't have to do this. Really," Tahki said. "I'll take the blame. If Dyraien doesn't want me working for him anymore, I can find a job someplace else." The words came easier than expected. The thought of losing his job scared him, but seeing Rye with that knife sent a wave of panic coursing so fiercely through his body that for a moment he genuinely didn't care if Dyraien fired him.

"People like Zinc are a lot like eastern jungle cats," Rye said. "Make yourself appear bigger and stronger, and they'll go tails-tucked back into the trees."

Tahki started to protest, but Rye moved quickly toward the town.

When they reached the underground tunnels, Tahki shivered.

"You sure you want to come with me?" Rye asked.

Tahki reached up and knocked on the door. The woman in red answered. She looked at Rye and gave him a seductive smile, but when her eyes landed on Tahki, she frowned and said, "Something I can do for you gentlemen?"

"Where's Zinc?" Rye said. Tahki could hear the anger clenched between his teeth.

The woman pursed her lips. "Probably stuck between the legs of some whore."

Rye shoved her aside and strode into the smoke-filled room. He walked to the nearest table and scooped up a handful of flickering lightning roots. Then he unlatched the knife from his side and sliced them open. They popped and bubbled, pink and blue light from inside draining onto the table, hissing and smoking as it touched the wood. The couple at the table jumped back.

"Are you out of your damn mind?" the woman in red said.

Tahki reached Rye's side and cringed. Lightning roots were highly toxic when cut open, which was why they'd been banned in most countries. If enough raw liquid hit the open air, a person could be poisoned from inhaling it. A root's outer case was thick, so leaks didn't happen often, but a sharp blade could puncture it. Rye held them with his bare hands like a bouquet of flowers, and then released the empty casings, reaching for a fresh handful.

"I'd hate for you to shut down your establishment due to air contamination," Rye said. "How much money do you suppose you'd lose? I hear it takes a month to properly cleanse the air and soil after a root leak."

"Now, now, let's all just calm down," said a slow, rough voice. Tahki turned and saw Zinc standing a few feet away. "Any friend of D's is always a welcomed guest here."

Rye let the roots fall. "Is this how you treat a friend of Dyraien's?" He gestured to Tahki.

"Not sure what the kid told you," Zinc said. "But it's your word over mine, and D and I were friends long before you entered the picture."

Rye stepped forward so he stood face-to-face with Zinc. "Dyraien isn't here now. It's just me, and I believe Tahki."

Tahki's heart palpitated. Rye looked strong, but could he take Zinc in a fight? The other man probably had no qualms about fighting dirty, and the sober-looking men and woman in the house had already formed a kind of lopsided circle around the two of them. Rye's knife hung visibly by his side, but he didn't reach for it.

Zinc rubbed his jaw. "Never understood what D saw in you. I told him long ago to drown you in the river. It's the proper way to dispose of a stray."

"You have your money," Rye said. "Now fill the order."

Zinc glanced to Tahki.

"Don't look at him," Rye said.

Zinc laughed. "You know, D said you never went to brothels. I always assumed you were some kind of eunuch. But I guess it wasn't about the parts a person had, it was about the color of skin."

"The order, Zinc. Fill it."

And then Zinc took a step back, put up his hands, and nodded. Tahki watched, surprised, because Zinc had no reason to back down.

"All right, calm down," Zinc said. "I'll fill the order." He snapped his fingers, and the woman in red came to his side. He nodded to her, and she vanished behind the curtain, reappearing a moment later with the order list. Zinc snatched the list and wrote something on the paper.

"Done," Zinc said.

The men and women around them returned to their tables.

Rye relaxed his shoulders. "Let's go," he said to Tahki.

Tahki turned, happy to leave. Before they made it outside, Zinc called, "Better stay close to that bodyguard of yours, kid." Tahki glanced back. Zinc grinned at him. "He ain't always gonna be around."

Rye grabbed Tahki's wrist and hurried him along. They made it outside, through the tunnels, and back to the gingoat before any words were exchanged.

"I didn't think he'd actually agree," Rye said.

"Then why'd you threaten him?"

He faced Tahki. "Because I couldn't let him get away with what he did to you."

Tahki felt himself blush and pretended to look at the sky. "Why do you think Zinc gave up without a fight?"

"I guess he realized Dyraien would find out and didn't want the trouble," Rye said.

Again, something didn't feel right. Though he could have easily overpowered them, Zinc seemed to fear Rye. Or maybe it hadn't been Rye who'd spooked him. Maybe it had something to do with how Dyraien would react if anything happened to Rye. But Tahki was too tired to think about it.

"Rye?"

"What?"

Tahki rubbed his wrist. "Thank you."

Rye shrugged. "It felt good to take Zinc down a peg."

"I don't mean only with Zinc," Tahki said. "Thank you for taking the fall for my design error. For getting me on the right path with my architecture. For watching out for me." It might be the painkillers, but his words, for the first time, sounded sincere.

This time it was Rye who blushed. He turned stiffly away. "We should get back to the castle before we're missed."

Tahki nodded. "Agreed."

Chapter 10

Two days had passed since his encounter with Zinc, and this morning was the first morning he hadn't needed to take painkillers. His head still hurt, but he decided he could tolerate the pain if it meant keeping a clear mind. Dyraien had asked about his bruises, and Tahki had told him a gingoat had kicked him. The prince offered to put the animal down, but Tahki begged him not to. Tahki had also told Gale he'd filled the order for her. He lied and said everything went fine, but she whacked him on the head with a wooden spoon anyway and said not to do her any favors. The paper for Sornjia's documents still hadn't come, and Gale reordered it. Tahki hadn't told her about Dyraien's visit, a risky choice, but Sornjia said he'd be extra cautious in case he stopped by again.

A few things still bothered Tahki about the incident in Edgewater. First, Gale claimed she'd never dealt with Zinc before, but Dyraien claimed she had, so one of them was lying. Second, when Gale dropped off lunch yesterday afternoon, Dyraien appeared agitated around her. Third, Rye told Dyraien Zinc tried to steal their money. He gave him a different version of the story so as not to condemn Tahki or Gale but made certain to emphasize the scam. Dyraien only shrugged and told him that that was the risk of hiring criminals. Tahki had expected him to be outraged, not indifferent.

Although these things troubled him, something good had come of the Zinc incident: his friendship with Rye. They hadn't spoken much the last two days, but every few hours Rye would happen by his room and glance in to see if his injuries were healing. This morning, Tahki had woken up extra early to help Rye lunge the gingoats, a task he hadn't enjoyed, but he liked spending more time with Rye.

He drew busily now at his desk, ideas popping into his head left and right. Though none of his designs were completed, a few of them showed potential.

Tahki leaned back in his chair and stretched his arms, careful not to strain too hard, when he heard a loud thump a few rooms down. He sat still in his chair and listened. Two more thumps sounded. The walls rang lightly from the vibration. The castle had been unusually quiet this morning. Not even the queen wailed.

Three more thuds knocked against the wall, and this time he followed the sound to the taxidermy room. The door was closed. He heard footsteps inside. Maybe Dyraien had brought his mother to pet the animals.

Something inside hit the floor with a *thunk*. Tahki knocked. "Dyraien?" No one answered. He pushed the handle slowly and slid his body through the gap in the door. A plume of dust rose among the animal heads and bodies. He looked around the room until his eyes settled on the great black cat in the center. Someone had pushed her over. The wind might have tipped her, but the windows were shut, and she looked too heavy to be brought down by a draft.

He stared at the great black beast. She looked so foreign here, contained in this small room. He wondered where she'd been caught, where the bullet had pierced her, taking away her last breath, and then he thought of Sornjia. His brother always sympathized with animals, even dead ones. One time he tried to save a few goats from the meat markets, but their father made him return them. Sornjia fasted and meditated for three days straight after that, and when he emerged, he said he understood that everyone must make their own choices in life, and he wouldn't interfere with the life of a shepherd again. Tahki hadn't understood what Sornjia meant at the time, but now he knew it was about choices. Sornjia chose not to eat or harm animals, but he couldn't make that choice for someone else.

Tahki started to leave the room, but the idea of leaving the cat on the ground seemed wrong somehow. He reached down to try to tilt her upright, but as he did, the faintest grumble rolled out from inside her throat.

He froze.

The cat lay still. He'd probably imagined it and reached for her again. When his hand touched her face, a jolt of energy surged through him, the way static moves, only it shot through his entire body.

Tahki jerked back. His body tingled, arms and legs feeling as though they were asleep. He rubbed his sides until his skin felt normal again and faced the creature. The dark walls of the castle felt too close. The air in the room tasted humid. He took a deep breath and then reached for the animal one more time.

The cat blinked.

Tahki stopped. "What?"

He stared as she turned her moist, reflective eyes his way. Before he could act, the black cat leaped off the floor, her paws catching him in the belly. She bared her long white fangs in his face. He squirmed beneath her, pain coursing through his body from his previous injuries. He kicked as hard as he could at the fur on her belly. The cat moved an inch, and he slid out from under her, scrambling to his feet.

She hunched in front of the door, claws extended. He ran to the other end of the room where hunting knives hung on the wall. He grabbed one with a red handle and faced her, his back pressed between deer antlers. The cat released a deep roar that drummed in his skull. Several boar heads fell off the wall. He wanted to scream for help, but her roar would bring everyone there.

The cat lunged. Tahki darted left and brought the knife into her shoulder. It didn't go deep, but it stuck. She knocked his body over with one paw the size of his chest. His breath left him and he gasped, falling to the floor as an explosion of pain tore through him.

The cat regarded the knife with an intelligent look of irritation. Tahki watched in horror as a nest of black, oily eel-like creatures erupted from the wound. They slithered like ink around the knife, formed a sleek black hand, and yanked it out. It fell to the floor with a clank. He had read stories and seen illustrations of gods and demons, but he'd never seen anything like her. She turned toward him and padded forward, her golden eyes flickering like the sun.

Tahki scooted back. He sat about ten feet from the door and stood slowly. The cat growled and lowered her head, muscles tensed, ready to pounce. Then he reached behind him and grabbed a taxidermy black-winged fox with both hands. Before she had a chance to attack again, he hurled the fox at her face and jolted for the door. The cat hissed and screeched, and he heard her paws leave the ground. He reached the door, slid into the hallway, and slammed it shut behind him, his body bracing against it for the expected impact.

Nothing hit the door. He waited and pressed an ear to the wood. No sound stirred inside.

"What are you doing?"

Tahki jumped. Dyraien stood in the hall, watching him.

"Aren't you a sweaty mess," Dyraien said. "What have you been up to?"

Tahki swallowed. "I... I was...."

"Yes?"

He studied the prince. Surely he'd heard the cat roar or wondered about the sounds of their fight. Tahki's hands shook, his teeth pressed together, and his knees buckled. Below them, he heard Rye sawing in his workshop. No one had heard, and he couldn't tell them about the cat. They'd think he was crazy.

"I just wanted to stretch my legs," he said in the most confident voice he could muster. "I guess I'm a little out of shape."

Dyraien raised an eyebrow. "You know there are at least a thousand acres of land outside to run around on. But you chose to do it in here?"

Tahki tried to shrug, but his muscles felt stiff with fear. "I wanted to be near my room in case I had an idea."

Dyraien smiled a little, but it was an impatient smile. "And how are your ideas coming along?"

Tahki needed to look inside the room to see if the cat was there or if it had been another hallucination.

"Actually," Tahki said. "I have a design. It might take me a few days to finalize it, but I think you'll be pleased."

Dyraien beamed at this. "That's good to hear, Tahki. That's very, very good." He opened his mouth, shut it, then opened it again. "I was beginning to think—well, never mind. I look forward to seeing your work." He walked away with a smile on his face, and Tahki wished he hadn't lied. None of his ideas were close to perfect. But he'd needed Dyraien to leave him alone so he could process the cat attack.

Tahki held his breath, turned to the door, opened it a sliver. Nothing stirred inside. The black cat was gone. The boar heads lay on the ground, the red-handled knife resting in the center. Tahki brought his hand to his chest and cringed. He lifted his shirt. A great red mark spread across his skin, tiny beads of blood dripping down from where the cat had pounced.

This wasn't right. The last time he'd hallucinated, everything had reverted to its original state. There had been no water in the halls, and his clothing had been dry. But now he bled, and the taxidermy room looked like a sandbull had been let loose inside.

Which meant it hadn't been a hallucination. But that was impossible. Dead things didn't come to life. And why had no one else seen it? Heard it? A cat that size couldn't simply vanish.

Tahki limped cautiously back to his room. This castle wasn't safe. Something was after him. Only him. He needed to tell someone, to get help. Whatever was happening to him, whatever this dark thing was that hunted and tormented him, he knew he couldn't ignore it any longer.

Chapter 11

"If you keep scratching, it won't heal," Sornjia said.

Tahki scratched the clawmark on his chest. The wound had swollen and pushed up red skin in three lines. He sat in Sornjia's room, if it could be called a room. The air tasted stale in the small space, like too much breath filled it. Sornjia didn't complain, not about the rickety bed that moaned like a dying dog every time you shifted your weight, or the musty odor of boiled clams from downstairs, or the unsettling old lady noises Gale's body produced on an all-seafood diet. But Sornjia was too much like their father. He took every unsavory situation as a humbling experience.

"So what are you going to do?" Sornjia said.

Tahki scratched at his wound. "I don't know. If I knew, I wouldn't have asked for your help."

He had told Sornjia everything last night: the dark shape in his room, the water, the black gates, Zinc, the cat. Sornjia hadn't ridiculed him, but that didn't make Tahki feel any better. He wanted his brother to tell him he was being paranoid, that it was all in his head, that he should see a doctor. But Sornjia had listened, both sympathetic and patient, never once calling his sanity into question.

Sornjia sat beside him. "You won't like what I have to say."

"How do you know?"

"You want me to say it's anxiety or something logical, something you can contain and control."

"Maybe it is."

Sornjia pointed at the marks on his chest. "Those don't look like a manifestation of an overworked imagination."

Tahki reached for his shirt and tugged it over his head. "Fine. What do you think happened?"

Sornjia curled his fingers into his palm. "I feel like a sparrow's wings are fluttering just under my eyelids."

"Sornjia."

"I have a confession to make," Sornjia said. "But you can't be angry."

"What kind of confession?"

Sornjia reached under his pillow and pulled out a handful of blue paper. Tahki stared at the paper. "It came a few days ago," Sornjia said. "Gale brought back a stack of letters from Edgewater. I found it before she sorted through the pile."

"Why didn't you tell me?" The encounter with Dyraien might have been avoided if Sornjia had told him about the document papers.

"I couldn't leave you alone," Sornjia said. "The castle, I think it's afraid of you."

Tahki sat on his hands so he wouldn't scratch. Though he should have been furious at Sornjia, it was nice to have someone to talk to, even if that someone spouted crazy theories.

"The castle isn't alive," Tahki said.

"Didn't you always say you wanted to give your drawings life? That you treat architecture like a living, breathing thing?"

"It's just an expression. Besides, I'm the victim here. That thing attacked *me*. Not the other way around."

"How big did you say the cat was?"

"It was the size of a sandbull, only slender."

"Right," Sornjia said. "And you just happened to get away because you're such a great fighter?"

Tahki frowned. "What do you mean?"

"If a creature that size wants to kill you, it will kill you."

"It *did* try to kill me."

"It barely scratched you."

"I thought you said you believed me."

"I do. But I think you're interpreting the events wrong. I think the castle is trying to tell you something, and you need to listen."

Tahki flopped back and the bed moaned. The cat had been real. He couldn't deny that. Did that mean the water had been real as well? Or the dark thing in his room? Had the cat visited him the first night?

"I think you should tell Rye," Sornjia said.

"Why would I do that?"

"You trust him."

"Which is exactly why I shouldn't tell him. He'll think I'm crazy."

"He helped you with Zinc. Why wouldn't he help you with these encounters as well?"

"Because Zinc is real. But these encounters? I'm not sure what they are. No one else has seen them or heard them or been bitten by them."

"Which is all the more reason to tell Rye," Sornjia said. "Trust is something that situates itself inside you and ties all your muscles and bones together. It's a feeling of wholeness, a feeling of control even when you have none. He'll listen to you, Tahki. He'll believe you."

Tahki pulled a pillow over his face and let out a muffled groan. "I'm not involving Rye." He threw the pillow on the bed. "And don't you try to involve him, either. He's not some merchant I upset in the market you need to apologize to on my behalf. Pretending to be me here could get us both killed."

Sornjia bowed his head. "If that's how you feel, I'll leave it be. But we can't ignore what's been happening to you. Dyraien is hiding something. I sensed something inside him when he came to the house, something unsteady, like he and I teetered on a thin piece of wood, trying to balance the other's weight. Maybe he has something to do with the strange encounters."

Tahki knew Dyraien wasn't telling him everything about the purpose of the castle, but it made no sense to bring Tahki here just to torment him. "Dyraien gave me my freedom. Where would I be if he hadn't hired me?"

"He has control over you, over the castle, over the people in the castle. And when people like that lose control, they become dangerous."

"Dyraien isn't dangerous."

"He's a prince about to lose his country. There isn't anything more dangerous than a person about to lose something."

A metal pot banged against the wall downstairs. "Make yourselves useful and set the table," Gale's raspy voice called.

They stood up at the same time. "What should I do, Sornjia? I can't tell Rye. I've caused him enough trouble."

"You need to find out what Dyraien is keeping behind those black gates."

Before Tahki could reply, Sornjia skipped out of the room. Tahki followed his brother downstairs into the kitchen. Gale had set out a plate of clams and a large bowl of rice.

"Too busy to help with lunch?" she asked.

Sornjia smiled. "Tahki is having nightmares."

Gale snorted. "Problems of entitled children are never problems."

Tahki picked at a clam. "You don't have anything else?"

"I have an old shoe you can suck on," Gale said. She stuck a glob of clam in her mouth and chewed in circles, the way a gingoat chews hay.

"Thank you for lunch," Sornjia said. He took a heaping pile of rice but left the clams. Apparently clams had feelings too and weren't on his list of things he could eat. Tahki was surprised he ate anything at all. Sornjia had said once that plants could talk and water could feel, like the entire world was a sentient thing.

Tahki rolled the clam in circles around his plate.

Gale sighed. "If you don't like it, you can fish in the river. Every year around this time the blue-headed trout make their way to the ocean. It's easy catching."

"I don't fish," Tahki said.

"Too good for that too?"

"He's afraid of water," Sornjia said.

"What a silly thing to fear."

"Our mother threw him in a lake when he was five," Sornjia said. "He almost drowned."

Tahki's pulse thumped in his throat. Sornjia had said it so casually, like it was nothing. Like the worst night of his life made for casual table conversation. Gale regarded Tahki curiously.

"You make her sound like a monster," Tahki said. "She saved my life."

Sornjia gave Gale a sad smile. "The palace caught fire. Father and I got out, but Mother and Tahki were trapped inside. She picked him up and threw him out the window into the lake below, but the fire was too fast. She couldn't get out."

The events played through Tahki's head in the same order they always did: drawing with his mother, the thick smell of ash, the burst of heat, the screams, the trembling arms that wrapped around him, the fall, the cold, the struggle for air, the blackness. He'd read once that people only remember a small portion of a memory, but Tahki would remember the fear he had felt that night for the rest of his life. His father had called it a miracle when Gotem rescued him. A one in a million chance that

Gotem had seen Tahki plunge. Sornjia said it hadn't been luck or chance, that Gotem had known. But if Gotem had known, why not stop the fire? Why not save his mother? Fortune-telling was a cheap trick used on the weak-minded. No one could know the future, just like no one could change the past.

Tahki glanced at Gale, expecting mockery.

"I'm sorry," Gale said. For the first time since meeting her, he saw something akin to pity in the hard lines of her face. Before Tahki could reply, a loud knock rattled the door. Sornjia scooted into his room without being told. Tahki wondered who it could be. Dyraien or Rye wouldn't knock, and no one was supposed to know about the location of the castle. Except Zinc. And possibly Zinc's people. And maybe half of Edgewater for all he knew.

Oddly, Gale didn't seem concerned. She sighed, shuffled to the door, pulled it open. Tahki followed her. A woman stood on the porch. Her long brown hair hung in damp clumps. She leaned her pale body against the rail and smirked. Tahki's eyes settled on her breasts, which were round and full and hardly contained under her tight blue shirt. He had never found breasts particularly interesting, nor had he found attraction in how curved a woman's backside was, yet he felt he couldn't look away from her. She was gorgeous. The kind of woman other men or women might buckle at the knees looking at.

"I thought you'd be taller," the woman said. "But you're prettier than I imagined. Guess D didn't exaggerate that part." It took Tahki a moment to realize she was talking to him, and another moment to realize he was still staring at her chest. He felt heat rise to his face and forced himself to meet her eyes.

Gale grunted. "I thought you weren't coming until next week."

The woman shrugged. "You know me. I'm full of surprises."

Gale wiggled her jaw. "When a gingoat surprises its rider by acting out, it usually wins itself a good beating."

"Charming as always," she said. "I got a letter from D. He's moved up the timeline and needed me to come early."

"He never mentioned anything to me." Gale folded her arms. "So why are you here?"

"I just told you. D sent for me."

"I mean, why are you at my house? You looking for handouts?"

Though Gale's tone was full of apparent loathing, the woman laughed. "I knew D wouldn't tell anyone, and I didn't want to surprise Rye. You know how he gets. Figured I'd stop in here first, let you soften the blow."

"I'd rather crap out a brick than do you a favor."

The woman pushed her way inside. "It's a favor for Rye. You and I are on the same team. We want the same thing. Might as well play nice, right?"

"If you wanted to play nice," Gale said, "you would have stayed in Edgewater."

Tahki cleared his throat.

The woman turned his way. "My name's Hona. I'm Dyraien's advisor. And you, you must be Tahki." She clicked her tongue. "Tahki. I like the way your name sounds. D talked a lot about you in his letters."

"Glad to meet you," Tahki said. He wondered what Dyraien had written about him.

Hona pressed a finger to her lower lip. "You look worn out. I hope D isn't pushing you too hard."

Tahki stifled a yawn. "No, he's been very generous with me. I had a late night, that's all."

Hona gave him a wry grin. Her expression reminded him a little of Dyraien. "Oh? And what kept you up so late?"

Tahki rubbed his wrist. "Work." And the fear of being eaten by a dead cat.

"Be careful," Hona said. "Too much time in that castle will drive you crazy."

Tahki forced a smile. It seemed the small circle of people who knew about the castle grew every day. At first, he had felt like he was part of something special. Now, the secret felt less important. Less exclusive. He wondered why Dyraien had been so adamant about Tahki's silence. Maybe it was the color of his skin after all. Though he'd been treated with respect, he was still a foreigner. He would always be a foreigner here.

"How's Rye?" Hona said.

Tahki shifted his weight. First Hona had mentioned she didn't want to surprise Rye, now she was asking about his well-being. Why would Dyraien's advisor be worried about Rye?

"Happy," Gale said. "No thanks to you."

"That's what Dyraien wrote." Hona folded her arms. "I didn't believe it. Happy and Rye aren't exactly synonymous."

"Fancy word use," Gale said.

"I've been practicing. Tuning my manners all ladylike." Hona wiped her nose with her arm.

"You're going to see him, aren't you?" Gale said.

"Of course. You don't ignore someone you love."

Tahki's mouth dropped a little. Love wasn't the kind of word you threw around the workplace. He had never seen Rye take an interest in anyone, but maybe there had been a reason for that. Maybe Hona was Rye's lover. Or wife. Rye never gave any indication he preferred men.

Hona scrunched her nose. "Does he talk about me?" Tahki pressed his lips together and waited. He didn't trust himself to speak.

"Why would Rye talk about you?" Gale said.

"Wishful thinking on my part," Hona said. "After almost a decade, you'd think he'd forgive his only sister."

"Sister?" Tahki blurted.

"Older sister," Hona said.

Relief washed over him. He tried not to let it show and took a deep breath. He wondered why Rye had never mentioned a sister. He'd never mentioned anything about his family. Tahki assumed he'd been an only child, maybe even an orphan.

"Have the kid take you up," Gale said. "I'm busy."

"If you say so." Hona turned to Tahki. "All right, green eyes. It's just you and me. I've been traveling all night and could use a bath and some ale."

As they walked through the afternoon fog, Tahki thought about the document papers Sornjia had hidden under his pillow. If Gale saw them, she'd throw Sornjia in a meat pot. He knew he should send Sornjia home, but what if the black cat returned and he needed to talk to someone? Hona's arrival proved he still knew next to nothing about Rye, so he couldn't confide in him.

"You're quiet," Hona said. "After spending weeks locked up in that castle, I thought you'd love the opportunity to talk to someone new."

"Sorry," Tahki said. He'd wanted to talk to her, but every question he thought to ask seemed intrusive, because they were all about Rye.

Hona flicked her hair. "I'm going to ask you something." It wasn't a question but a statement, like she was preparing him.

"All right," Tahki said.

Hona licked her lips. "Are you and Rye involved?"

Tahki felt a twist in his gut. "What do you mean?" He knew what she meant.

"I mean, are you two having sex?"

The question was so absurdly blatant. He wanted to appear casual, like he wasn't embarrassed or upset or confused, but a lump rose in his throat and the hairs on his arm felt like tiny needles, and he knew his voice would shake when he spoke. "No. We're not… involved."

"Why not?"

Tahki pinched his brow. Her voice sounded strangely petulant. "I don't know how to answer that," he said. They were almost to the castle, and he hurried his pace.

Hona matched his speed. "You like him, don't you?"

"Why would you think that?"

"D told me you've taken a liking to Rye."

"We work together, that's all."

"D also said he's taken a liking to you."

No one back home would dare mention these things out loud. The entire conversation left him feeling exposed. Yet a small part of Tahki delighted at the idea Rye might be attracted to him.

"I'm making you uncomfortable," Hona said as they reached the front doors. "Listen. Things are going to get unpleasant when we go inside, but no matter what happens, I need you to know that I love my brother, and all I want is for him to be happy."

Tahki didn't have time ask questions. She walked inside the castle and held a high-pitched note for five seconds, calling Dyraien's name.

A minute later, Dyraien jogged down the steps.

"I've just put Mother to bed," he said. His tone sounded more impatient than angry.

"How is Old Loopy doing?"

"Please refrain from calling the queen 'Old Loopy.'" Dyraien ran a hand through his hair. "She's getting sicker each day. How is the council?"

"Impatient."

"How long do we have?"

"A month."

"Shit."

"They would have given you to the end of the year, but you missed the last meeting. They're going to ask for the queen's resignation."

"They've become bold in her absence. I remember a day when just the mention of my mother's name would send them cowering under their desks." Dyraien sighed. "Do they suspect anything?"

"It's been almost ten years since Queen Genevi has done anything noteworthy. When someone with such a fierce reputation suddenly vanishes, all people have is their suspicion. It's only thanks to her reputation they've stalled this long."

Dyraien drew in a slow breath. "What about my people?"

"The people want an election. They like the idea of voting for a leader. There are already three candidates lined up."

Dyraien appeared calm, but Tahki didn't know why. If he'd followed the conversation correctly, Dyraien only had a month to complete the castle to try and get in good standing with the council before a new leader would be elected.

"You still want to go through with this?" Hona said.

Dyraien held his head up and flicked a strand of blond hair from his eyes. "Of course. You're not getting out of this that easy."

For a second, Hona tensed. "I wasn't trying—"

Dyraien gave her a cruel grin. Hona fell silent, and again Tahki felt like a wide-eyed child watching his parents argue over a matter he couldn't understand.

"Nothing has changed," Dyraien said in a soft voice. "Do your job, and don't ever second-guess me." He looked at Tahki for the first time since they'd started talking, and his expression lightened. "Tahki, would you join us for dinner tonight?"

He'd never been invited to dine with Dyraien before. It caught him a little off guard. "I'd be honored."

"Excellent. We can hear about your progress."

Tahki felt the area under his rib cage flutter with anticipation. He had made no progress and doubted he would anytime soon, not with the black cat roaming the castle.

"You can use my bath," Dyraien said to Hona.

Hona shook her head. "Not before I see him."

"Do you think that's a good idea?"

"I think it's a horrible idea, but I'm going to see him."

Dyraien shrugged. "Very well. But behave yourself."

Though Tahki wasn't invited, he followed as Dyraien took her to Rye's workroom. If they minded his company, they said nothing.

The overturned boat blocked part of the doorway. Tahki startled when Dyraien spun around, grabbed his shoulder, and pushed him not so gently into the room first. Rye was reading a newspaper at his table but looked up when Tahki stumbled in. Their eyes met, and Rye grinned. Tahki smiled back. But then Rye's face twisted into a horrible frown.

"I don't get a smile?" Hona said.

Tahki stepped out of the way.

Hona touched the underside of the boat. "Looks nice. Think she'll be water-ready by next spring?"

"Get out," Rye said. "Get the fuck out of here."

The hatred in Rye's voice surprised him. He'd never heard Rye use foul language before, not even when they'd gone to see Zinc.

"Let's keep it civil," Dyraien said.

Rye stood and faced him. "You did this on purpose."

"What ever do you mean?" Dyraien asked.

"You knew what bringing her here would do to me."

Dyraien held up his hands and repressed a grin, like he got some pleasure out of this. "She insisted. There was nothing I could do."

"Come on, Rye," Hona said. "We all work together. I'm trying my hardest to make amends. Why can't you do the same?"

Rye barked a cold laugh. "You want me to be more like you?"

Hona stepped forward. "I didn't say that."

"You did." Rye's voice was steady now. "All right. I'll be more like you." He laid the newspaper on the table, pushed in his chair, and walked gracefully out of the room without looking back. A moment later, Tahki heard the front door open and close.

Tahki made to go after him, but Dyraien grabbed his arm.

"Trust me," Dyraien said. "You don't want to be around him when he's like this."

"Why?"

Dyraien released him. "Help me with dinner. We'll prepare something nice for Hona. And then we three can sit down and have a talk."

TAHKI WATCHED Dyraien slice a row of carrots in a series of quick jabs. The tick of the knife against the wooden cutting board was the only sound in the kitchen. His skin felt clammy from standing over a steaming pot of boiling potatoes. The scent of honeyed pork filled his nose. Dyraien had done most of the work preparing the meal. He chopped every vegetable with a kind of showy elegance, as though a court full of people watched and applauded him. His fingers moved almost too rapidly to follow. Once, he threw a potato in the air and it landed across the blade of his knife directly in the middle.

Tahki wondered exactly how much of his upbringing had been traditional. Did Dyraien know how to sword fight and shoot a pistol? Could he dance? Hunt? Did he know about taxes and diplomacy?

The potatoes bobbed up and down. Tahki swirled them around the hot water with a spoon. He didn't mind helping with dinner. A month ago he might have, but he found a certain satisfaction in these small tasks. He also found Dyraien's kitchen tricks and princely smiles charming, and at that moment, he felt guilty for suspecting Dyraien had something to do with the Zinc incident.

"You like to stare when you think no one's looking," Dyraien said.

Tahki moved his eyes back to the potatoes.

"It's all right," Dyraien said. It sounded like he was smiling. "I don't mind you staring at me. I'd like to know you better, Tahki. I'd like to know about your family. Your upbringing. What you want out of life."

"I want to complete the castle," Tahki said.

Dyraien laughed. "It's comforting to know you share my goal."

"I'm sure Rye shares it too."

Dyraien stopped cutting. "Rye doesn't know what he wants."

It seemed pompous to speak for Rye, but Tahki didn't dare challenge him. Dyraien had known Rye for almost ten years.

"Your ears must have been itching," Dyraien said.

Tahki peeked up at Dyraien, but his eyes were focused on the door. Rye slouched into the kitchen. He leaned forward slightly, shoulders tense, dark circles under his eyes. He stood across from Dyraien.

"Can we talk?" Rye said to the prince.

"You know you never have to ask," Dyraien said. He glanced at Tahki. "Will you run and fetch flour from the dry storage?"

It was an obvious busy chore. If they had wanted privacy, they could have just asked. But Tahki obeyed and left the room. Instead of fetching the flour, however, he slid into the room next door. He didn't want to spy on them, but he needed to know more about Dyraien and Rye if he wanted to figure out the mysteries of the castle. At least that's what he told himself.

A thumb-sized hole cracked the wall where he could see into the kitchen. Tahki pressed his eye against the smooth obsidian. It cooled his forehead and sent a brief chill across his face.

"You're angry with me," Dyraien said. He diced a clove of garlic without looking at it.

Rye slid into a chair and rubbed his temples. "Why didn't you tell me?"

"Because you dwell and brood and mope like it pays to be depressed. If I had told you Hona planned to arrive early, you would have gone to stay in Edgewater, and I need you to keep working here."

"That wasn't your choice to make."

"I hired Hona because I thought it would be good for you," Dyraien said. "You're not the only one with a shitty childhood, you know."

"I will not make amends with her," Rye said. "So stop interfering."

Tahki had never heard anyone talk to a prince that way. What surprised him more, Dyraien didn't seem upset by his tone.

"And you call me a stubborn ass," Dyraien said.

"You know what she did, and you know how I feel about her."

Dyraien scraped the garlic into a bowl and set it aside. He laid his knife on the table, walked over to Rye, then brought their foreheads together. Rye's jaw clenched, but he didn't pull away.

"I'm sorry," Dyraien whispered. "I didn't mean to hurt you." He removed his head and kissed Rye's brow. Oddly, the gesture didn't stir any feelings of jealousy. The way Dyraien touched Rye was different from his usual flirtatious touches. It wasn't sadistic or deviant or manipulative. It was brotherly, kind, sincere. Possibly the most genuine emotion Tahki had seen Dyraien display.

Embarrassed by his intrusion, Tahki moved away from the wall and went to fetch the flour.

TAHKI SET the polished wood table with white plates and silver utensils, and then Dyraien reset it properly, amused that Tahki had put the knife on the wrong side. They ate in one of the larger rooms with a big red rug in the center. The table sat six people, but there were only four chairs. A tray of pork and garlic potatoes covered half the table. Dyraien also supplied two bottles of wine and three glasses. Hona joined them, but Rye had gone to Edgewater. Whatever Hona had done, it must have been bad, because Tahki remembered Rye saying he wanted to avoid the town when he could.

Tahki glanced around the room in search of the black cat.

Dyraien cracked a handful of lightning roots and set them upright in a clear vase. They all helped themselves. Hona ate fast and in large forkfuls. Dyraien held his fork between his thumb and index finger and took small bites. Tahki knew the proper way to hold a fork and knife but decided not to show his manners. He still had a persona to keep, and that persona hadn't been raised in a palace.

He bit into a modest hunk of sweet and salty pork. On top of charming, Dyraien was also a brilliant cook.

"I'd like to purchase a piano," Dyraien said.

Tahki swallowed. "A what?"

"A new musical instrument unlike any I've heard before. A piano's sound is so complex, so elegant. I've been in love since my last visit to the capital. It's amazing the kind of emotions a person's fingers can produce. You've never heard one, Tahki?"

Tahki shook his head. "I think I remember reading about them."

"You cannot read about music, just like you cannot taste the grapes in an oil painting. Music is something to experience. On my next visit to the capital, you'll have to join me. We'll see a performance together."

"Thank you," Tahki said. "I'd like that very much." He resumed eating, but Dyraien's eyes didn't leave him.

"Tahki," he said. His voice was calm and kind. "I need a date."

Tahki peeked up from his potatoes. "A date?"

Dyraien set his fork down. "I need to know when I'll have the design."

Tahki remembered the promise he'd made after the cat attack. "Right. Tomorrow. I should have something tomorrow." He felt a stab of guilt. There was no way he'd have anything by then.

"That's excellent." Dyraien beamed. "And it will be better than your last attempt?"

Tahki felt his face flush. "Of course. I think I was nervous the first time. Too eager."

Dyraien flicked his hand dismissively. "It was Rye's fault."

Another jab of guilt. Tahki cleared his throat. "About my first design. I may have pushed Rye to accept it. I don't think he liked the design, but I insisted. It wasn't his fault."

Dyraien raised a brow. "Rye should have known better."

"Still," Tahki said. "Please don't be angry with him."

Dyraien frowned slightly. "I could never be angry with Rye."

Tahki looked down at his food.

"You seem very concerned about my brother," Hona said. She licked the tip of her fork.

Tahki shrugged and tried to seem casual.

"You look like you're going to explode," Hona said.

"Excuse me?"

Hona pursed her lips. "All those questions bubbling up inside you, and they'll pop if you don't ask."

"Don't ask what?"

Hona laughed. It wasn't a pretty laugh, like he expected her to have, but choppy, like a hiccup. "You want to know why Rye hates me."

Dyraien reached for one bottle of wine and uncorked it. "Is that really appropriate dinner conversation?"

"Just look at the kid," Hona said. "He's bursting to know."

Dyraien poured the wine. Tahki wondered why he didn't want him to know more about Rye. Was it for Rye's protection or some more possessive reason?

"It's none of my business," Tahki said. He didn't like the uncomfortable air that had settled over the table.

Hona twirled her wine and slid her tongue along the edge of the glass. "If I choose to share part of my life story with you, that's my business."

"But it's not your story," Dyraien said. "And I don't think Rye would like you airing his past to just anyone."

Tahki wasn't just anyone, was he? How could Dyraien act so kind to him one moment and in the next pretend like he was a stranger at his table? Dyraien handed Tahki a glass of wine. It smelled bitter. A dark crimson color stained the top of the glass when he took a polite sip. He'd never had more than a few sips before. If the wine was good or bad, he couldn't tell. Wine all tasted the same to him. He took a larger gulp, and it burned his throat a little.

"Come on, D," Hona said. She made a sad face and slid her body forward, her arms stretching across the table like a relaxed cat. "I think he's earned it. Don't you?"

Dyraien sipped his wine. "Do as you wish." His words were tight, confined.

Tahki shivered. He wished a fire burned. Though lightning roots were brighter and gave off no odor, they didn't provide any warmth.

Hona leaned back and rolled her neck. "Tell me, Tahki. Do you come from a good family?"

Tahki blinked. "A good family?"

"Are you well off?"

Tahki took another gulp of wine. His lips felt thick and heavy with residue. "I guess."

"You guess," Hona chimed. "You have no idea what it's like to be hungry."

That wasn't true. Tahki had been hungry just before dinner. He hadn't eaten breakfast and skipped the clam lunch.

"Hunger and pride don't make good company," Hona said. "Rye was always too proud to beg. As kids, we were dragged around by our mother. During the day, Rye and I would find safe places to sleep, and during the nights, we'd follow our mother around from bar to bar, carrying her sad sack of bones across town after she'd pissed herself drunk. That woman could drink ten men on shore leave under the table. It was actually quite impressive."

Tahki had wanted to know about Rye, but this felt wrong, intrusive.

Hona went on. "Don't think I'm looking for sympathy or pity, and don't think Rye is, either. We were poor, but so was everyone in that part of town. Our mother was a worthless drunk, but at least she didn't beat us or anything."

"Maybe you would have better manners if she had," Dyraien said.

Hona laughed, despite the seriousness of his voice. "Maybe. And maybe Rye would have had the sense to leave her behind." Hona slouched in her chair. Her voice sounded a little hoarse, like she'd been screaming. She traced the edge of her glass so it hummed. "Rye was ten and I was fifteen when I left."

"When you left?"

Hona scrunched her nose. "Ran away, I guess you could say." She looked over to Dyraien. Tahki noticed the prince's eyes narrow ever so slightly. "I told myself I'd find a job and bring them money, but I was lying. I abandoned Rye, left him with our alcoholic mother."

Tahki's heart beat fast. The wine made him feel warm, but Hona's words chilled him. He pictured a young Rye, shivering in the cold outside some bar.

He thought about when he'd been ten. The fine meals he ate with his father, the beautiful imported silk clothing, the expensive toys he played with once or twice. Hona had been right. He didn't know what it was like to be hungry. To rely on the pity of strangers for a meal.

"Anyway," Hona said in a sad voice. "I came back years later, but I was too late."

"Rye's mother left him shortly after Hona," Dyraien said. "Left him to fend for himself. He was all alone. When I found him and took him in, he had no one. No one who'd ever offered him so much as a kind word. But I fixed all that, and we have each other now. What more could he want?"

Tahki watched the lightning roots flicker pale light across the table. His eyelids drooped. Rye's story made him tired and depressed, and he wanted to be alone, away from the glances he didn't understand, away from the people who kept him an arm's length away, who only told him part of the truth.

"Maybe we should retire to our rooms," Dyraien said. "We'll clean up tomorrow."

They all stood, but as Tahki walked from the room, Hona grabbed his arm.

"I tried to make it right," she said. "I tried to fix things between us."

Tahki pulled his arm out of her grip. He wanted to be away from her. Away from anyone who had caused Rye grief.

"Let him go, Hona," Dyraien said, his voice sharp.

Tahki walked from the room, a slight sway in his step. He knew Rye's past now, but Rye knew nothing about him, and that wasn't right.

Tonight, he'd tell Rye who he was and where he was from.

WHEN HE arrived in his room, Tahki sat on his bed, still a little fuzzy-headed from the wine. Hona's words stuck in his mind. He had learned so much about Rye. It was only fair Rye learned about him now.

He took a deep breath. Tonight, he'd tell Rye everything. If Rye kept his secret, their bond would grow. But if Rye couldn't, what would he do? Rye wouldn't turn him over to Dyraien, that much he knew. Worst scenario, Rye would tell Tahki to leave.

It seemed worth the risk for a chance to finally tell Rye the truth.

With this resolve in mind, Tahki left to find Rye, hoping he'd be back from Edgewater. He tiptoed down the stairs. Everything looked distorted in the dark. Walls crawled upward forever. The banisters curled beside him like long, outstretched fingers. The white marble appeared to move as clouds swept in front of the moon. As he reached the bottom step, the sound of plates clattering echoed through the hall. For a moment, he pictured the black cat crouched and ready to pounce, but then he heard voices. Dyraien, Hona, and someone else. He followed the chatter to the dining room. The door was cracked only half an inch, but he could see inside.

Dyraien and Hona sat at the table, speaking lowly to a man across from them. A man with short hair and a pointed chin.

"Must be nice," Zinc said. "Living here all cozy and comfortable. Do I ever get invited to dine with you? Don't think so. And why would that be? Not good enough for you? Not a large enough vo-cabulary?"

"Not clean enough," Dyraien said.

Zinc ate from the tray of leftover pork, tearing off meat with his hands and chewing loudly. "Right, right. Or maybe you don't love the people of Vatolokít as much as you say you do."

Dyraien leaned back in his chair, arms behind his head. "Tell me, Zinc. How much money would I need to pay your people to have them tie you to a rock and throw you in the ocean? Twenty notes? Thirty? I suspect the number is pretty low."

Tahki pressed closer. He could see Dyraien now. His eyes appeared dark and threatening, like at any moment he might swipe a knife from the table and lodge it in Zinc's throat.

Zinc must have sensed this, too, because he swallowed and said in a tense voice, "You can't blame me for what happened."

"I think I can," Dyraien said. "A perk of being a prince. I can blame anyone for anything."

"Fuck, D. I figured you sent the kid."

"Why in the eight hells would I do that?" Dyraien said. "He's my lead architect."

Tahki's palms started to sweat. They were talking about him.

"No idea." Zinc burped. "It's not like you—what's that word you like to use—*di-vulge* your plans to me."

"You're a piece of goat shit, Zinc," Dyraien said.

Zinc straightened his back. "Now hold on. Just you hold on a minute. I held up my end of the bargain."

"You confused a pretty foreign boy for a seventy-year-old alcoholic judge. And what's worse, you involved Rye."

"Wasn't my fault Rye showed up. You told me you'd scalp me bloody if I ever touched him," Zinc said. "What was I supposed to do?"

"You were supposed to do your job," Dyraien said.

Hona sighed. "Wouldn't it be easier to just tell Rye the truth?"

Dyraien shook his head. "He wouldn't understand. Not until the castle is complete. Besides, there are other distractions now, things I fear might make Rye difficult to control."

"You mean the kid?" Hona said.

"Of course the kid." Dyraien ran a hand through his hair. "We can work around this. We can still achieve what we set out to do, so long as Tahki completes the castle and you two get me the parcel."

"We will," Hona said. "It should arrive tomorrow night. We'll bring it in back so Rye doesn't see."

Tahki felt a lump in his throat, maybe from the wine, from the confusion, from the way it seemed every time he learned something about this castle and these people, new complications arose. He heard the front door push open and moved away from the dining room out into the hall. He saw Rye heading to his workroom.

Tahki approached, sweaty and light-headed. "Rye?"

Rye turned. "What's wrong?" The concern in his voice sounded warm and genuine. Tahki wondered if he should tell him about Zinc first but then thought better of it. He didn't need any added complications. Whatever was going on between Dyraien and Zinc, Rye knew nothing about it.

"I need to talk to you."

Rye opened the door, and they stepped inside the room that smelled of pine and cedar. Wood dust lay on the floor. A few lightning roots flickered. Tahki reached out and touched the bottom of the boat.

"Your eyes are red. Have you been crying?" Rye said.

Rain tapped against the window. A few drops, then a few more. The downpour thumped against the obsidian roof, ringing like a sad song.

Tahki's eyes felt swollen. "I think it's just the wine."

In the dim light, he saw Rye's face tighten. Hona had said their mother was a drunk, and he'd never seen Rye touch alcohol. Wine probably brought back bad memories.

"Gods, Rye, I had no idea," Tahki said.

He thought about Rye's childhood, about how alone he must have felt. Tahki had lost his mother, but his father worked hard to compensate for the loss. He never realized just how hard his father had tried to fill the void their mother's death created. He worked full-time but still managed to play with and teach his children. He didn't shove them into the arms of some servant and forget about them. And Sornjia had been there too. As much as Tahki resented his twin, he couldn't count the number of times he'd gone to Sornjia for help, or confided in him, or asked his brother to cover for him.

"Tahki, what's going on?"

Tahki met his gray eyes. "I can't imagine what you went through."

"What I went through?"

"When you—" Tahki hesitated. No secrets. That's what he promised himself. "Hona told me about your childhood."

A pained look crossed Rye's face, and he turned away.

"I think she just wanted me to know more about you," Tahki said.

"She had no right." Rye's voice was barely a whisper. When he faced Tahki, his eyes were wide, his breath rapid. "You should have asked me if you wanted to know about my life. Instead, you went to her. You heard it from her."

Tahki frowned. He *had* asked Rye about his life, but Rye always changed the subject. "I didn't ask her to tell me. She just did."

"And you listened." Rye balled his fists, his voice growing louder. "You could have walked away, but you didn't."

"I'm sorry," Tahki said, taken aback. "We were eating dinner. I thought it would be rude to leave." Maybe he'd misread Rye all along. Rye clearly didn't want him to know about his past.

"Stop lying," Rye said, his voice booming off the walls. "All you care about is yourself. You think everyone needs to tell you everything because you deserve to know."

Tahki shook his head. He was no stranger to tantrum throwing and knew firsthand what it was to overreact to a situation, but he didn't understand why Rye reacted so hysterically.

"I'm sorry," Tahki said again. The conversation escalated too quickly. He needed to end it. "You're right. I should have asked her to stop. It was an honest mistake. Can we just forget I said anything?"

"Forget? Are you just going to forget that I'm some sad sob story? That I was neglected and abused? That my mother was an embarrassment, that my only sister abandoned me?"

Tahki shifted uneasily. "If you want to talk about it—"

"I don't," Rye snapped. "Not with you. Not anymore." He put his hand over his mouth a moment, shaking lightly. "When I first met you, I thought you were just some pretentious kid. But then I saw your work, your passion, your imagination, and I thought maybe you were someone I could talk to, could relate to."

Tahki nodded. "I am. You can."

Rye laughed, a dark noise. "I know Dyraien isn't always the best company, but at least he never pitied me or went behind my back." His words came fast, and Tahki's head twirled.

When he spoke again, Tahki's voice sounded winded and desperate. "I'm not pitying you, and I didn't go behind your back. I didn't want secrets between us, so I came to tell you something. Something about me. Something important."

Rye shook his head. "Whatever it is, I don't want to hear it. Stay away from me, Tahki." Before Tahki could say more, Rye pushed past him, out of the room, and vanished into the dark.

Tahki stood, braced against the boat, heart rapping violently. All that progress he'd made with Rye, gone in an instant. He'd never seen

Rye act so frantic. At Zinc's, Rye had been angry, but his anger had still been contained. This Rye tonight was new. A person Tahki never knew existed.

And Tahki had been the one to bring that person out.

He paced the room and slammed his fist on Rye's worktable. His knuckles throbbed. He kicked the chair, shoved a pile of books to the floor, sent the newspapers fluttering. Why had Hona told him? Why hadn't Dyraien stopped her? Maybe it wasn't Hona who'd truly done the damage. Sornjia had said Dyraien liked to control people. Had he planned this? Set up these events knowing Tahki would tell Rye, knowing Rye would hate him for it, so Dyraien could have Rye all to himself? Or had the restless nights made Tahki paranoid?

He fell to the floor and leaned against the wall. Something crinkled beneath him. He peeked down. Black words stared back at him: the newspaper Rye had been reading. It was dated the day after he left the fair. The headline read: Disaster: Steaming Chaos at the World Fair.

Tahki frowned. He spun the paper around to read.

Thomisan Corrine is being held in contempt after his Steam Locomotive exploded during a demonstration, killing seventeen and injuring over fifty. A third of the Innovation Hall has been destroyed.

A series of speculative interviews followed. They determined the tragedy to be the result of negligence. An expert—someone he didn't recognize—claimed the coal source had been accidentally swapped for a similar black mineral that released a toxic gas when heated. The pressure had built inside the steam chamber and it had burst. Investigations were being held at the capital, and no one was allowed to leave the country until they ruled out foul play.

Tahki marveled in horror at the tremendous power that a seemingly small mechanism had. The power of machines was extraordinary. The locomotive sounded more effective than most modern weapons. If the steam machine had been larger, it might have leveled half the city.

Rain streamed down the window. His eyes followed the wet lines. Explosion. Power. A machine.

After weeks of muddled thoughts, Tahki saw the design in his mind with greater clarity than anything he'd seen before. He'd studied the locomotive in person at the fair and knew the basic components.

He hardly felt his feet carrying him to his room or his hands as they cracked all the lighting roots he could find. He yanked out a sheet of paper, gripped his mother's pencil, and then sketched rapid lines. He worked in a fevered rush. All other thoughts faded.

Steam was the solution.

Dyraien had been right all along. The river was a power source. All Tahki had to do was convert the water to steam.

Nothing mattered but this. He forgot about Hona, about Dyraien, and even about Rye. He saw only black lines and hard edges. Architecture filled his mind more completely than it had in weeks, in months. More fully than it ever had. He couldn't just see the design in his mind. He could feel it. Every part of it, a grand, functioning thing, and as he drew, it was as though he breathed life into it. It came alive before his eyes.

Outside, thunder rumbled. A hard sleet roared against the roof. The world cried, flashing brightly, forcing itself over the castle like it meant to bring it down.

Tahki didn't stop. Not when his hand cramped, not when he felt nauseated from the wine, not when his head pounded so badly he felt his eyes might bleed. He ignored the pain and worked until his blisters popped and exhaustion forced his head to the desk in a dreamless sleep.

Chapter 12

He woke in a puddle of drool and charcoal. Warm light trickled on his face, and for a moment he forgot where he was. As he squinted into the light, he realized the sun had broken through the fog.

Tahki sat up. A paper stuck to his cheek. He gently tore it away. His head throbbed and his hand cramped. For a moment he'd forgotten why his rulers and pens and papers were scattered all over the place. Then his eyes found the design, and with shaky hands, he looked over his work. He'd never designed anything like it before. No one had. It was a product of pure ingenuity, and he knew then that if Dyraien didn't like it, he'd be finished here, because this design had pushed his architectural abilities to their limit.

He stumbled out of his chair, eager to find Rye, when the events from last night treaded into his mind. His hand held him steady in the doorway. Though his fight with Rye still stung, there were other more concerning matters that plagued him.

Tahki took a breath and thought. So far, he'd lumped everything that had happened to him over the weeks as a series of unrelated events, but what did he really know? One, there was something strange about this castle. He'd hallucinated twice, and then a dead cat—a nonhallucinated dead cat—had come back to life and tried to kill him. Two, Dyraien had attempted to scam Gale, or it seemed that way, and might be hiding his true intentions for this castle. But he had no reason to believe the strange occurrences and Dyraien's suspicious behavior were connected. In fact, last night Dyraien had been angered by Zinc's treatment of Tahki. Even if Dyraien wasn't honest about what he planned to do with the castle, he looked out for Tahki's well-being. Why he tried to scam Gale wasn't clear, but there could be a number of explanations. Gale was an admitted alcoholic as well as a washed-up judge. Maybe she had committed some crime against him, and this was a kind of petty revenge.

Maybe he could ask Rye about Gale once things between them mended, and showing he'd come up with a good solution was the first step.

He clutched his design and left to find Rye.

The boat room was empty, so Tahki tried his bedroom, but there was no answer when he knocked. Tahki bit his lip. Maybe Rye had gone to Edgewater to stay the night.

He jogged to the stables to see if all gingoats were accounted for. The morning air felt brisk against the bare skin of his arms. His boots sloshed through the puddles from the storm. The air smelled rich with rain, and he filled his lungs. The reflective sun off the pale ground hurt his eyes, so he shielded them from the rays with his papers and stepped under the slanted wooden roof of the stable.

He found Rye beside a gingoat, brushing her fur with a comb. Even before Rye looked up, Tahki felt an awkward air shift between them.

He didn't have friends back home. Sornjia did, but not him. He played with the daughters and sons of visiting diplomats and joined the empress's daughter for a swim in the oasis on occasion, but he hadn't felt connected to them. He hadn't been able to talk to them the way he talked to Rye. But Rye clearly had his own problems to sort through and needed space, so it would be best to keep things professional for now.

"I think I have something," Tahki said. "A design idea."

Rye glanced at the papers. For a moment, Tahki thought he might not take them, but he set the brush aside and tugged them free. Then he stepped from the stables into the light and examined the paper.

Thirty seconds passed. A minute. Two minutes. Rye held the designs high toward the castle, as though to overlay the pencil marks with the real thing. Finally, he folded the paper and turned to Tahki. Tahki wished he was better at reading faces, because a complicated emotion seemed to fill Rye.

"How did you...." Rye ran a free hand through his messy hair. "What makes you think this would work?" The words didn't sound harsh but inquisitive. Cautious.

"I read about the steam locomotive last night after—" Tahki paused. "Well, the idea came to me last night. I saw the locomotive at the fair, and after reading about the explosion, I realized steam power might be the answer. If we could convert it into a conduit system, we could turn the entire interior of the castle into a power source. I want to use pipes to funnel steam, but not bamboo pipes. Copper pipes. By forcing steam into a series of metal pipes, we'd be able to bring energy to any part of the castle."

Rye pinched his brow. "A steam conduit."

Tahki nodded. "The center, here, is the power source. The castle will become a mechanism that could do anything from launch projectiles to send concentrated steam jets across enemy lines. With the river below us, we have an endless supply of energy."

"We'd use a firebox to fuel the distillation," Rye said. His eyes grew wide with excitement.

Tahki swallowed. "So, is it good? Will it work?"

One of the gingoats snorted and swished her tail. Tahki reached up and scratched behind her ear. She didn't try to bite him this time but instead leaned into his touch.

Rye rubbed his jaw. "It's good. It's really, really good. I've never…."

Tahki couldn't repress his smile, or the wobbly feeling in his knees, or the way the skin on the top of his scalp tingled. But he'd be foolish to get too excited. Dyraien still needed to approve it.

"Dyraien is leaving for Edgewater soon," Rye said. "We need to show him this now."

Tahki nodded, and together they walked back to the castle in silence.

They found Dyraien in his mother's room. Rye told Tahki to wait outside while he went in to fetch him. A strange wail sounded beyond the door. A mix between the wind inside a tunnel and the yowls of a cat. He shivered.

When they emerged, Dyraien grabbed the design with both hands. He mulled over it, his eyes darting quickly from corner to corner. Tahki held his breath. Dyraien looked to Rye, a little wide-eyed, like he was afraid to question it. Rye nodded slightly, and relief flooded Dyraien's face. He turned and yanked Tahki forward by the shoulders, drawing him in for a firm embrace.

"This is brilliant," he whispered. "You are brilliant."

When he pulled away, Tahki was left flushed. After weeks of doubting his skills as an architect, he'd proved himself.

Yet as Dyraien started babbling about logistics, Tahki couldn't help but wonder what the design would really be used for. Sornjia said Dyraien was dangerous, and Tahki had just handed him a powerful weapon. What if they somehow used it to attack another country? What if that country was Dhaulen'aii? But all Dyraien had ever talked about was how he loved his people, how he wanted to protect them. The castle wasn't designed to attack; it was designed to defend.

"You know," Dyraien said. "I almost doubted you. I'm ashamed to admit it, but I thought you'd lied to me last night when you said you had an idea. But now I see I was a fool to doubt you. I can't tell you how proud I am of you, Tahki."

Tahki smiled, but he couldn't take his eyes off the design Dyraien held. Now that he'd earned his praise and the initial excitement had worn off, an unwanted feeling of doubt settled over him.

"But we can't celebrate just yet," Dyraien said. "I will write up the order list and send a message to the capital to have the parts forged. In three days, I want you two to travel to Edgewater to see the delivery is complete and up to our standards. Understand?" Tahki and Rye nodded. Dyraien smiled at both of them, a childlike giddiness on his face.

Dyraien said, "I want you to know that my mother would be very pleased with both of you. No matter what happens after this, you should both feel proud today. Together, we will accomplish something great. Together, we will change the world."

THREE DAYS inched by, and Tahki helped prepare the castle for the installment of the conduit system. Dyraien said most of the parts would come preassembled, so all they'd need to do was secure everything in its proper place and it would be ready to test.

As he worked, he expected to feel confident, to feel victorious, but those feelings had only lasted a moment, and then they were gone. This should have been his golden moment. The moment he'd yearned for. The moment someone—not someone, but the Prince of Vatolokit—had acknowledged him as a brilliant architect. After weeks of stress and constant rejection, he'd come up with a solution. But his thoughts were stuck on Dyraien, the way his thirsty eyes moved over Tahki's work. No one got that excited over a gift.

Still, he knew nothing for sure.

He visited Sornjia once, but his brother only spouted more nonsense about danger and black clouds and dark ravens. He wanted to mend things with Rye but didn't want to force conversation. Tahki needed to be patient. If he'd learned anything over the last few weeks, it was that rushing things never helped.

When the day finally arrived to leave for Edgewater, Tahki felt better, like he had a goal to focus on again. After stuffing down a quick breakfast of apple cobbler and sweet cream, Tahki found Rye holding the reins of two gingoats outside the front door. Rye had avoided him since he'd approved the design but hadn't protested traveling with Tahki, which gave him hope.

They mounted their goats and headed for the high road. Mudslides from the storm three days ago had blocked the lower trail, so they'd been forced to take a less traveled path that followed the river. A thin layer of clouds shadowed the sun, but the day still felt warm. He had missed the sun. Maybe not the intense heat of home, but the world looked better in the bright light of day. A few mothsnails even crawled out of holes in the sand.

The muddy path sucked and splattered as they tromped along. Tahki's mount threw her head and snorted. He hadn't ridden her in a while and forgot to lunge her this morning.

"Calm down, girl," Tahki said. He yanked left on the reins. Usually Rye helped him when she acted up, but not this time.

Tahki relaxed his shoulders. "Easy, girl. Easy." He petted her neck gently and she calmed. He noticed Rye glancing his way, but when Tahki looked up, Rye kicked his mount into a trot and sped ahead.

As they traveled farther, his gingoat grew restless again, agitated by something he couldn't see. It was almost as though she sensed a predator nearby. Tahki fought with the reins, so immersed in his struggle with the beast he forgot about the Misty River, until spray dampened his skin and he looked up. The gingoat stopped ten paces from a wooden bridge.

The river thundered by. The dark bridge looked slick from the toiling white waters and only wide enough for one goat to cross at a time. If he threw a stick in the water, it would be carried down, all the way back under the castle, until it dropped a hundred feet over the waterfall.

Tahki tried to swallow but couldn't. His mouth felt dry, and his breath left his body in ragged huffs. He had thought he could manage the river crossing, but he hadn't expected the bridge to be so long, the river so dangerous. It wasn't nearly this vicious by the castle.

When he looked up, he saw Rye had made it across already and was stopped on the other side, fiddling with his bag. Rye didn't look back or try to make eye contact, but he was delaying, the same way he'd delayed the first day they'd met, on the hike to the castle.

Tahki needed to cross. He'd overcome worse these last few weeks. The bridge in his path was nothing. It might take him five seconds to cross if he ran. Five seconds, and they'd be on their way again. He took a breath and dismounted his gingoat. With her acting up, he didn't want to be on her back while they crossed. He stepped toward the bridge, sliding his feet as though the ground was made of ice. Every inch closer drew out another bead of sweat across his forehead. The instinct to run throbbed through his legs. He tried not to think about the night he'd almost drowned, but the harder he pushed those memories from his mind, the stronger they appeared.

Another foot closer. River water splashed on his lips and he licked it away. Rye had made it across just fine. He could see his outline through the spray but couldn't hear him over the howls of the river. He focused on bridge, now within reach. All he needed to do was reach out and grab it.

With one shaky hand, he grabbed for the railing, eyes focused on the dripping wood.

And then his gingoat reared. The reins tugged free, and the animal stumbled back. Tahki felt himself start to fall, but his hand flailed and grabbed the railing. He fumbled a moment and then found his balance. His heart pounded, eyes wide as he glanced into the river he'd almost fallen into. He breathed deep and then shoved away from the bank toward his gingoat. She pranced, fearful of him.

"Easy," he said. She wouldn't calm down. "Come on, girl." He jerked forward and grabbed the reins before she could bolt. A breath escaped his lips, and he rubbed his face. After he composed himself and his mount, Tahki turned back toward the bridge.

He froze.

The black cat stood in front of the bridge, as real and clear and absolute as the river.

Tahki stared, stunned. The leather reins slid from his hands. Air caught in his throat. It was as though a spell had been cast on his legs. A numbness settled over him as he looked into the cat's eyes. They swirled like the heavens, like stars colliding. His nose tingled. The scent of spiced curry bread filled his nostrils. The sound of the river became the chatter of people, hundreds of people, like he stood in the middle of a crowded foyer and listened as they spoke of the weather, of fishing, of the land and the sea. He felt pine needles brush his skin and coral rub against his teeth. His stomach bloated like it was Dunesday and he'd just eaten an entire baked lamb pie. The sensations had a dreamlike realness to them, pleasant and nonthreatening.

It wasn't until the cat stepped around him that the strangeness shattered, and he was left with crippling fear in its wake. The black beast did not roar or pounce or lunge. She moved her sleek body like the sun moved shadows, a lulled pace that took both a lifetime and a second to reach him.

She stood beside him now, her body more massive than he remembered. He felt strangely at peace.

But it didn't last.

The cat lowered her massive head and growled. Then with the same fluidity as before, she raised one giant paw and shoved Tahki's chest. The motion felt both controlled and forceful, so quick he hardly had time to let out a scream as he fell down the bank and into the river.

The water consumed him. He fought to find the surface, propelled by the swift and violent force. Cold water filled every part of him. He couldn't see, couldn't breathe, couldn't move. The current thrust him forward, pulled him under. He scrambled to find anything to push off from with his legs, but the water moved too fast. He tried to fight it as fire tore through his body. His lungs burned, and blackness seeped into his mind. First his arms stopped moving, then his legs stopped kicking, and suddenly none of his limbs worked.

He couldn't fight it.

And then he felt his body resist the tug of water. Something dug into his flesh, and he pictured the black cat clawing at him. It had jumped into the river to finish him off. But then he realized the burning had stopped.

He felt hard ground beneath him. Somewhere, a voice yelled, but he couldn't make out the words. Something warm pressed against his face, against his ears and nose. There was pressure on his stomach and chest, rhythmic and a little painful. He wanted it to stop, but it persisted, until he felt the river churn inside him. Suddenly, his body convulsed and he threw up water. He coughed and spat and gulped in air. At first he couldn't see, but as his eyes adjusted, he noticed dirt and rock walls on every side.

When he turned, he saw Rye hunched over him, eyes wide with panic. Tahki tried to pull himself up.

"Don't," Rye said. He set his hand on his chest. "Don't try to move." Tahki obeyed. Rye's hands shook a little. He wiped his nose. "What kind of idiot falls in a river?" He tried to smile, but it came out a trembling grimace.

"Sorry," Tahki whispered. His throat felt raw.

"Sorry?" Rye repeated. He shook his head. "You weren't breathing."

"Sorry," Tahki said again. He couldn't think of anything else to say.

Rye laughed a humorless laugh. "You really do have a thing for the dramatics, don't you?" His voiced sounded thick. His entire body shook, his eyes full of fear.

As Tahki regained consciousness, he pieced together what had happened. The black cat had pushed him into the river. Rye had not seen it, but he'd probably heard Tahki scream. He must have jumped in after him, and the river had towed them somewhere dark, maybe under the castle. But one certain thought stuck in his mind.

Rye had saved his life.

He felt dizzy. Rye wasn't angry at him anymore but fearful, which wasn't any better. With each day that had passed since Tahki had come to live at the castle, his relationship with Rye grew more complicated, more confusing. But at that moment, Tahki needed simplicity. He needed clarity, and he knew no words could express his feelings.

So Tahki reached up, his back still firm against the ground, and locked his arms over Rye's neck. He drew Rye down to him, curling his fingers in his hair, and brought their lips together. The kiss felt soft and cool, and both their bodies relaxed against each other.

But the trauma of the river had been too much. Tahki's arms fell to the dirt, and his mind slipped away into darkness.

HE WASN'T asleep, but he couldn't open his eyes. His limbs refused to move just yet. It still felt like his body was caught in the tow of the river. He could almost feel the current moving over him, the water so cold it burned, and he wondered if his mother had felt the same way when the flames devoured her.

She had been brilliant, loved, respected. She would have become famous had she saved herself instead of Tahki that night. All he'd wanted to do since the day she'd died was make it up to her, follow the path she would have taken. If he became a famous architect, his success would be hers. His father had never understood his obsession with fame, that if the world saw what Tahki could do, they would get a glimpse of what his mother might have achieved. This castle had been his chance to prove to her that he had been worth saving, but someone or something clearly didn't want him to succeed.

The numbness faded, and he rubbed his eyelids gently until they unstuck. He opened his eyes to Rye's muddy face. His hair looked clumped and damp, his lips parted slightly, his brow furrowed.

Tahki's stomach twisted at the thought of the kiss. He'd wanted to kiss Rye for a long time now, but not like this. The kiss hadn't even been consensual. Rye would be furious with him, maybe even refuse to talk to him. Although the people of Vatolokít might view a stolen kiss as romantic and whimsical, Tahki had been raised to understand that kissing someone without their permission was wrong.

He took a deep breath. This place looked dark and smelled heavily of dirt and minerals. Moisture clung to the rock walls around him. Only a faint glow bloomed from beneath a slate wall where the river flowed in.

He rubbed the bumps along his skin. His wet clothing felt slimy and heavy against his body. He wanted to take it off and curl up next to Rye and feel warm again, but the thought made him flush. Instead, he tried to look around for an exit.

Rye stirred, and his eyes blinked open.

Tahki swallowed. He wondered if Rye would even remember the kiss. Maybe saving Tahki from the river had left his mind raw and fuzzy.

"You should have woken me," Rye said. His voice sounded groggy and harsh, like he'd swallowed a handful of gravel.

"I just woke up," Tahki said.

Rye rubbed his head. "We're under the castle."

"I noticed, but where?"

"The river carried us to an underground cave." Rye rose, stumbled, and steadied himself. Tahki had never seen him look so unstable. "Dyraien said there were natural tunnels below the castle, but I was too focused on breaking free of the river to notice our location."

Tahki hugged himself. "Rye?"

"What?" Rye stretched his muscles and cringed.

"Thank you."

Rye didn't look at him. Maybe he'd call Tahki a moron again. Maybe he'd yell at him for delaying work on the castle. Maybe he'd tell Tahki to stay away from him.

"You shouldn't thank me," Rye said. He still wouldn't look at him. "Those things I said to you, that night Hona told you about my past… I didn't mean them."

Tahki swallowed. "I was out of line."

"No, it wasn't your fault. I overreacted. I shouldn't have said all those horrible things." Rye looked at him now. "It's not that I didn't want you to know about me. I just wanted to tell you myself, but I was afraid."

"Afraid?" Rye didn't strike him as the kind of person who feared anything.

"I was afraid you'd treat me different, either pity me or think I wasn't a worthy friend, that I wasn't good enough because my family was a disgrace." Rye sighed. "I should have apologized sooner, but I was ashamed by my behavior and didn't know how to approach you."

Tahki thought a moment. For the last few weeks, he had been the one fighting to prove himself. He never considered Rye might be trying to do the same. "I would never pity you or think you unworthy. You're amazing, Rye. You've overcome so much, and you never complain about anything. Besides, wasn't it you who told me not to try so hard to impress people?"

Rye smiled. "I guess I did." Then he said in a slightly timid voice, "When we get out, maybe we can talk more. I'd like to hear what you wanted to tell me that night."

Tahki thought of the kiss again. He wanted to bring it up, but that might ruin the moment. Instead, he nodded and said, "Is there a way out?"

"The room is sealed," Rye said. "I walked around last night but couldn't find any exit. We're surrounded by dirt walls on every side, too thick to dig through by hand. I'll have to dive under the wall, swim to the other side." Tahki felt sick. Rye must have sensed this, because he said, "You stay here. I'll get Dyraien and some supplies, and we'll knock out the wall."

"All right," Tahki said. It would be easier if he just swam with Rye, but he couldn't swim, and going against the current would be too difficult for Rye to manage with him hanging on.

Without another word, Rye stripped off his shirt and boots. Tahki forced himself to watch, a wave of dizziness overtaking him as Rye took a deep breath and dove in. Tahki shivered as the icy water splashed onto the dirt by his feet. He picked up Rye's damp shirt and boots and sat in the dirt. Tahki hugged the clothing for comfort, brought his knees to his chest, shut his eyes, and chanted a silent mantra to the gods.

Something splashed in the water, and his eyes flew open. He expected to see Rye, but no one was there.

"Hello?" Tahki called. Maybe Dyraien had seen them struggling in the river and come to rescue them.

As he peered into the dim light, a low growl rumbled through the cave. Tahki stood slowly and turned his body toward the sound. He knew what he would find before his eyes rested on the dark mass crouching beside the river. The black cat hunched an arm's length away. There was no place to run, so he faced the animal, his back pressed tight against the rock wall. But the cat didn't attack him. She moved away from the water, toward a tunnel that hadn't been there before. He squinted. Maybe the tunnel was another trick.

The cat trotted a few paces and then looked back at him. Another throaty growl escaped her. He could hear Sornjia's voice telling him to follow her, but he didn't move. The cat was a monster who'd tried to kill him just hours ago. He searched for anything he might use as a weapon, but the only thing he had on him was his mother's pencil. It hadn't fallen out in the river, but a small pencil wouldn't do much good. He'd lodged a hunting knife in the cat's side before and it hardly made a scratch.

The cat swished her tail and growled again, this time loud enough to shake his bones. Tahki couldn't retreat, and there was nowhere to hide and wait for Rye. His only option was to go forward, so he took one hesitant step. The cat moved on, but when he didn't follow, she stopped. He gripped Rye's clothing and took another step. The cat also stepped forward. They moved like this down the tunnel, one choppy step at a time, the cat always a few paces in front of him. She padded through the dirt, leaving behind paw prints larger than both of his feet put together. Her shoulders bobbed up and down in a hypnotic rhythm, and all he could think about was how her jaws could crush him in one bite.

The light faded, and for a time he could hardly make out her shape. With every step, he grew a little bolder. He could actually study the cat now without anxiety overpowering all his sense.

"Where are you leading me?" He felt ridiculous talking to a cat and even more so when she didn't reply.

The pathway finally opened up, and Tahki found himself in a room where natural lightning roots glowed in the dirt walls. Something glinted in the light. He saw a handle, dark wood, and iron bolts.

A door.

He rushed to it and tugged, but it didn't budge. With a sigh, he backed away. The door looked massive, the rings the size of his chest. Tahki swallowed. He didn't recognize the room. A stone pool with black water sat in the middle of a wide, circular floor. The ceiling looked twenty feet tall.

He was standing inside the black gates.

A low moan escaped the cat, and Tahki turned just in time to see her body collapse onto the ground. Light faded from her eyes, and she went still. Tahki watched her a moment, and when she didn't revive, he turned to the black gates and tried tugging again, frantic to escape before she woke. He pulled and twisted and pounded on the wood with his fist.

"Rye? Dyraien? Anyone? Let me out! I'm down here!"

A low groan came from behind, and he turned toward the black pool. The water inside boiled, and he watched in horror as eels twisted their bodies into an oily knot. A shiny black hand emerged from the bubbling heap, then a head, then a body, and legs.

Tahki dropped Rye's boots and shirt and slid his back against the gate, caught between fear and fascination. He wanted to run down the tunnel, but he couldn't move. The figure twisted, its body convulsing as it emerged. Its arms extended, stretched upward, and then it became deathly still.

"You...," a soft, breathless voice called. "You are...."

Tahki swallowed. His entire body trembled. A scream inched its way up his throat, but he couldn't get it out.

The figure bent forward. "You are... a moron!"

Tahki stared, not sure he heard right.

The black water drained away to reveal a young woman no older than him. Her skin was bronze, almost golden, her hair white as cloud marble. Her naked body radiated beauty. It took his brain a moment to realize she had spoken Dhaulenian.

"Well?" the woman said. "Are you just going to sit there all day shivering like a naked dog-rat?"

Tahki didn't move.

The woman rolled her eyes. "I thought Nhymiicha would have raised you better."

Hearing his mother's name broke his fixation. He slid his back up the gate but didn't step forward. "Who.... What are you?"

The woman made a sour face. "Your brother wouldn't waste time with stupid questions. He'd ask something smart, like, how did you possess that cat's body? Why are you stuck in that filthy black water? How do you keep your hair so nice and shiny when you're dead?"

Tahki stared. "Dead?" His religion taught him spirits were real, but he'd never believed it. He'd never really believed in the gods, either, yet just moments ago he'd prayed to them. "You've been the one haunting me? Attacking me?"

The woman pursed her lips and blew air at him. "*Piscgiia!*" She used the word to describe a small, hairless rodent that infested the slums of Dhaulen'aii, an insult commonly shouted at disrespectful children. "*You* were the one who attacked *me*."

Tahki's hand moved to his chest where the cat marks throbbed lightly.

"Oh please," the woman said. She spoke with large sweeping motions of her hands. "You always have to make it about yourself, don't you? Here I am, a dead woman, kidnapped from her home, tortured and sacrificed, and you still make it about you."

Tahki's back stiffened. He had no idea if he should feel afraid or insulted or tricked. "How do you know my mother's name?"

The woman put her hands on her hips. The eels in the water thrashed around her legs. "Tahki." She said his name the way an upset parent might. "I am your great-grandmother."

Her words didn't shock him. His brain had already been shocked enough, like when you keep hitting the same tender spot on your elbow and it eventually goes numb. But he averted his eyes, because if she really was his great-grandmother, he didn't want to see her naked.

"Piscgiia, you're such a prude. That's your father's side of the family," she said. "Your mother's side always welcomed free skin."

"Stop calling me piscgiia," Tahki said. He glanced back at her. "What do you want from me?"

Her face softened a little. "I want you to listen to me. I need your help, Tahki." Her desperate tone made her less frightening.

He remembered his mother painting their family tree on a giant wooden canvas. The finished product had been hung in his parents' bedroom. Tahki used to lie on their bed and study the names. He pictured the tree now and mentally followed the black branches on his mother's side: His mother, grandmother, great-grandmother. He saw her name in his mind.

Niivrena. Her name was Niivrena. He remembered his mother calling her Nii, but all she'd ever told him about her was that she'd vanished without a word when she was young. His father told him Nhymiicha's family had always been flighty and unpredictable. They were people who spoke to the sands and listened to the wind, rarely settling down for long.

"All right," Tahki said. "I'll listen." He took a cautious step forward but gave the lifeless black cat a wide berth.

"I'm sorry about your chest," Nii said. "Possession isn't an exact art. You never have total control over the creature you take the body of, even if they're dead. But I didn't have a choice. You ignored all my illusions. I had to take corporeal form, which is very dangerous for a spirit."

Tahki frowned. "Illusions? You mean the thing in my room and the water?"

Nii nodded. "I tried to bring you here. I can only appear in this body and talk to you when I'm in this pool."

"Why?"

"Because this is the place I was murdered." The eels in the water flared up, nipping at her knees. Tahki wasn't sure where Nii ended and where the eels started, if they were a part of her or keeping her captive. She seemed to ignore them.

Tahki rubbed his wrist and asked, "Who killed you?"

She didn't hesitate. "A woman named Thronis. Dyraien's great-grandmother."

"Why did she kill you?"

"Tahki," Nii said. "I've been watching you. I know what I'm about to say is going to be hard to accept, not because you're a logical person, but because you like Dyraien. You like this castle. You're going to want to resist my words."

She was right. He'd already started reasoning against what little information he had.

Nii bent down and drew a circle in the black water to calm the eels. "Do you know the history of the river you fell in?"

Tahki watched the black water twirl. "You mean the Misty River, the river you tried to drown me in?"

Nii looked him up and down. "You seem fine to me."

"Thanks to Rye."

Nii pursed her lips. "I had a hunch he would save you."

"A hunch? What if you'd been wrong?"

"Then there is always your twin." She gave him a smile. "Now, unless you want to stay here for an eternity arguing with me, tell me what you know of the river."

Tahki rubbed his eyes. If he was going to learn anything, he needed to comply. "I know the river runs from the Calaridian Sea through Vatolokít all the way across Dhaulen'aii. It connects the two oceans."

"But do you know the spiritual history of it?"

Tahki nodded. The Misty River, what in Dhaulen'aii was called Wairupok'ae—the river of souls—was sacred to his people. It was said the river spirited souls from the world of the living to the Dim, the world of the gods.

"This spot here," Nii explained. She wiggled her arms and fingers in a showy manner, like a magician putting on a show for children. "This spot, where the water falls into the white sands, is an entryway, a sacred area where mystical energy gathers. Our ancestors would travel for miles to pray here. It is where the first mystic was born."

Tahki started to ask what a mystic was, but Nii shushed him.

"I know," she said. "So many questions. Give me time to explain, Piscgiia. Mystics are Dhaulenians born with a special connection to the Dim. They are conduits for the gods. The word of the gods travels through them. Because of this connection, it is said the soul of a mystic is so powerful it can open a pathway between worlds. Are you listening to my words, Tahki?"

Tahki nodded.

"But you don't believe them, even after all of this?" Nii kicked her feet and the eels slithered around her legs.

Tahki swallowed. "I don't know what I believe."

Nii rolled her eyes. He'd never actually seen anyone roll her eyes as much as she did. She seemed a little dramatic.

"Listen," Nii said. "Dyraien Királye is not what he claims to be. The Királyes have lied for generations. They have a conquest sickness in them."

Tahki almost jumped to Dyraien's defense, but Nii gave him a hard look and he kept quiet.

"Ambrusthin Királye is Dyraien's great-great-grandmother. She grew up in a temple not far from here, raised by Dhaulenian monks after her father abandoned her. The monks taught her our religion, our ways. One day, a mystic showed up at the temple, a young girl come to learn from the abbot. Ambrusthin befriended the girl, and together they set out on a quest to open the Dim. Ambrusthin was obsessed with the idea of gods and the world of the immortals. The monks did nothing to stop them, as it seemed like harmless child's play. I assume you know what happened next."

Tahki didn't.

Nii looked irritated. "They opened it."

"Opened what?"

"How is it you inherited your mother's talent but not her wit? They opened the Dim, Tahki. Ambrusthin found a way to do it by using the young mystic girl. They saw the Dim with their own eyes. But the pathway did not stay open. It closed as they entered, and both of their bodies were thrust unnaturally back to our world. The mystic girl was killed instantly. Her soul had been the payment for opening it. As for Ambrusthin, her sanity was taken. But not immediately. She grew older, married a prince, killed him when he became king, and took over the country. She had children and told her child what she knew of the Dim before she completely lost her mind. Since then, every generation of Királye has tried to open it and keep it open so they may enter. None have succeeded."

"But why open the Dim?"

"Why do humans do anything? For power. They are searching for the immortals to unlock their secrets. The Dim appears in many cultures, though it's not called the same thing. Many believe it's an afterlife and that the gods are beings of infinite power. Emperors, queens, bishops, they all seek larger armies, deadlier guns, heavier bags of gold. But no family has gone to such length to obtain power as the Királyes have. They are willing to tear the world apart for it."

Tahki swallowed again and again. His throat felt dry and hot. He tried to absorb her words, tried to sort out the lies from the truth.

Nii continued. "The Királyes have pushed for technological advancement in order to find a way to keep the pathway open. They claim they want the world to evolve. Every time a new power source emerges, they use it to try and open the Dim. They capture a mystic and try to keep the path open. I was taken from my home. From my bed by a Királye lackey. They brought me here, bound me, bled me, and forced the pathway to open through me. It was so violating I welcomed death when the pathway collapsed. At least I drove one of them insane." She spat.

Tahki's head spun. "Dyraien would never do that. He's... he's intelligent. He's logical. He would never believe in something like this. He's not like his mother or grandmother or great-grandmother. He's different."

Nii's mouth curved into a cruel smile. "Yes, he is different. But not for the reasons you think."

Tahki felt cold.

"Ten years ago," Nii said, "Dyraien's mother opened the Dim. Dyraien was with her when it happened. She entered and the pathway collapsed. Her body returned to this world just like her predecessors. But this time was different. This time, something was taken from the Dim. The queen stole a piece of the Dim before the path fell. Something the gods want returned to them, because they fear what is to come. Tahki, are you listening?"

Tahki held his breath.

"This is why I am here, Tahki. This is why the gods allowed me to return. For the first time since this world was born, the gods are fearful. Fearful of Dyraien, for he is the first living human to lay eyes on the Dim and keep his sanity. He has witnessed the power the Dim holds, he has discovered its secrets, and he will find a way to bring back that power and use it for his own conquest."

Tahki shook his head. "I've never heard Dyraien mention the Dim." Nii had him all wrong. And yet, Dyraien had looked so obsessive when he saw Tahki's design.

Nii raised an eye brow. "Tahki, what purpose did you think this castle, built over a sacred river in the middle of nowhere, would have? Dyraien wants a weapon. A weapon that will be used to keep the pathway open long enough for him to get what he wants."

"It can't be."

The eels pecked at Nii's side. A high-pitched screech filled the room.

"Tahki," the eels screamed. "You must destroy the castle."

He grabbed his ears.

"Listen to my words," Nii said. "Ten years ago, the monks uncovered the Királyes' plot. Dyraien closed the borders and silenced all who knew the truth."

Tahki forced himself to look at her.

Her eyes swelled with rage. "Dyraien will find a mystic and use this castle to open the Dim. He will destroy both worlds. The Dim must not be opened! You must destroy this castle!"

"I can't!" Tahki yelled.

The eels simmered, and a hush fell over them.

"The castle means everything to me," Tahki said. "You tormented me. Tried to drown me. What if you're just some evil spirit? How do I even know you're my great-grandmother?"

"Because you feel my words are true," Nii said. "Deep inside, you know something is wrong with this castle. The gods have brought you here for a reason."

"My skills as an architect brought me here." He stood a little straighter. "If you want the castle destroyed, why not just take the cat's body and do it yourself?"

"I can't do it alone, Tahki. The cat's body is vulnerable, and illusions only work for so long. It takes a great deal of energy to possess something. If the cat is destroyed, my spirit won't be strong enough to take another. And even if I did manage to kill Dyraien, there are others who know of his plan. So long as this castle stands, there is always a risk. More innocent people will be killed in the Királye conquest."

"But I've worked so hard," Tahki pleaded. "I finally proved myself."

Nii looked suddenly tired. "I know you will do the right thing. I know you will become the man your mother says you are."

Every inch of Tahki's skin crawled. It only struck him now to ask the obvious question. "If you really are a spirit, and you have a connection to the Dim, then I want to see my mother."

Nii looked down into the water. "It does not work like that."

"Why not?" Tahki said. "Why are you here and not her?"

"Because the gods wish it so."

"The gods." Tahki laughed. "If they're all-powerful, why not have them destroy the castle?"

At this, Nii hesitated. "The gods are not what you think. They need your help."

"They took my mother from me. They burned her alive."

Nii's body appeared shorter. She sunk slowly into the pool. "Tahki." Her voice sounded weak. "I know you are hurt and confused, but you must do what is right. You must push aside your doubt and find the courage to save your people, to honor your fallen ancestors. It is up to you now." A faint black mist evaporated off her body. Tahki tried to ask more questions, but she fell into the pool with an unceremonious splash. The eels slithered beneath the surface. The water rippled for a minute and then stilled.

Only Tahki's shallow breath filled the room. He approached the pool and stared into the black waters. Nii's words bounced across his mind, but one sentence stood out: You must destroy the castle.

A grunting noise drew his eyes to the body of the black cat. Her paws twitched, then her whiskers, and then her tail swung outward, catching him in the gut, knocking him over. She rose, stretched, and yawned as though waking from a nap.

Tahki stood. "Nii?"

The black cat looked at him.

"Can you understand me?"

The cat didn't move.

"Blink once if you can understand."

The cat didn't blink.

Tahki buried his face in his hands. "Gods, this isn't happening. This can't be happening." They lived in such an advanced world. A world where science and logic outranked religion for the first time in decades. And now he was forced to think about gods and spirits and other worlds. He knew he needed to do something but wasn't sure what that something was. He couldn't destroy the castle, but he couldn't ignore what Nii told him, either. He'd have to find the piece of the Dim Queen Genevi supposedly brought back.

A creaking noise drew his attention. The cat rolled her head on the ground near the black gate, twisting and turning in the dirt.

"What are you doing?"

The cat ignored him. Tahki saw a small brass lever, something he'd missed before, click forward, and the gates opened an inch. Tahki ran to them. He set his hands on the sturdy wood and heaved. The gate gave way just enough for him to fit his body through. He fetched Rye's clothing and squeezed out. The cat wiggled through as well. He found the stairs and started up. The cat followed.

Tahki halted. "They can't see you. You'll send everyone in a frenzy."

The cat swished her tail and continued upward.

"Listen," he said. "If you want me to help you, you need to stay out of sight."

At this, the cat stopped. She regarded him with a humanlike irritation. For a moment, he thought she might bite him. Instead, she slunk back down the stairway and vanished. After he was sure she was gone, he headed up, unsure how he'd explain his escape to Rye.

Chapter 13

He found Rye, still wet and gathering supplies for Tahki's rescue, and gave him his clothing, explaining that he'd found a thin part in the wall and dug through. He said he'd ended up on the other side of the black gates and was able to open them and come through.

"So what's behind there?" Rye asked after Tahki changed into dry clothing.

"Where?"

"The black gates. You were wondering about them, weren't you?"

"Oh. There isn't anything, just a dirt room." Tahki hesitated, and then said, "Would you mind not telling Dyraien I was in there?"

"Why?"

Tahki shrugged. "It just seems like somewhere he wouldn't want anyone to be. I'd rather not upset him after I've already thrown us off schedule."

"I don't think Dyraien would mind," Rye said. "But I won't say anything, if you don't want me to."

"Thanks." Tahki sat on his bed and rested his head against the wall.

"Dyraien and I will ride to Edgewater to check the order. You should rest."

"All right," Tahki said. Physically, he felt better and should have gone with Rye, but he needed to sort out what Nii had told him.

Rye hesitated and then said, "When I get back, let's have that talk." He left before Tahki could reply.

A few moments later, Dyraien appeared in his doorway, dressed for riding.

"Rye said you felt guilty about falling in the river," Dyraien said, posed with his hand against the doorframe. "I wanted to tell you not to worry. We've only been delayed half a day. Nothing to fret over."

"I'm sorry I've delayed our work," Tahki said.

Dyraien's blue eyes drifted over Tahki. "We have a busy next couple of days, and I'll need you fresh and ready to work when I return."

Tahki forced a nod.

It felt strange talking to him, pretending like nothing had changed. Of course in Dyraien's mind nothing had. But to Tahki, the prince's eyes appeared darker, his golden hair a little less lustrous. Tahki had known from the first day something was off about Dyraien's plans for the castle, but could he really be trying to open the Dim? It sounded too unbelievable. And yet, wasn't everything that had happened to him unbelievable? The castle flooding. A resurrected cat. Talking to a spirit. It was all too much. Nii expected him to act, but his mind spun in so many different directions, he could think of nowhere to start.

Tahki thought about confronting him. All these secrets and games hurt his head. They were civilized humans, weren't they? What would happen if he outright asked Dyraien about his family, about the Dim, about the true purpose of the castle? It wasn't like Dyraien had royal guards waiting to arrest him.

But he didn't know anything for sure, except that Dyraien was hiding something, and he couldn't risk both his life and possibly Sornjia's by exposing himself.

Dyraien lingered. "You really need to be more careful, Tahki. We can't have you drowning on us now, can we? Not before the rebirth of our castle." He said "our castle" like he and Tahki were having a child together.

"I'm excited to see her completed," Tahki said.

"You should be." Dyraien smiled. "You've worked so hard, and soon you'll be repaid for all your efforts. I promise."

AFTER DYRAIEN and Rye left for Edgewater, Tahki took a long bath, washed the mud off his face, dressed, and went to find Sornjia. The sun dimmed, and a low haze covered the orange and pink sky. Evening approached.

Before he reached the bottom of the cliff, he heard heavy steps behind him. He glanced back. The black cat followed at a distance. He didn't try to chase her away.

When he reached the house, he told the cat to wait outside until he made sure Gale was gone, but the cat ignored him and pushed inside the home with her snout.

"Hold on a minute!" Tahki whispered. "If she sees you—"

"Gale?" Sornjia called from the kitchen. "Did you forget something?"

Sornjia stepped into the room and froze at the sight of the black cat. The cat looked even more monstrous inside the house. If she stood on her hind paws, her head would break through the low ceiling.

Tahki hadn't seen his brother surprised by much. In fact, he couldn't remember his brother ever looking so shocked. It felt like a small victory.

"That's her?" Sornjia said. "The cat who attacked you?"

Tahki nodded.

"She's beautiful," Sornjia said in a breathless voice.

"Beautiful?" Tahki frowned. "She's a monster."

"I want to pet her."

"What? No. Sornjia, she tried to drown me."

Sornjia reached out a hand. Instead of growling or snapping or clawing at him like she'd done to Tahki, she leaned gently into his touch. The eels peeked out from under her skin and reached forward like long blades of grass turning toward the sun. Sornjia tensed but didn't pull away as they hissed and curled around his fingers. They disappeared back into her fur after a few seconds. Sornjia smiled.

"You can't be serious," Tahki said. "Aren't you the least bit shocked by her? Even you can't deny she's the creepiest thing you've ever seen."

The cat turned to Tahki and snarled. He took a step back.

"People are scared of darkness and shadows," Sornjia said. "But shadows have never hurt anyone."

Tahki gave up. He'd expected a little more resistance from Sornjia. A little more questioning. A little more *something*. Sornjia acted like Tahki had brought home a stray street cat.

"Tell me everything," Sornjia said.

"What if Gale comes back?"

"She won't. She's gone until tomorrow morning on a fishing trip. Sit. Speak."

Sornjia settled himself on a wobbly chair by the table, and Tahki sat across from him. The cat hunched by Sornjia's side, her head now at eye level with them.

Tahki spoke with clear and precise words, recalling as much detail as he could. He started with his near-death experience in the river, even confessed his kiss with Rye, and then talked about Nii. As he spoke, Sornjia stroked the cat's head as though she were nothing more than a playful kitten. He knew Sornjia believed in the gods. He meditated and worshipped as adamantly as their father. But even their father would have had difficulty accepting the cat's existence.

When Tahki finished, Sornjia fetched him a glass of water without being asked. Tahki drank it in three large gulps. It cooled his raw throat. The water here tasted more heavily of minerals than the water back home.

"Are you going to do it?" Sornjia said after Tahki caught his breath.

"Do what?"

"Destroy the castle."

"No."

"Why?"

"Because I have no idea what I'm up against." Tahki rubbed his eyes with his wrists. "I need to find proof. I need to know for certain what Nii said about Dyraien is true."

He couldn't ignore what Nii had told him, but the weight of what she said about the castle felt like a boulder pinning him down. He'd worked so hard on his designs, overcome so much failure to find success. And how would Rye react if he took down the castle without proof? He didn't even know how to destroy it. They had no explosives, and obsidian wouldn't burn. He might be able to get Rye behind the black gates, let him talk to Nii, but that was a huge risk. Rye might run at the sight of the cat or think it was a trick. One thing he knew for sure, if he tried to bring down the castle or Dyraien without solid proof, Rye would never forgive him.

"Pooka," Sornjia said.

"What?"

"Pooka," Sornjia repeated. "That's what I'm going to call her."

Tahki looked at the cat. "She isn't a stray. You can't name her. Besides, shouldn't we call her Nii?"

Sornjia rubbed behind her ear. She shut her eyes and made a low throaty noise that sounded like a deep purr. "I don't think it is Nii," Sornjia said. "Not entirely. I think Nii's spirit is in there, but these bones, those muscles, her teeth and claws and tail, they all belong to the cat."

The black cat—now unarguably named Pooka—rolled her shoulders and yawned. If he understood correctly, she was more wild animal than possessed spirit. Nothing prevented her from turning them into an afternoon meal.

Tahki scooted away from her. "Sornjia, I need to find proof of what the Királyes have done. I need something I can show Rye and Gale to convince them I'm not crazy. I'll need their help if I want to expose Dyraien."

Sornjia smiled. "Then we search for evidence."

When Sornjia smiled, it always touched his eyes. They were identical, but Tahki could never smile like that. Sornjia had a genuine selflessness about him, a mindful nature that seemed unreachable to Tahki. It was wrong to ask his brother for help. Sornjia's life might be at risk. He should insist he leave. Yet he knew his brother would not go. Tahki might be able to force him, drag him across the border, but that would leave Rye here alone to withstand whatever Dyraien planned.

Tahki said, "All right. Where do we start?"

Sornjia sat forward in his chair. "We need to find what Dyraien's mother took from the Dim."

Tahki chewed the inside of his lip. "If he had anything, it would be in his room."

"You'll have to search when he's away."

Tahki nodded. "He's in Edgewater now. What about you?"

"Dyraien mentioned a parcel. I'm going to try and find out what it is. From what you overheard, it sounds like Zinc and Hona will be delivering it to the castle. I'll hide out on the high road and wait for them."

Tahki took a breath. "Promise me you'll stay away from Zinc. I think he's waiting for an opportunity to get me alone."

Sornjia smiled wider. "It will be just like when we played Alabaraiin as children."

Tahki thought back to all the trouble they'd caused as kids, stealing curry pies and spying on their father's diplomatic meetings as they reenacted adventures of their favorite storybook hero. In those stories, there was always some great evil to vanquish. A villain with a scar across his left eye and an evil laugh. Tahki wished things were as straightforward in real life.

They walked outside. Stars flickered above, a rare clear night. He hadn't noticed how different the constellations were here. It looked like purple dust had been sprinkled across the sky.

"I think this is where we wish each other good luck," Sornjia said.

Tahki rubbed his wrist and faced his brother. "You don't have to do this. I'm the one haunted by spirits. You should be home, meditating with the monks. I bet they miss you."

Sornjia pointed to the sky. "I'm right where I'm supposed to be. All the stars are shining their light on us, a thousand brothers and sisters wanting us to succeed." With that, Sornjia headed down the road, Pooka trotting beside him with eerie fluidity, and for the briefest moment, Tahki felt as though some terrible fate awaited his brother.

THE CASTLE appeared darker than usual. He'd never been inside it alone before. Of course he wasn't alone. Not with the queen locked up, a prisoner in her own home. She'd been so silent the last few days he'd almost forgotten about her.

It felt intimate, walking up the white stairway, heading through the black halls with no sound but the clack of his boots on the hard marble. The walls pressed around him; the floor curved to meet his feet. He reached out and ran his hand along the fine obsidian. The walls weren't flat but bumpy, imperfect. A gem that hadn't been cut. A few pillars below had crumbled, shards of obsidian scattered on the floor. He had dreamed of completing the castle for weeks, picturing what she would look like whole. Now he wondered what it would take to demolish her. He tried not to think about it and instead set his eyes on Dyraien's door. When he reached it, he pressed an ear against the cold wood, but no sound stirred inside.

"Dyraien?" he said. No answer came. He pushed the handle down and walked inside, closing the door behind him as he looked around.

His senses flared as he entered the room. His ears strained to hear the sounds they hadn't caught before: the low sleeping wails of the queen in the next room, the scrape of dry sand against the windowpane, the tick of a tall clock in the corner.

It didn't look like the room of a prince. There were no lavish decorations, no tapestries or golden statues or bearskin rugs. But it was still the nicest room in the castle. His bed was large with royal blue sheets, puffy pillows, and four oak bedposts. The walls were lined with books on every subject from human anatomy to modern architecture to objective journals on world religions. Some of the books were about Dhaulen'aii. But he had books on many other cultures too. A few titles he didn't recognize. He pulled one out and saw pictures of people in sexual positions. Quickly, he shoved the erotic covers away and felt himself flush.

The room smelled heavily of rosewater and some kind of citrus fruit. No dust lay on the floor, which meant he wouldn't leave any footprints. His search started at the bookshelves. In stories he'd read, secret items—a poison knife or loaded pistol—were always hidden inside a carved-out book. There were too many books to go through, so instead, he flicked each one by the spine to see if any rattled. After that, he went to the windows and patted the curtains. He moved counterclockwise around the room, tapping the marble floor with his boots to see if any area felt hollow or wobbly. Every piece of clothing was unfolded and refolded. He skimmed schematics and letters stacked on the writing desk. He even opened up the mechanism in the clock.

He had no idea what a piece of the Dim looked like.

At one point, he found his design for the steam conduit system tucked neatly in one of the drawers. Dyraien would be suspicious if he found it missing, but he decided to take it anyway. He swiped the paper, folded it until it fit in his pocket, and felt immediately better. Dyraien might have already ordered the supplies, but at least if they destroyed this castle, he wouldn't be able to make another. He continued to pace the wall, feeling for drafts or cracks, and when he found none, he checked Dyraien's bath chamber with the same scrutiny.

Half an hour later, Tahki collapsed onto Dyraien's bed. His eyes felt heavy with sleep, and his arms hurt. He let out a sigh and rubbed his temples, feeling foolish. He hadn't found so much as a harsh letter. Maybe Nii had been wrong. Dyraien wasn't hiding anything. He wasn't following in the footsteps of his mother. Maybe this castle was some kind of cover-up for her mistakes, that all along he'd sought to make things right, give up the throne and give the council an apology gift.

He put his hand on the bedpost and heaved himself up. As he did, the post wobbled and something clunked inside. Tahki stared at the wooden post. He wiggled it, and it rattled again. It felt loose and hollow.

With quick fingers, he unscrewed the knob at the top and peered inside. The post was indeed hollowed out, and something glinted inside. He reached in with his index and middle finger and grasped something. It took a moment to maneuver the item up the sides. When he finally freed it, he stepped to the window to examine it.

A stone the size of his palm lay in his hand, but he couldn't really call it a stone. It looked more like glass, and beneath the smooth, clear surface, the night sky shined back at him.

He couldn't tear his eyes away.

The stone hummed slightly. He'd seen stars through telescopes and read about bright lights that appeared in the northern sky. The stone in his hand reminded him of those lights. Purples, blues, and greens all mixed together, dancing as bright white specks flowed into one another. A small fleck shot across the surface like a shooting star. It circled the stone once and then erupted like a firework.

As he turned the stone over in his palm, mesmerized by its beauty, he noticed it wasn't a stone, but a piece of something, like it had been broken off a larger part. But he'd never seen anything like it. In his head he listed all the minerals he knew, but none of them possessed properties like this. If it didn't feel so sturdy, so real, he would have thought it to be an illusion.

The stone captivated him so entirely he didn't hear the footsteps until they squeaked against the marble a few doors down.

Tahki spun around. The footsteps stopped right outside. He shoved the stone back in the post and loosely twisted the knob. As the door handle turned down, he dove under the bed, pulling his feet in as someone entered the room. He recognized Dyraien's muddy white boots.

Sweat broke out across his brow. Had he seen Tahki dive under the bed? Did he notice the crumpled bedsheets? Had Tahki put everything back in its rightful place? Dyraien seemed like the kind of person who would instantly know if someone had rummaged through his things.

Tahki's throat pressed against the hard marble, and he could feel his pulse beating. He tried to swallow, but the cold floor constricted his airway. Dyraien walked across the room, sat down on his bed, and released a sigh. The mattress curved downward and pressed against

Tahki's back. He watched Dyraien's boots fly off, dirt skidding across the floor as they landed.

Tahki held his breath. A strange laugh caught in his throat, and the most unusual need to cry out struck him. How would he explain himself if he was found? Dyraien was paranoid about spies, especially foreign ones. And here Tahki was, hiding beneath the prince's bed. He couldn't look guiltier if he tried.

He felt Dyraien lie back onto the bed. The posts shook, and the knob Tahki hadn't secured jiggled and fell to the floor with a loud clank. The knob rolled in a circle inches from Tahki's face.

Silence.

Every hair on Tahki's arm pricked upward. The pressure from the mattress lifted, and Dyraien stood above the knob, his bare feet close enough to touch.

Dyraien reached down and scooped up the knob. If he looked to his left, everything would be over. But his motions were fluid, his blond hair only bobbing into sight a second. The smell of ale and smoke wafted over Tahki. Again there came no sound.

This morning had been one of the proudest moments of his life. The feeling of accomplishment and success had overwhelmed him. He had thought things would finally go his way, that his life from that point on would be a series of consecutive wins. Now he wondered if these were his last moments of freedom. But no, Dyraien wouldn't imprison him. Tahki would be considered a traitor and killed.

He heard the stone slide down the post and the knob turn. The mattress curved against him again. Dyraien had put the stone back, perhaps figuring the loose knob had been his own error.

At least Tahki prayed he had.

Tahki lay still on his belly for countless minutes, until Dyraien's snores became audible. Then he crawled out from under the bed and slid across the floor, his face low, his palms slippery with sweat against the marble. He dragged his body slowly so it wouldn't squeak against the floor. The door lay only an arm's length away when Dyraien coughed and the bed creaked.

Tahki froze. He didn't dare turn to see if Dyraien watched him. The moonlight had dimmed, but the marble was so white that Tahki's body formed a stark silhouette. He tried to hold his breath, but his lungs ached too much. Then a few prayers later, Dyraien's snores filled the room again.

This time Tahki scrambled forward on his knees. Dyraien hadn't shut the door tight, so it was easy to sneak through. It wasn't until he was out in the hall and making his way down the stairs that he took a deep breath. His legs quivered like a thin wire bearing an elephant's weight.

At the bottom of the stairs, he stopped. He should have taken the stone with him. But the stone alone wouldn't have been enough to condemn Dyraien. It did, however, prove that Nii had been telling the truth, because nothing like that stone existed in this world.

Tahki made for the front door. He needed to find Sornjia and see what kind of item the parcel was, and if it would tie into the stone somehow.

"Tahki?"

Tahki startled.

Rye stood in the doorway of his workroom. "I thought you were resting."

"I was," Tahki said. "My legs hurt from sitting around all day. I thought I'd go for a walk."

Rye ran a hand through his hair. "I'm glad you're feeling better." He turned back to his workroom, then hesitated. He faced Tahki and said, "Actually, if you have time, there's something I'd like to talk to you about."

Tahki remembered the promised talk, but now wasn't the time to tell him about Dhaulen'aii or who he was. Or maybe it wasn't about that at all. Maybe Rye had remembered the kiss and wanted to tell him he wasn't interested. Either way, Tahki didn't have time for a long—and most likely uncomfortable—talk. He needed to find out about the parcel.

"I'm a little tired," Tahki said.

"I thought you said you were going for a walk."

Tahki rubbed his wrist. "I was, but suddenly I don't feel all that good."

Rye's eyes lowered. He shrugged one shoulder and said, "I understand. We'll talk later. When you feel better." He turned to go, and Tahki couldn't stand it. Rye sounded so disappointed.

"A minute," Tahki said. "Just a minute, and then I should get to bed."

Rye nodded. "Let's talk in my room."

DESPITE HIS previous apprehension, Tahki felt a wave of calm upon entering Rye's room. He'd come to associate the smells of linseed oil and coffee with comfort and safety.

When the door closed behind them, Rye spoke. "I'm not great with talking about stuff like this." Tahki wasn't sure what "stuff like this" meant, but Rye clearly had more to say, so he kept quiet. "But these last few days have been so confusing, and I can't sort it all out in my head, so I need to say it aloud."

Tahki situated himself on the bed, ready to listen.

Rye paced a little, fidgeted with one of his brass compasses, and then straightened his shirt. He must have become aware of his fidgeting, because when he spoke again, he folded his arms into each other as though to keep them still. "It's about what happened at the river."

Tahki tensed. "The river?" He thought of the black cat, of Nii, of the kiss.

Rye's arms broke free and he rubbed his jaw. "I—" He swallowed. "I know you were traumatized, and you didn't know what you were doing. But I don't want you to avoid me, or act weird around me. We can just pretend it never happened, if that's what you want."

Tahki frowned. "Avoid you?"

"I know it didn't mean anything."

"What didn't?"

Rye met his eyes with apparent effort. "You kissed me."

This time it was Tahki who looked away, though he didn't feel ashamed of what he'd done.

"It's all right," Rye said. "I know it was a mistake. It's why you didn't mention it, why you acted scared when you saw me just now."

Tahki couldn't tell him he had looked scared because he'd been sneaking around the prince's bedroom.

"Rye, you don't understand."

"I do understand," Rye said. Every muscle in his body tensed. "We're isolated out here, and the isolation can get to you in more ways than one. Even if you don't feel the same way I feel about you, we can still be friends."

Tahki sat stiffly. "Even if I don't feel the same way?"

Rye swallowed. "No one has ever made me feel so confused, so angry, so nervous and excited as you do." He took a breath. "It frustrated me that someone I hardly knew could make me feel all that. Then you kissed me, and I thought you felt the same. But I understand you made a mistake. We're adults. It doesn't have to be awkward."

Tahki felt lucid then, a warm sensation dissolving through his body as he realized what Rye was telling him.

"Say something," Rye said.

But Tahki had nothing to say, because the feelings Rye had described were exactly how he felt too. He smiled, picturing Rye practicing this speech, trying to sound both diplomatic and indifferent but instead coming off flustered and shy. Rye looked a little hurt, probably thinking Tahki was mocking him.

So Tahki rose from the bed, stood directly in front of Rye, grabbed his face between his hands, and drew their lips together. He had to crane his neck upward to reach. The kiss was sloppy, but he didn't care. He pressed into Rye, and Rye pressed back. He wrapped his arms around Rye's neck and pulled their hips together. The embrace felt both painful and passionate, like their need for each other turned all other sensations into ones of pleasure.

When they broke apart, Rye pushed Tahki's shoulders gently, and he fell onto the bed. Rye removed his shirt. Tahki tugged his shirt off, too, but suddenly felt self-conscious. He'd never thought about the appeal of his own body. His adolescence had been spent closed in a dark room drawing. He'd immersed himself so deeply in architecture that things like sex and physical attraction hadn't mattered. He'd been called pretty before, but pretty wasn't what he wanted. Pretty was flowers and sunsets. No one ever craved pretty, not the way they craved lean muscles, a strong jaw, and disarmingly dark eyes like Rye had.

But Rye's desire was apparent, and Tahki relaxed a little. No one had ever looked at him with such want. Rye ran his fingers along Tahki's collarbone. A line of goose bumps rose in their wake. Tahki let out a small gasp and dug his fingers into Rye's hair. He never thought another person's hands could feel so good, could make his body react so strongly. He wondered if Rye felt the same pressure building in his lower abdomen.

Rye leaned down and kissed him. This kiss was skillful. Tahki parted his lips and their tongues met. A delicious humidity passed between them, sweat rolling off their bodies. Each kiss touched something deep inside Tahki, a buried passion he hadn't known existed. Rye's breath came in hot, ragged waves. His skin was smooth and pale in the light, his muscles flexing with each small movement.

Then Rye started to move down Tahki's body. He kissed him on his neck, his shoulders, his chest, and his belly. Tahki tried to reciprocate, but each time he sat up, Rye pushed him gently back down. When Rye started to unbutton Tahki's pants, Tahki lifted his legs a little, which prevented Rye from continuing. Rye pushed his legs down, but Tahki drew them back up.

Rye stopped. "Is something wrong?"

"No. Everything feels right." Tahki panted lightly.

"Then why do you keep stopping me? Don't you want this?"

Tahki frowned. "Of course. But you're not letting me touch you the way you're touching me."

"What do you mean?"

"Every time I try to do something to you, you push me down. I just want to make you feel the way you're making me feel."

Rye lowered his eyes a little, uneasy now about something Tahki didn't understand. He wished he'd kept quiet, let Rye do what he wanted, how he wanted.

"Right," Rye said. "I guess that's how it's supposed to be, isn't it? Two people together, trusting each other."

Tahki didn't know what he meant, but before he could ask, Rye grabbed his shoulders and yanked him up. He rolled over, so Tahki was on top now, Rye on his back.

"I'm all yours," Rye said.

Tahki didn't move. He straddled Rye, uncertain what to do. Clearly Rye felt uncomfortable letting Tahki have some control, and this was a gesture to show his trust. Tahki didn't want to mess it up.

Rye watched him patiently. His hand slid up and down Tahki's arm, stroking the skin in a gentle, sensual way. Tahki had no idea he could be aroused by such a simple touch.

He unbuttoned Rye's pants and slid his hand in. It gave him a boost of confidence when he felt Rye's arousal. He moved his hand quickly and kissed Rye's neck. Rye moaned and unbuttoned Tahki's pants.

"Like this," Rye whispered in his ear. With maddening slowness he touched Tahki, only his motions were different, more rhythmic.

Tahki mimicked, and for a time they melted into each other, their bodies entwined, burning like fire. Or maybe it was like water flowing. Or mountains colliding. Or wind sweeping across an endless plain.

The pressure inside Tahki grew and grew until his insides shook and shivered, and the release tore through him so strongly he bit his own lip and tasted blood before it was done. Beneath him, he felt Rye go through the same motions, and they collapsed next to each other, panting.

Tahki breathed deeply, his entire body relaxed, and he thought if he could have Rye like this, he wouldn't need fame, or the castle, or the approval of a prince. If Rye could be his from now on, he would ask for nothing more.

Chapter 14

When Tahki woke the next morning, he tried to keep his eyes pinched shut. Morning meant work, and work, for the first time in his life, wasn't something he wanted to think about. After weeks of pressure put on him because of the castle, the hauntings, the conspiracies, his entire body begged him to let this moment last just a little longer.

He arched his back and felt Rye's body behind him. After a moment of debate, he turned to face him and kissed the tip of his nose.

Rye smiled but didn't open his eyes. "You smell like graphite."

"I didn't know graphite smelled."

"It does. Like dirt and lead and a little like static electricity."

"You can smell static electricity?"

"I have a great sense of smell."

"What else do I smell like?"

"Sweat. Salt. And…." Rye opened his eyes. He drew his face near Tahki and took a deep breath. "A little like wet cat."

Tahki thought of Pooka and wondered if Sornjia had found out anything about the parcel. But then Rye's hand moved from his back to his shoulder to his belly, and those thoughts faded. Rye's hand rested on his stomach a moment before traveling downward. Tahki shut his eyes and leaned into Rye's touch. They hadn't had sex last night, only touched each other with their hands. Tahki didn't want to rush things, but his body craved more.

Rye kissed his neck and whispered, "When the castle is done, I want to take you sailing."

Tahki laughed. "Not going to happen."

"It's not?"

"It's not."

"Why?"

"I'm terrified of drowning."

Rye sat up a little and looked him in the eye.

Tahki hadn't wanted them to stop kissing, but he didn't want to miss an opportunity to tell Rye something about himself, either.

He told him about his mother, about the fire, how he'd almost drowned, leaving out obvious details like how he'd lived in a palace, how it had been a monk who'd saved him. It didn't feel like the right time to tell him everything, not when his world felt so perfect.

"I'm sorry about your mother," Rye whispered. "Maybe when the castle is finished, I can take you out on a lake. Start small, work up to the big blue."

Tahki shook his head. "No force in this world will get me on a boat."

Rye smiled. "Sounds like a challenge. I might not be as persuasive as Dyraien, but I'm patient."

"Why is sailing so important to you?"

Rye shifted on his side. "The only time I really feel like myself is when I'm out on the ocean. When Dyraien and I first met, I didn't trust him. He saved me, but deep down I thought it was for some selfish reason. What prince offers a slum child safety and asks for nothing in return? I stayed suspicious, until he took me sailing for the first time. He taught me how to navigate, how to test the wind, how to predict storms. No one had ever done anything like that for me. It changed my life."

"You and Dyraien are really close, aren't you?" Tahki asked.

"Dyraien is my family. I know he's not perfect, but he's a good person. He's my brother."

Guilt nested in the pit of Tahki's stomach. Rye considered Dyraien his brother, and Dyraien seemed to have similar sentiments. It would be difficult to convince Rye of the prince's intentions. Rye clearly didn't know the Királye history. He might be able to prove Dyraien had lied about the castle, but Tahki would need some irrevocable piece of evidence beyond a shiny stone if he planned to get Rye on his side. One thing he knew for sure, no matter what happened next, he would not leave the castle without Rye by his side.

Tahki turned to kiss him when the door flew open. It banged against the wall and Tahki jumped. Dyraien strode in, his face focused on a paper in his hand.

"Rye," Dyraien said. "The order is set to arrive in one hour. We need to push everything up to accommodate for an early drop and clear the—" And then he caught sight of them. A rare look of confusion crossed his face. It seemed like he was about to ask a question, but then his eyes narrowed slightly. He probably realized what was happening. Or what had happened.

"What needs clearing?" Rye said. His voice sounded calm, unashamed.

Tahki didn't know why he felt guilty. They'd done nothing wrong. Yet the way Dyraien watched them—or watched Rye—made Tahki's skin flush with shame. Dyraien didn't look at him. He kept his eyes on Rye.

"The entryway," Dyraien said. The cold edge to his voice sent a chill down Tahki's back. "We'll need to unhinge the front door."

Rye nodded. "That shouldn't take me more than ten minutes. We'll be ready for the supplies."

Dyraien stood still. His lips pressed into a thin line, like he was trying hard to contain himself. "Keeping to the timeline is crucial to our success. Distractions are our enemy." With that, he turned and strode out without closing the door behind him.

Tahki released a breath. "He looked angry."

Rye yawned. "Angry?"

"I don't think he'll like me so much after this."

"Why would you think that?"

Tahki thought about how Dyraien needed control. How he seemed so possessive of Rye, and hated the unexpected. Seeing the two of them in bed together had probably been quite a shock.

"I just wish you had locked the door," Tahki said.

Rye frowned. "Are you ashamed of what we did?"

"What? Gods no."

Rye grabbed his hand. "Don't worry about Dyraien. He's the one always telling me I need to bed someone."

Tahki kissed his shoulder. "I'm starving. Make me breakfast."

Rye shoved Tahki's head away. "How about you make me breakfast this time?"

"All right. How do you want your bread? Baked or fried?"

"Honestly," Rye said, "what would you do without me?"

Tahki considered this. Had it not been for Rye, he would have been fired, lost, drowned, and who knew what else.

"I owe you a lot," Tahki said. He hoped it came out sincere, because he'd never thought anything as genuinely as he thought this. "More than I think I'll ever be able to pay back."

Rye swiveled over the side of the bed. "You really have a way of turning lighthearted conversations into something dramatic, don't you?"

"I think I get that from my mom's side."

"How about we both make breakfast? Omelet on fried bread."

"I can manage that."

They dressed and went to the kitchen. Rye cracked a few eggs in a bowl while Tahki buttered some bread at the table. The wind tapped at the window behind him. He couldn't stop smiling. After weeks of stealing glances, Tahki could finally stare openly at Rye. The wind rapped gently again. Tahki watched Rye grate cheese into the pan where the eggs sizzled. He knew it wouldn't be easy convincing Rye about Dyraien's secret, but he needed to try. The supplies were to be delivered any moment. He was running out of time.

The wind knocked at the glass behind him, three consecutive beats. Tahki glanced back and nearly fell out of his chair. Sornjia stared back at him, one hand on the glass, eyes wide, positioned to the left of the window so only his head could be seen. Tahki stood so quickly the chair tumbled back and crashed to the ground.

"Something wrong?" Rye asked, his eyes on the eggs.

Tahki put his back to the window. "What? No. No, nothing's wrong."

"I thought you'd be more excited," Rye said. "They'll be delivering the order today. You'll finally get to see one of your designs come to life."

For an instant, the thought sent a wave of joy through him. Seeing one of his designs come to life—he didn't count the temple, since it had fallen apart—had been a dream since he first started sketching. He didn't know anything about the gods, if they controlled a person's fate, but if they did, it was cruel and unjust to give him a taste of success and then take it away before anyone could see him shine.

He walked over to Rye. "Listen, I completely forgot, I promised Gale I'd stop over. She had a question about the installation of the conduit system."

"We can go together, after breakfast," Rye said.

Tahki rubbed his wrist.

Rye rested the spatula against the pan. "What's the matter?"

"Nothing." Tahki smiled.

"You're rubbing your left wrist. You only do that when you're nervous."

Tahki let his hands drop to his side. "Have you met Gale? I don't want to incur her wrath. I need to run down there, now, but there's no sense in both of us going. I'm sure Dyraien needs your help with unhinging the door, and I'd prefer not to upset him again."

Rye shrugged. "If that's what you want."

Tahki started to walk out of the room, but Rye grabbed his wrist. He tugged him close and kissed his mouth. When they pulled apart, Rye gave him a gentle shove out the door and said, "I'll see you tonight."

"Have you lost your mind?" Tahki said. "Gods, Sornjia, what were you thinking coming here? What if someone had seen you?"

They moved from the castle into the thin mist. Sornjia stayed a few paces ahead of him, his hands clenched into fists.

"Sornjia, slow down." Tahki had to jog to keep up with him. "What's going on? Where's Pooka? Talk to me." He grabbed his brother's shoulder and spun him around.

"There's no time," Sornjia said.

"Sornjia, you're scaring me."

Sornjia continued toward Gale's house. "I knew something awful would happen. I could feel it turning in my gut, but I never thought it would be this."

"What? What happened? What did you see?"

Sornjia kept quiet until they reached Gale's. The old woman hadn't returned from her fishing trip, but she might be back at any time.

"How long until the castle is complete?" Sornjia asked.

"The supplies have probably arrived by now. They'll install everything today. Dyraien hired some outside contractors to help." He knew the contractors were Zinc's people, those who could be paid for their silence.

Sornjia grabbed his head. "I'm sinking. I'm stuck in a black bog. The more I wiggle, the deeper I fall."

"Enough with the doom and despair," Tahki said. "Just tell me what you saw."

Sornjia gulped. He seemed to struggle a moment and then said, "They have Gotem."

"Gotem?"

Sornjia nodded. "The parcel wasn't a thing. It was a person. It was Gotem. They've captured Gotem, Tahki."

"That's impossible. Gotem is back home in Dhaulen'aii."

"They're going to do something terrible to him."

"Why would they capture Gotem? They don't even know him."

"I waited on the high road until I saw them," Sornjia said. "Hona and Zinc, driving a buckboard. I followed them to the castle. They went around back, met up with Dyraien, unloaded a large box from the back."

"You went back to the castle? What if they had seen you?"

"I was careful. Listen, Tahki, they pried open the box, and there he was, tied and gagged."

Tahki's mouth felt dry. "It couldn't have been Gotem."

"It was him."

"How close were you that you were able to distinguish him?"

"Tahki, don't you understand what this means?"

Tahki shook his head. He couldn't stop thinking about what would have happened if Sornjia had been caught.

Sornjia put his hand on Tahki's shoulders and looked him in the eye. "Gotem is a mystic, Tahki. They're going to use him to open the Dim."

Tahki stared back into his brother's green eyes. Sornjia spoke with such certainty. "You're sure you saw Gotem?" It wouldn't have mattered if it was Gotem or not. Someone had been captured. If Tahki could find him, it might be enough to prove Dyraien's guilt.

"Pooka and I saw him," Sornjia said. "She looked so angry, but I told her not to be rash. She's waiting for us out on the sand field."

"Waiting for us to what?"

"To make a plan," Sornjia said. "We need to rescue Gotem, destroy the castle, and expose Dyraien. It's up to us to set things right."

Tahki watched his brother's eyes flare with purpose. If Dyraien had caught Tahki in his room last night, Sornjia would have been stuck here, unable to get across the border. His brother had traveled to Vatolokít of his own volition, but he'd only done so because of Tahki's recklessness. He'd been irresponsible, impulsive, and above all else, selfish. This castle might have proved his talent to his mother's spirit, but all the talent in the world wouldn't mean a thing if Sornjia got hurt or killed.

"The plan," Tahki said. "The plan is to get you out of Vatolokít."

Sornjia bit his knuckle, studying him, like it was Tahki who spoke in riddles now. "I don't understand," he said.

"There is no *we* this time, Sornjia," Tahki said. "I'm going to forge the documents for you. You'll go to Edgewater and take a southbound carriage to the border."

"Have you been listening? They abducted Gotem. We can't leave him."

Tahki straightened his back. "I won't leave Gotem. Once you're gone, I'm going to find him. He's the proof I need to convince Rye and Gale. After I have them on my side, we can work together to expose Dyraien."

"That will take too long," Sornjia said. "We need to act now."

"We can't just barge in there. Aren't you the one who said we can't be rash?"

"That's before I knew how soon they'd complete the castle." Sornjia stepped closer to him. "We can use Pooka as a distraction. She'll cause a ruckus, and we'll find Gotem and rescue him, and then we'll destroy the castle."

"We don't even know where Dyraien took him."

"Rye will help us. I know he will. If we can just—"

"Stop, Sornjia," Tahki yelled. "You're not going anywhere near that castle. You're going home."

Sornjia stared. "Tahki, I know you always tell me to speak normal, to be clear about what I say, so please listen closely. If you do this alone, you will die."

Sornjia had never been so specific with his precognitions. Normally, when he predicted dark clouds and stormy weather, his eyes would glaze over, a part of him lost somewhere. But now he looked alert, his eyes brighter than Tahki had ever seen.

"This is not up for negotiation," Tahki said. "It's either you leave alone, or I drag you across the border, and then Gotem will be left behind." It was a bluff. He wouldn't leave Gotem, and he wouldn't leave Rye. But he also couldn't put his brother's life in danger again. For once in his life, he would be the one thinking of Sornjia's safety, instead of the other way around.

"Please, Tahki. Don't send me away."

Tahki didn't answer. He went to Sornjia's room, retrieved the blue papers from under his pillow, and walked to the front door.

"I'm going back to the castle now," Tahki said. "My supplies are there. I should have these forged in an hour."

"Tahki?"

"Swear to me you'll leave." Tahki turned to him. "Swear you'll go home when I return with the documents."

He expected his brother to argue, to spurt out some condemning metaphor. But Sornjia looked relaxed, his shoulders loose, body no longer posed for a fight.

Sornjia stared at him through half-lidded eyes, the fire in them now extinguished. And then, in a calm voice, he said, "All right. If you want me to leave, I'll leave."

"You swear?"

"I swear on the trees and the sky and the sea."

"Good." Before his brother changed his mind, Tahki jogged out the door, across the damp sands, and up the narrow path where the castle waited for him in the silent fog.

THIRTY MINUTES after he'd returned to the castle and started forging Sornjia's documents, he heard a loud commotion downstairs.

The supplies had been delivered.

The queen wailed in her room, but Dyraien didn't see to her. It was unlike the prince to ignore his mother's cries. Tahki knew he should hate the queen for what she'd done to his people, but he remembered how pitiful she'd looked that first day in the castle, and he felt a little sorry for her.

He let the documents dry, fanning the rough paper back and forth so the ink wouldn't smear, and then he folded them carefully into his pocket and walked to the stairs. Once his brother left, he could search for Gotem, or whoever it was they'd captured.

From the top of the steps, he saw two buckboards outside, the front doors spread wide, unhinged. Men and women heaved wooden crates and stacked them inside the open doors. He recognized a few of Zinc's people from the gambling house. Most of the crates were six by three, the exact size of his conduit chambers. But the second buckboard was stacked with circular containers three times that size. He had no idea what might be inside. None of the parts needed to be that large.

Dyraien was nowhere to be seen. Rye stood near the entrance, clipboard in hand, checking off the boxes as Zinc's people brought them in. Tahki didn't know how to search for Gotem without appearing suspicious.

Rye looked up as Tahki reached the bottom step. "Tahki?"

Tahki walked over to him. "Sorry I'm late. I was in my room rechecking a mistake I thought I made on my schematics. Everything's fine, though, but I have to run back to Gale's. I left some supplies behind."

Rye frowned. He stared at Tahki in an unnerving way. "Tahki?" he said again, cautious and confused.

"Be careful," Tahki said. "My name is one of those names where if you say it too many times, it starts to sound strange."

Rye looked behind him. He turned to the left, to the right, and then stared straight ahead. "I don't understand."

"Don't understand what?"

Rye appeared dazed. "I just saw you a second ago."

"What?"

"You and I, we were just outside together. I called your name, but you ignored me."

"Are you sure it was me?"

Rye licked his lips. "Is this a game or something?" He squinted. "And how did you change your clothing so fast?"

Tahki almost smiled, almost laughed at how Rye had mistook him for one of Zinc's men, but then his feet went cold, then his legs, arms, all the way up to his neck. The sounds of the men and women became a faint ringing in his ears. Rye's face blurred, his lips moving a centimeter a minute. Rye hadn't mistaken him for one of Zinc's men.

Sornjia was here. Sornjia had come to the castle.

"Are you all right?"

Tahki blinked. "Where did you say you saw me?"

"While it's nice to learn you have a sense of humor," Rye said, "do you think this is an appropriate time for jokes?"

"Rye. Where did you see me?" He nearly yelled it. One of Zinc's men eyed the two of them.

Rye gave him a concerned look. "Outside. And then you headed down to the basement. I tried to catch up, but they needed me here." He hesitated and then said, "I guess I saw wrong."

Panic swept through Tahki. "Where is Dyraien?"

"Haven't seen him."

A crash outside drew Rye's attention. "Dammit," he said. "That's the third one." He looked back at Tahki. "I don't know what's going on with you, but we'll talk later."

Tahki nodded, and Rye jogged over to a fallen crate. Tahki darted left, grabbed the door down to the basement, yanked it open, and sprinted into the dark. When he reached the black gates, he stopped. They were pulled shut, and he feared they might be locked, until a cool draft brushed his face. The gates were opened. Only a crack, but enough to see through. Tahki pressed an eye to the slit and peered into the circular dirt room.

Dyraien and Zinc stood in the center. Tahki pushed the gate open an inch more so he could see better. The sound of the rumbling river was enough to block any creaks. He viewed the entire room, but his eyes fixed on Zinc.

There, grasped tight in his thick hands, Sornjia slouched. He was forced to his knees, his head lowered, not resisting.

Tahki's heart thudded fast.

"I told you he was trouble," Zinc said. "Knew the first moment I seen him he was a spy."

"Let's not be hasty," Dyraien said. "I'm sure he has a good explanation for doing what he did."

Sornjia stayed quiet but glanced to his left.

Tahki pressed his eye closer. In the corner of the room he saw a dark heap: a man. His arms and legs were tied, his face bruised, his eyes crusted shut. He wore red and gold robes. His bald head bled a little.

Gotem. Sornjia must have tried to rescue him but was caught in the process. How he'd known where to look, Tahki didn't know.

Dyraien followed Sornjia's gaze to Gotem. "That man tried to sabotage my castle." He knelt down, grabbed Sornjia's chin, and raised his head. "What concerns me is how you knew about him and why you tried to free him."

Sornjia kept his lips pressed tight.

"It's in your best interest to speak," Dyraien said. "Here I am, accusing you of something very serious, and you haven't said a word. I'm giving you a chance to explain yourself, Tahki." Zinc dug his knee into Sornjia's back.

Tahki felt sick. There was no more planning, no more wondering how he'd confront Dyraien, no more worrying how he'd explain himself to Rye. His time was up. Sornjia had been captured. Now, both Dyraien and Rye would know the lies he'd told.

Dyraien released Sornjia's face. "You know, I hadn't noticed it until now, but your skin, it looks like his, slightly golden, a trait specifically belonging to a certain region of the world." He motioned toward Gotem. "Which makes me want to ask if you're from Dhaulen'aii. If you came here to gather information about the queen and bring it back to your people."

Sornjia didn't look at him.

"Answer him," Zinc said, and twisted his arm in an unnatural angle. Tahki had never felt such a burning desire to take someone's life before.

Dyraien held up his hand. "His silence tells me everything I need to know. Tie him up with the monk."

"You're a crow," Sornjia said.

Dyraien faced him. "I'm a what?"

"A crow," Sornjia said. "A liar. A trickster. You climb into shadows and turn day into night."

Dyraien stared. "The way you talk. It's like before, when I saw you at Gale's."

Tahki dug his nails into the wood of the door. He had no idea how he'd get Sornjia free without being seen. He could attack them, but he had no weapons.

"You need to stop this, Dyraien," Sornjia said. "Your family has done wrong, but you can stop the wickedness. I know deep down you're not like your mother."

Dyraien smirked. "You don't know anything."

With a straight, calm face, Sornjia said, "I know you're trying to open the Dim. I know Gotem isn't a spy, he's a mystic. You've stolen him from his home and are going to use him to open the Dim, just like your mother and grandmother and great-grandmother and great-great-grandmother. You turned the castle into a weapon in order to keep the pathway open."

Tahki watched as the persona Dyraien had played over the weeks crumbled. The charming, well-to-do prince shattered, and he was left gaping, his eyes wide, his face frozen in shock. If the world could see him now, Tahki wouldn't need Gotem or the stone to prove Dyraien's guilt.

"This some kinda joke?" Zinc said. "How does he know about the plan, D? You said only you, me, and Hona knew. D? How does he know?"

"Shut your mouth," Dyraien said to Zinc. "Just shut up. Shut up!" He ran his hand through his hair. A wild panic set in his eyes. "You can't know that. There's no way you could possibly know that."

"There's still time to make this right," Sornjia said.

Dyraien eyed him. "Who are you?"

"I'm someone who can help you."

For a second, a look of defeat, or maybe it was relief, flashed in Dyraien's eyes. Tahki thought he might actually release Sornjia. But then his face hardened. "You're trying to trick me. Distract me. I don't know who sent you, but I don't play other people's games. I'm the one in control here."

"I don't think you're as in control as you think you are," Sornjia said.

Dyraien made a fist and brought it hard against Sornjia's jaw. Tahki heard bone meet bone and cringed. If it hurt, Sornjia didn't show it. Tahki'd never seen Dyraien look so unsuppressed. So out of control. His hair hung in clumps over his eyes; his breath came in ragged waves, like something had broken inside him. But a moment later he composed himself. He brushed his hair back and took a deep breath.

"We need to act now," Dyraien said to Zinc.

"Now?" Zinc licked his lips. "But they ain't done putting the castle together."

"It needs to be now," Dyraien said. "We have a real traitor to blame."

Zinc hesitated a moment and then flashed a yellow-toothed grin. "What about Rye?"

"Rye will believe what I tell him." Dyraien clenched his teeth and looked at Sornjia. "Family always forgive one another, no matter how terrible a crime they commit." He faced Zinc. "Go."

Zinc cracked his knuckles. "Won't be long." He used his belt to tie Sornjia's hands, and then he walked toward the door. Tahki jumped under the wooden stairs and crouched in the shadows. Zinc ran up and out of sight. Tahki wanted to follow, fearful of what the man might do, but hated the idea of leaving Sornjia alone with Dyraien. He crept back to the door and peered inside. Even with Zinc gone, he didn't think he could take Dyraien in a fight. If he was caught too, what good would he be to his brother?

"Tell me something," Dyraien said to Sornjia. "Your passion for architecture, all those times your eyes flared with excitement when I spoke to you about the project, your constant need for approval... was it all a lie? An act?" He bent down, reached out, rested his hand on Sornjia's shoulder. "How could you be dishonest with me, after all I've done for you?"

Sornjia stared back at him. "Your words fall from your mouth the way acid rain falls in the jungle."

Dyraien stood. "I liked you, you know. I don't like many people, but your passion for technology impressed me. I thought you would understand what I'm trying to achieve."

"You know what you're doing is wrong. It's why you didn't tell Rye. You knew he'd try to stop you."

Any chance to reason with Dyraien faded. A fierce defensiveness came into his voice. "Rye is my brother. Mine. If you think he'll choose you over me just because you opened your legs for him, you're going to be thoroughly disappointed."

And then Dyraien stepped back and coughed hard. He rubbed his eyes vigorously, ruffled his hair into a frantic mess, and proceeded to slap himself across the face again and again and again, until his cheeks burned bright red.

Tahki watched, both curious and horrified at the prince's odd behavior. Sornjia, too, appeared at a loss as to why Dyraien beat himself. By the time Zinc returned, Dyraien looked crazed and fevered. Zinc, unaffected by his dishevelment, grabbed Sornjia and shoved a rag in his mouth.

"Done," Zinc said.

Dyraien panted. "Good." And then said in a hesitant voice, "Was it quick?"

Zinc shrugged. "Does it matter? What's done is done."

Dyraien nodded, more to himself than to Zinc. "And Rye? He didn't see you?"

"Everyone is on the third floor," Zinc said. "They've started the isolation."

"You mean the installation," Dyraien corrected.

"Tomato, potato." Zinc spat.

"Very well. Let's get on with the show. Give me two minutes, then bring him up."

"Alive?"

"Of course alive."

Tahki hid again as Dyraien left the black gates and limped upstairs. This time, Tahki followed him. He waited a moment and watched as Dyraien moved into the center of the entranceway. When his back was turned, Tahki darted behind a partially broken pillar. He barely had time to take cover before Dyraien's voice rang through the halls. "Rye! Gale! Anyone! Come quickly!"

It didn't take long for Rye and some of Zinc's men to appear. A few pieces of obsidian cut Tahki's leg as he kneeled. He ignored the sharp pokes.

"What's wrong?" Rye said as he reached the bottom step. "What happened to you?"

Dyraien's body shook. "Mother, she… she…."

"What?"

Dyraien swallowed. "She's been killed."

Tahki felt cold.

Rye stared. "The queen is dead?"

Dyraien nodded. "She was killed. Murdered in her own bed."

Rye darted up the staircase. Tahki didn't dare think what Zinc had done. What Dyraien had told him to do. But Rye reappeared a moment later, a look of shock on his face, and Tahki covered his mouth with his hand. It didn't make sense. Why would Dyraien have his own mother killed, after going to great lengths to keep her alive and take care of her?

"Who would have done something like this?" Rye said. He put his hand to his forehead and took a deep breath. "Zinc. It had to be Zinc." Tahki felt a surge of gratitude toward Rye. He wanted to jump out and tell him it was true, Zinc had killed Queen Genevi, but he wouldn't risk it with Sornjia still held hostage.

"It wasn't Zinc," Dyraien whispered.

"How do you know?"

"Because I saw who did it."

"Who? Who did this?"

Dyraien's jaw trembled. "I trusted him. He was so smart, so kind. I never thought he was capable of something like this."

"Dyraien, who are you talking about?"

All the blood seemed to drain from Tahki's body. He felt lightheaded, a surreal sense of place and time drifting over him. He crouched only a few meters away, close enough to hear every sharp inhalation Rye took, every false sob Dyraien sputtered.

"He fooled us both," Dyraien said. "With his pretty face and clever designs."

Rye didn't move. "No."

Dyraien sniffed and wiped his eyes. "I saw him, Rye. Saw him leave her room with a bloody knife. He sliced her neck. I didn't know what he'd done until I saw her, dead on the floor."

Rye shook his head rapidly. "You're wrong. It wasn't him. It wasn't Tahki."

"It wasn't me," Tahki whispered.

Dyraien grabbed Rye's neck and drew their foreheads together. "I know how you felt about him. I know you wanted to trust him. But you still have me, Rye. You and I, we're never alone, so long as we have each other."

Rye pulled away. "Tahki didn't do this."

"He did," Dyraien said. "He's already confessed his crimes."

Then as though queued like an actor in a theatrical performance, Zinc stepped out of the basement, dragging a tied and gagged Sornjia behind him. Zinc shoved Sornjia to the floor in front of them.

"He's from Dhaulen'aii," Dyraien said, loud enough for Zinc's men on the third floor to hear. "He's a spy, sent here to kill the queen and sabotage our plans."

The men and women above murmured among themselves. Witnesses, Tahki realized. People who would support Dyraien's claim. And if he could get Rye to believe him, Rye would convince Gale, and everyone would blame Tahki.

"That makes no sense," Rye said. "Why would he help us with the castle if he was a spy?"

"Authenticity," Dyraien said in an exasperated tone. "He used it to get us to trust him. To confide our secrets to him."

"Untie him," Rye demanded. "I want to hear his story."

"So he can lie and manipulate you?"

"So he can explain himself."

"He really has you wrapped around his sad little finger, doesn't he?" Dyraien said. "My mother's corpse rots in her room. He is a traitor. And you know what happens to traitors."

Zinc pulled a knife from a sheath and crouched down beside Sornjia.

"No!" Rye yelled. Two of Zinc's men descended from above and restrained him. Rye brought his elbow into the chest of one and slammed his fist into the face of the other. Three more men and two women fell on him, shoving his arms behind his back, grabbing any part of him they could hold.

Tahki couldn't move. Everything knotted up.

Zinc brought the knife to Sornjia's throat. The silver blade glinted in the light. Zinc smirked and licked his lips. He was going to cut Sornjia's throat. Sornjia was going to die. No one would save him, and it was all Tahki's fault.

Every part of him screamed: *Go. Run. Act.* Black obsidian pressed around him, reflecting his body at every angle. His breath caught in his throat. The scent of sweat and blood and death moved across him like a shadow, and he saw his brother's blood spill in his mind, a lake of red.

Tahki gripped a cool obsidian shard from the floor. He grasped it so tightly the sharp sides bled his palm, a warm sensation running down his fingers. Zinc pressed the blade into Sornjia's neck, and Tahki leaped from his hiding spot. He cleared the room in five wide strides and swung the obsidian across Zinc's head before anyone could react. The glasslike stone shattered as it cut into his head. Zinc cried out, stumbled back, and writhed on the floor.

Tahki stood over Sornjia and untied him. "Are you all right?"

Sornjia nodded.

Once Sornjia was free, Tahki spun around. Every face in the room turned his way. Rye and Dyraien looked shocked and confused. Zinc cursed. Zinc's people looked to their leader for direction.

"How are there two of you?" Dyraien said.

"There's only one of me," Tahki said. "This is Sornjia, my twin brother."

Dyraien looked from Tahki to Sornjia. "Proof. This is proof! Proof he lied to us! Proof he killed the queen!" He faced Rye, obviously trying to turn the situation to his advantage. "Don't you see now? Don't you see he lied?"

Rye didn't move, his expression unreadable.

"You're wrong," Sornjia said. "My brother didn't kill anyone. You killed your mother, Dyraien, and tried to frame him."

"Liar," Dyraien said. "Rye, we've been fooled. Tahki is a spy from Dhaulen'aii. Him and his doppelgänger."

"Why don't you tell him, Dyraien," Tahki said. "Tell Rye the true purpose of this castle. Tell him how you planned to kill a man in order to open the Dim. Tell him about the Királye conquest."

Dyraien faced Rye. "Do you hear him? He's mad, Rye. He's a liar and a traitor and he's mad!"

Rye looked from Sornjia to Tahki, and Tahki wished he'd been honest with him from the start. But before any explanations could be given, a cry erupted from behind.

"You little shit!" Zinc said. He stood now, a pistol in his hand, blood clumping on the side of his head. "I'll blow both your fucking brains to the seventh hell!" Zinc aimed the pistol at Tahki's chest and pulled the trigger.

Tahki blinked. Gunpowder filled his nose. Bells chimed in his head. He wasn't sure if he heard someone scream or if he had screamed. He didn't know if his eyes were open or shut. The ends of his fingertips tingled, and he felt a heavy weight tremble against his body. He looked down, chin pressed against his chest, teeth grinding against one another.

Sornjia's body leaned into him. Blood dripped from his brother's shoulder onto his arm. The white marble beneath them turned crimson. He could feel every heave his brother took, and as he felt the rise and fall of his chest, as he watched his brother's eyes blink rapidly, he understood.

Sornjia had put himself in the bullet's path.

"Sornjia!" Tahki cried. "Sornjia…. Sornjia, look at me!"

"I'm all right," Sornjia said, dazed. He looked at the blood trailing down his arm. "So much red."

Tahki heard Zinc's people rush forward. Rye held them back, but Tahki could see he'd be overpowered at any moment. Sornjia squirmed in his arms.

"Don't move," Tahki said. He heard the click of the pistol as it cocked again. Tahki looked up. Zinc stood five feet away, blood dripping down his skull into his eyes.

"I won't miss this time," Zinc said.

"She'll see," Sornjia muttered. Tahki turned his body so his brother would be shielded.

"Don't watch," Tahki said and moved his hand over Sornjia's eyes. This was it. There was nothing more he could do. They would die here.

"She'll come," Sornjia said again.

Zinc squeezed the trigger.

Tahki felt a powerful thrust of wind rush by them, black and sleek and deadly. Instead of the crack of a bullet, Zinc's cry burst through the castle. Pooka hunched over them, a mass of fangs and fur, Zinc's body caught in her mouth. She swung him back and forth like a limp doll and then released him. His body skidded across the floor and stopped at Dyraien's feet. Blood flowed from a deep gash in his stomach, and he howled in pain. The cat let out a deafening roar, and everyone froze.

Dyraien stumbled back. "What is that thing?"

Most of Zinc's men fled to nearby rooms like a herd of startled deer. One man drew a pistol and pointed it at Pooka, but the cat leaped quicker than he could pull the trigger. Pooka tore at his arm, bit down, and threw him against the wall. She lowered her head and growled again.

Rye tried to move toward Tahki, but Dyraien grabbed him and said, "That thing will kill you!"

"Tahki." Sornjia's voice. "Run."

This time Tahki didn't hesitate. He heaved Sornjia and moved for the door, but his brother's body was too heavy, and Sornjia had trouble walking on his own.

"Pooka," Sornjia said. "Help."

The cat appeared at their side, and Tahki rested Sornjia against her. She looked terrifying, her fangs red, her claws extended, her eyes searching to find prey. Even Tahki felt disturbed by the wild animal inside her, but once Sornjia was secured and they started moving, he felt relieved she'd come to help them. With Zinc's men too intimidated to fire at them, it left a clear path to the front door. They moved across the marble, out into the fog. The air tasted wet and heavy. Tahki tried to concentrate on everything real. The cold air. The warm blood. The scent of gunpowder. Anything that would keep him moving, keep him alert and awake, keep his mind from shutting down completely.

"Tahki!" Rye called.

Tahki faced the castle. Rye stood in the doorway. In Rye's eyes, he saw confusion, disbelief, and a deep, deep hurt. But he couldn't stop now. Sornjia needed him.

He turned away as the sounds of Zinc's men stirred behind them. Dyraien was a prince trained for leadership and battle. Pooka might have surprised him, but he would recuperate quickly and send someone after them. The fog gave them cover enough to flee, but men on gingoats would hunt them. With the cat's help, Tahki moved Sornjia far and fast from the castle, not looking back to see the chaos they'd left in their wake.

Chapter 15

He jogged alongside Pooka, holding Sornjia steady. They ran hard for a time and then walked when it became apparent no one trailed them. Tahki found the ruins, the first place he'd felt a connection to Rye. Dyraien probably figured they'd run to Edgewater, try to find medical help. He must know Sornjia would bleed out unless the wound was closed. And he was right. Though they'd put the castle far behind them, they were trapped. Sornjia needed help, but they couldn't risk traveling to Edgewater.

They entered the ring of tall stones. Tahki eased Sornjia against a thick gray slab of rock that jutted out of the ground like a giant spearhead. Pooka settled herself above him on a flat rock and stretched her muscles. She lowered her head beside Sornjia, and he reached up to pet her. His eyes appeared dim, his breath shallow. The wound bled badly. The moist fog kept it open, and the bullet was still lodged inside. They had no tools, and Tahki doubted he could sneak back into the castle to get some.

Tahki stripped off his shirt and held it to Sornjia's shoulder. "The wound isn't bad." The white shirt turned bright red.

Sornjia smiled. "Liar."

Tahki swallowed. "I'm going to the river to get some water. Do you think you can hold my shirt here?"

Sornjia nodded, clumsily grasped for the shirt, and shut his eyes.

Tahki walked to the river, and when he was far enough away, he cried. He sniffed and coughed into his hands. Tears blurred his vision, but he didn't wipe them away. The river here was calm. He knelt and splashed his face and then removed one of his boots and plunged it beneath the water. Goose bumps rose on his skin, and he shivered.

He had never felt so powerless in his life. He needed a plan, some way to heal Sornjia. He could sneak back to Gale's house, but she might not help them now that Sornjia had been exposed. Edgewater was too far, and Zinc's men would be on the lookout for them. He might be able to return to the castle and bargain with Dyraien, offer to take the blame for killing the queen if Dyraien promised to save Sornjia, but who was to say he wouldn't kill him on sight?

Even with Pooka, he'd never be able to get into the castle without help. And Rye? He didn't want to think about him. By now, Dyraien would have fabricated some elaborate story about Tahki, and Rye would believe him, because there was no explanation for Sornjia or Pooka.

Feeling defeated and without options, he wiped his eyes and returned to Sornjia with his boot full of water.

"Hold still," Tahki said. He moved his shirt and poured the icy water onto Sornjia's wound. It occurred to him that cleaning the hole to prevent infection would prove useless so long as the bullet was still lodged inside.

"Tahki," Sornjia said, his eyes still closed. "We have a visitor."

Tahki frowned. "A visitor?"

Sornjia pointed behind him.

Tahki turned. At the edge of the ruins, Rye stood straight and stiff. He stared at them both, and then took a cautious step forward. Tahki watched him a moment, until he caught a glint of a knife in Rye's hand. He lurched forward to block him.

"Rye, stop," Tahki said. "Whatever Dyraien told you, he's lying. I know you don't have a reason to trust me, but Sornjia is innocent."

"Tahki," Sornjia said. "Let him pass."

Tahki glanced at his brother.

Rye walked around him and mumbled, "You're so dramatic." When he got to Sornjia, he stopped and stared at Pooka, who stared back with her large sky-filled eyes.

"She won't hurt you," Sornjia said.

Rye didn't move.

"Pooka," Sornjia said. "Can you leave for a minute?"

Pooka inclined her head and nudged Sornjia. He smiled and patted her snout, and then the cat rose to her full height and vanished into the ruins. When she was gone, Rye knelt beside Sornjia. Tahki joined them, ready to defend his brother if needed. But Rye only dug through the leather bag at his side and took out several medical tools. The object he carried wasn't a knife but a surgical scalpel.

"We need to get the bullet out," Rye said. "It's deep. I didn't have time to grab anything to numb it. It will hurt."

"I'll be fine," Sornjia said.

Rye nodded and leaned forward.

"Rye," Tahki said.

"Let me work," Rye said. "Or he'll bleed to death." His voice was calm but stern.

Tahki dug his fingers into the cool soil as Rye pressed the knife to Sornjia's shoulder. Sornjia's face remained placid as the knife cut his flesh. Tahki's own shoulder throbbed just at the thought of the knife. He realized, after a moment, that Sornjia was meditating. He'd seen monks sit for hours and hours, putting themselves in a deep trance, able to block out pain and hunger and all other sensations. For the first time, Tahki understood meditation wasn't a waste of time. It was a way to train your mind, to strengthen your mentality, to control your body when outside forces threatened you.

Something clinked against a rock. The silver bullet fell to the ground, bloody and misshapen. Tahki flinched but also marveled at how something so small could do so much damage. Rye stitched Sornjia's arm shut and wrapped it in a white bandage. Tahki tugged his bloody shirt over his head and gagged at the smell, but it was too cold not to wear it.

"He needs rest," Rye said. He gathered his supplies and put them back in the brown leather bag.

"He'll survive?"

"So long as he doesn't tear it open, he should be fine."

Tahki nodded. "Rye, if you'll just give me a chance to explain."

"I just said your brother needs rest," Rye said. He stood and motioned for Tahki to follow. They found a group of rocks far away from Sornjia so they wouldn't disturb him but could still see him.

"How did you find us?" Tahki asked.

Rye watched Pooka slink over the rocks. She curled her body near Sornjia, her massive form shielding him from the wind. "I followed her paw prints."

"Won't Zinc's men do the same?"

"I told Dyraien I saw you heading toward Edgewater. He sent a few men out that way but wanted everyone else working on the castle." Rye didn't take his eyes off Pooka. "What is she?"

"I'm not sure you'll believe me if I tell you," Tahki said.

"That's for me to decide."

Tahki swallowed. "I think… I think she's my dead great-grandmother."

Rye turned his head slowly back to Tahki. "All right. You have my attention."

Tahki sat against a rock and sighed. "I'm not sure where to start."

"How about tell me who you are, where you're from. Start with things that are true, and then we can move on to the lies." Rye pulled a match from his bag and busied himself by starting a fire.

"Won't someone see the smoke?"

Rye shook his head. "Not in the fog." He glanced at Tahki. "Are you going to talk, or should I just take Dyraien's word as the truth?"

Tahki rubbed his wrist. "What did Dyraien say?"

"He said you killed the queen. That you're a spy." Rye hesitated. "I said I'd bring you back to him."

"And will you? Bring me back to him?"

Rye held his eyes. "Tahki, tell me the truth. I want to hear it from you."

Tahki sighed. "My full name is Tahki'jie. My father is Lord Aumin'jie."

Rye frowned, like the name sounded familiar but he couldn't place it.

"My father is royal ambassador to the Empress of Dhaulen'aii." He studied Rye's face, watching every subtle inclination of his eyebrows, every slight tilt of his mouth, every narrowing of his eyes. "I came here without my father's permission. I forged documents and snuck across the borders, but I'm not a spy. Rye, I swear. I only wanted to enter the fair for a chance to win. I never thought I'd get offered a job by the queen's son. I know it wasn't smart, but after I lost, I felt like I'd go home a failure. When Gale offered me this job, I couldn't believe it. I thought I actually had a chance to become famous."

Tahki spoke, and Rye listened. He talked in great detail about the thing in his room, about the illusions, about his fight with Pooka. He spoke about the conversation he'd heard between Dyraien and Hona and Zinc. When he got to Nii, Tahki hesitated.

"I need to show you something," Tahki said. He rose and walked to where Sornjia rested. Rye followed but stayed at a distance. Tahki reached out a hand to Pooka. She growled and he retracted.

"I need to show him," he said to Pooka.

Pooka lowered her head but still growled. Tahki extend his hand and ran it across her shoulder. The eels boiled up around him, their long, oily bodies forming tiny hands at the tip. They grabbed Tahki's fingers, swaying and drawing him in. He pulled away before the black hands reached up to his elbow. A shudder ebbed through his body, but he repressed it. Rye couldn't know how unsettled Pooka still made him.

He walked back to their spot and sat down, resisting the urge to wipe off his arm where the hands had touched him.

Rye looked tense, and his eyes flicked back to her with a kind of enchanted horror. "That's not possible."

"That's what I've been telling myself for weeks."

"I've never seen anything like her," Rye said. It pleased Tahki that he sounded more fascinated than fearful. At least he'd keep an open mind.

"I needed to show you, because what I'm about to say is going to sound crazy." Tahki told him about Nii, about the Királyes history. He finished with Gotem, with what Sornjia had done, and how Dyraien had sent Zinc to kill his own mother.

By the time he finished, dusk had settled over the ruins. When Tahki said his last word, he felt lighter, like he could finally take in a full breath of air. If he had known confessing everything would feel this good, he would have talked a long time ago.

He gave Rye time to contemplate. The fire popped and spat, and the fog cleared a little.

"You're right," Rye said. "It does sound crazy."

"I don't have any proof, other than Pooka," Tahki said.

Rye raised an eyebrow. "Pooka?"

Tahki motioned to the cat.

"Pooka," Rye said. "As in Cuddle me Pooka, the popular child's toy? That's what you named her?"

"I didn't name— You're missing the point. I know you don't believe me, but she's proof there's something wrong with Dyraien and his family. If we could get to the black pool again, maybe Pooka could turn back into a human, and you'll see I wasn't lying."

"I never said that," Rye said.

"Said what?"

"That I didn't believe you." Rye ran a hand through his hair. "Why didn't you tell me this sooner?"

Tahki shrugged. "It never seemed like the right time."

"The right time was the moment before we spent the night together."

Tahki cringed. "You're right. I'm sorry. Rye, please believe me when I say I'm sorry."

Rye sighed. "It just doesn't make any sense. I know Dyraien doesn't want to lose his country, but he's not a bad person."

"He tried to kill me," Tahki said.

Rye hesitated. "He must have thought you were a spy."

"You know he didn't."

"I can't just condemn him without evidence."

"I thought you said you believed me."

"I do. I believe something strange is happening here, and Dyraien hasn't been honest about it."

"So let's go to the capital. Expose Dyraien's plot."

"I can't do that."

"Why?"

"Because I can't betray him like that. Dyraien saved me, Tahki."

"I know, he took you in off the streets. But one good deed doesn't excuse murder."

"You don't understand," Rye snapped. "He didn't just take me off the streets. After my mother left, I had nowhere to go. The authorities picked me up. I know you think Vatolokít is modern, is advanced and civilized, but the truth is, the city is corrupt. Orphan kids are placed in one of two places: in the factories for hard labor or in the brothels for a life of depravity."

Tahki stared. He was about to ask which one Rye had been sent to, but he already knew. It was why Rye had avoided the brothel in Edgewater, why he'd been so experienced in bed, and why he'd been so uneasy about letting Tahki touch him.

"Don't look at me like that," Rye said. "I didn't sleep with anyone. But these brothels, they train you until you're thirteen. Then they put you out for sale. I lied about my age when I went in, said I was younger than I was, so they kept me in training for a few years. When I turned fourteen, though, they said I was ready to work. I don't expect you to have the slightest idea what it was like for me, surrounded by twisted perverts, watching children my age exposed to horrible sexual acts."

Tahki could only shake his head.

"But I didn't have to work for them. I ran away to the upper cites one night, but the authorities caught me. They would have returned me to that awful place, but Dyraien saw what was happening and saved me. He took me in, gave me an education. He taught me how to fight, how to shoot a pistol, how to ride a gingoat. He gave me a home. Tahki, I owe Dyraien everything."

Tahki felt gratitude toward the prince, but only for the prince who'd rescued Rye, the prince who hadn't tried to kill him. He knew he wouldn't be able to convince Rye that Dyraien was a bad person. Maybe Dyraien had saved Rye, maybe it had been the only kind thing he'd ever done. Even with that knowledge, Tahki still couldn't forgive him.

"Gotem is Dyraien's captive," Tahki said. "Believe what you want about him, but Gotem is like family to me. I have to save him."

"And I'll help you," Rye said. "But I still want to talk to Dyraien. I know I can reason with him. I have to give him a chance to admit to his crimes. I owe him that much."

"And if he tries to kill me again?" Tahki asked.

"I won't let that happen. Tahki." Rye moved next to him, put his hand on his face. "I won't let him hurt you or your brother. And...." He leaned in and brought their lips together. They held each other a moment before pulling apart. "And I forgive you for lying to me because I trust you. But you have to trust me now. Trust me that Dyraien can be changed."

Dyraien could not be reasoned with, Tahki knew that, but Rye needed to see it for himself. If Rye wasn't totally committed to stopping Dyraien, they would fail, and Dyraien would be free to unleash whatever he planned upon the world.

THEY SLEPT curled in the dirt, wrapped around each other for most of the night. When the sun rose, Tahki woke to quiet chatter. He inhaled and immediately coughed as his nostrils filled with something that smelled like burnt hair. Tears filled his eyes and he had to plug his nose as he rose and approached the fire where Rye and Sornjia sat.

"What is that?" Tahki said, holding his nose. Rye roasted what looked like black carrots over the fire.

"Cho root," Rye said. "You can dig for it under the soil. It smells bad and tastes bland, but it's full of nutrients."

Tahki stuck out his tongue. "No thanks."

Rye removed the sticks he'd been using as skewers and handed one to Tahki. With a begrudging look, Tahki took it and nibbled on the tip.

"How's your shoulder?" Tahki said to Sornjia.

"Fine," Sornjia said.

Rye smirked.

"What's so funny?" Tahki said.

"You two look alike, but you aren't very similar," Rye said.

"Why do you say that?"

"If the situation were reversed," Rye said. "You wouldn't stop complaining until the whole country knew you'd been shot."

Sornjia smiled. Tahki didn't.

"Your smile is different too," Rye said.

Tahki watched Rye observe Sornjia, and the most ridiculous feeling of jealousy overtook him. He and Sornjia were identical. If Rye was attracted to him physically, he would be attracted to Sornjia too. And personality wise, Sornjia had always been the more likable one.

"But Tahki has something I'll never have," Sornjia said.

"What's that?"

"Ingenuity."

At that, Rye smiled. "I guess he can be clever, when he wants to be."

Tahki felt his face flush. "Where's Pooka?"

Sornjia gestured vaguely.

"Does she listen to you?" Rye said. "I mean, she can understand you, can't she?"

"I have no idea," Tahki said.

Rye leaned forward. "Because we could really use her to get inside the castle. She could scare away Zinc's men."

"She won't," Sornjia said.

Rye frowned. "Why not?"

"She knows you want to reason with Dyraien," Sornjia said. "She wants the castle destroyed. You have other plans."

Rye chewed his root slowly.

"Rescuing Gotem is our priority," Tahki said. "Dyraien can't open the Dim without him. Once Gotem is safe, we'll figure out what to do about the castle and Dyraien."

"We should get moving," Rye said. "Sending some of Zinc's men to Edgewater will have slowed the installation, but even at half staff, they'll complete it today."

Tahki nodded and stood. He went to the river and splashed his face, the cold water waking him up. He felt better after eating the root, more alert. When he returned, Rye spoke lowly with Sornjia.

"Are you ready?" Tahki said.

Rye glanced up. "Yes."

"You'll be fine here, won't you?" Tahki said to Sornjia.

Sornjia touched his middle finger to his thumb, the sign for *everything is all right*, a common Dhaulenian gesture Tahki hadn't seen since leaving home.

With that, they departed for the castle, the sun draped across them. It felt strange for the day to be bright and beautiful when such a dark task awaited.

"What did you and my brother talk about?"

Rye glanced at him. "Dyraien, mostly. I talked about our life together. All the things Dyraien did for me."

"And just now? What did my brother say to you?" And then he felt the need to add, "You don't have to tell me, if you don't want."

Rye smiled. "I think he told me to keep you safe."

"You think?"

Rye shrugged. "He says things in an odd way."

"Well, you did a better job deciphering him than most people do."

THEY FOLLOWED the lower road and scaled a small part of the cliffside when they neared. Rye had to help Tahki several times when they came to a particularly steep area. Tahki wasn't afraid of heights, but the river raged below them, and he couldn't help but look down with every step, despite Rye telling him not to.

When they breached the top of the cliff and the black spirals came into view, Tahki felt a strange draw to the castle, a kind of addictive pull. He hadn't built her, but he felt a connection. For the last month she had filled his mind. An odd sense of possessiveness fell over him as they crept closer to the obsidian walls. He felt like he was betraying an old friend.

They snuck around to where the waterwheel turned. The wheel collected water from the river and deposited it to a funnel that carried it into the castle.

"Look," Rye said. He pointed to the kitchen door. A man stood, arguing loudly with a short old woman.

"Gale," Tahki said.

"Wait here." Rye moved from their spot before Tahki had time to question him. He darted quickly and knocked the man in the back of the head. Gale gaped as Rye beat the man until he stopped moving. From books, Tahki always thought a man could be taken down with a single blow, but the reality was much more gruesome. He moved to Rye's side.

"What in the hells are you doing?" Gale said, and narrowed her eyes at Tahki. "Do you have any idea what Dyraien told me about you?"

"I'm sorry, Gale," Tahki said. "Dyraien killed the queen. He tried to kill Sornjia too. He lied about the castle, about everything."

Gale looked to Rye, who nodded.

"You really are going to be the death of me," Gale muttered.

"You should get out of here," Rye said.

"And go where?"

"Find Hona," Tahki said. He ignored the look of disgust Rye gave him. "She knows what's going on. Get her to talk."

Gale covered her eyes with her hand and sighed. "They're looking for you. Both of you. Dyraien gave orders to bring you to him right away. The inside is crawling with Zinc's people."

"Then we'll have to find another way," Rye said. He headed toward the north side of the castle.

"I'm sorry for all the trouble I've caused you," Tahki said before sprinting after Rye. He followed him up the road a little way, far enough they'd be out of sight, until they stopped near the river. Tahki shook his head, dread filling every part of him. Water sloshed over the bank, flowing down. Mist beaded on his face.

"This can't be the only way in," Tahki said.

"It is."

"I don't think I can do it."

"Tahki." Rye grabbed his hand. "I won't let anything happen to you."

Tahki's body shook. "What if we go over the waterfall instead?"

"We won't."

Tahki tried to step back farther, but Rye held him.

"Close your eyes," Rye said.

"No."

"Close your eyes, count to ten."

"No."

Rye pulled him closer. "Trust me."

Tahki thought back to the conversation he'd had with Sornjia after Pooka had attacked him. Sornjia had said trust was a feeling of wholeness, a feeling of control even when you had none.

Tahki put his hand on Rye's chest and took a deep breath. "Don't let me drown, or I swear I'll come back as an evil spirit and haunt you."

Rye smiled but didn't reply. Instead, he grasped Tahki's hand so tight it felt like his finger bones might bruise. It happened fast after that, so fast Tahki didn't have time to contemplate his decision, which was probably what Rye had intended. Rye pushed Tahki in and held on, and they both remained submerged a moment as they drifted under the castle. The cold knocked the breath out of Tahki, but Rye's arm drew them to the surface and kept them afloat. It was dark beneath the castle. Tahki didn't know how Rye managed to find the bank and pull them out, but he did, and they rested in the dirt on their backs, taking deep breaths.

"Eleven," Tahki panted.

"What?" Rye said.

"You said count to ten, but it took eleven seconds."

Rye shoved Tahki's face gently away with a wet hand and smiled. He looked like he was about to say something when a hard hand struck Tahki's shoulder, and then he was flying upward, out of control. He flailed and stumbled, his arms twisting so painfully behind him he feared they might break.

"Dyraien said you might try something like this," Zinc said. "I didn't think you'd be stupid enough."

They fought to break free. Rye, too, had been restrained. It took two men and a woman to hold him back. Tahki couldn't believe he'd risked jumping in the river only to be caught immediately.

"After you," Zinc said with a bow. He shoved them down the dark tunnel lined with lightning roots. Zinc breathed heavily. He walked with a more pronounced limp, and his sides had been bandaged where Pooka had bitten him. The only way he could possibly stand would be if he'd taken drugs to ease the pain, which meant they might be able to overpower him.

But when Tahki glanced to Rye, he didn't appear to struggle, and a moment later they found themselves behind the black gates. This time, instead of Nii in the black pool, Gotem sat tied and gagged. Water came up to his chest. The monk's eyes were only a sliver, but when he caught sight of Tahki, they opened wide in fearful recognition.

"Gotem," Tahki said. If he hadn't run away, if he hadn't completed the castle for Dyraien, Gotem would be safe back home, meditating in a temple.

"Let him go," Dyraien said to the three holding Rye. He stood a few feet away from Gotem.

Rye yanked free of their grasp. He stepped forward, his eyes traveling all over the room. Tahki, too, observed the differences from his last visit. He saw the ceiling had been opened up and noticed a brass ring had been set in the dirt, like a giant gaping mouth above them.

And there were other differences. Unlike last time, blue lanterns had been hung all around, illuminating the space in an eerie light. Tahki also noticed a ring of stones in the center of the room. He squinted and discovered they weren't stones but minerals. A collection of minerals from all over the world. Some he couldn't remember the names of, and a few he didn't recognize. Some minerals were the size of Tahki's head, others the size of his small toe. Some of them gleamed in the blue light; others reflected a dozen colors. A few absorbed light. Others blended in with the dirt. Someone—Dyraien, he guessed—had arranged them in a specific order. The pattern appeared ritualistic. In the center of the mineral circle, pieces of obsidian formed a human-sized X.

"Dyraien," Rye said. "What is all this?"

Dyraien pivoted on his heels and strode slowly to Rye's side. He laid a hand on his shoulder and squeezed. "I'm not angry with you, Rye. He's manipulating you, so it's not your fault. But everything he has told you is a lie."

Rye glanced to Gotem. "It doesn't look like a lie."

Dyraien released his shoulder. "So that's all it takes? All someone needs to do is spread their legs for you, and you'll kick me into the gutter and forget all I've done for you?"

"That's not true," Rye said. "I came back for you. To give you a chance to explain yourself."

Dyraien laughed. "Me explain? You're the one who betrayed me, Rye."

Rye stepped closer. "Did you do it? Did you have your mother killed?"

"Is this how it's going to be?" Dyraien said. "His word against mine?"

"Answer the question, Dyraien."

"Tell me where the cat is first."

Tahki saw him tense as he spoke of Pooka. Zinc and his people also looked around the room, nervous at the mention of the cat.

"She's outside," Tahki said. "Waiting for my command to attack."

Dyraien hesitated and then looked to Rye. "Is he telling the truth?"

Rye said nothing.

"We're giving you a chance here," Tahki said. "Let Gotem go, and I won't call her."

Dyraien studied him. There was no telling what went through his head. Tahki still wasn't totally sure what Dyraien wanted from them.

"Call the beast, then," Dyraien said. "Because I have no intention of letting the monk go. Not until I get what I want."

"And what do you want?" Rye said.

Tahki looked around for anything that might aid in their escape, but they were trapped. Why would Dyraien humor them like this? Why not just lock them up and do whatever it was he planned to do? Dyraien was intelligent. He didn't seem like the kind of man to play with his food before eating it.

"Do you ever consider the life you'd be living now if I hadn't saved you?" Dyraien said to Rye. "You'd probably be sucking on the tits of some woman. And look at all the gratitude you're showing me now. I thought we were family, Rye."

"I thought we were too," Rye said. "You say I'm your brother, but I feel more like a prisoner."

Tahki had never seen Dyraien look as dangerous as he did then. Dyraien's jaw clenched, his fists quivered, and his eyes deadlocked on

Rye. And that's when Tahki understood why they hadn't been locked up or killed.

Dyraien needed Rye.

He wanted him on his side. He'd been deeply hurt by Rye's actions, by the fact Rye believed Tahki over him. Dyraien saw Rye as his brother. If Sornjia had chosen to believe a stranger he hardly knew over Tahki, Tahki would feel indignation, embarrassment, betrayal.

For years Tahki thought he couldn't stand his family. But now he realized those feelings of irritation had been a luxury. He had no idea how he would have survived had it not been for his father and brother. Though his father had taken architecture away, it was only because of his father's love that he'd been able to study architecture in the first place. Most noble borns would force their son into politics or a more respectable field. But Tahki's father had given him freedom. And Sornjia had always been there for him too. He'd always been on Tahki's side. Never in Tahki's life had he ever felt alone. Misunderstood, maybe, but never alone. Even though he was a prince, Dyraien had no one but Rye. Rye knew this too. Even though Rye had Tahki now, he still considered Dyraien his brother.

"The cat isn't here," Rye said. "That's the truth. Now it's your turn."

Dyraien said in a flat voice, "Yes. I had my mother killed."

Tahki felt a small relief at the confession.

Rye shook his head, slow and steady. "Why?"

"I saved her," Dyraien said. "She was suffering. You have no idea the kind of madness that consumed her. It wasn't the kind of crazy you see on the streets. It was crazy from another world. Inside her mind, she was stuck in the eighth hell."

"But why now? Why kill her now and frame Tahki?"

"Because I needed her death in order to rule," Dyraien said. "Tragedy brings a country together. My people will feel sympathy for me. The poor prince, first his mother was murdered by a foreign spy, then the evil council tried to take his country away. I will spearhead an expedition for justice, use her death to rally outrage among my people toward her killer. My people will flock to me like chicks flock to their mother. They will obey everything I say."

"You did all this because you want to rule?"

"I did all this because I know what's best for my people. This isn't selfish, Rye. I'm doing this... *all this*... for them." Dyraien turned to

Gotem. "My family's history is dark. But I'm going to change that. I'm going to bring us all into a new age of enlightenment."

Dyraien walked over to Gotem. He shoved the monk's head back and cleared gunk from his eyes with his thumb. "You awake?"

Gotem murmured. Dyraien pulled out his gag.

"Foolish boy," Gotem said. "You don't know what you're doing."

Dyraien shushed him, the way a mother might shush a finicky child. "You have work to do."

Rye was at his side. "Dyraien, let that man go."

Dyraien glanced to Zinc. Without a word, the men and woman who had previously held Rye restrained him again.

"Dyraien," Rye said. "Don't do this."

"You won't listen to me," Dyraien said. "Not until you see it with your own eyes. Not until you see what I'm fighting so hard to obtain."

Rye struggled. "How can you believe in all this? How can you think this place you're trying to reach is real?"

"Because," Dyraien didn't turn to him, "I dragged my mother's body out of it when she entered ten years ago."

He took out a knife, and in one swift motion drew the blade across Gotem's forehead. The monk didn't cry out like Tahki expected, but he clenched his teeth and cringed as blood covered his face in a red curtain. Tahki felt sick with horror.

"Are you mad?" Rye yelled.

Dyraien ignored him. "All right." He spoke in an upbeat voice. "We have the minerals. I've arranged the circle. The monk's blood has mixed with sacred water." Dyraien raised his arms. "Now, open!"

Tahki shut his eyes and held his breath. The entire room fell silent.

Nothing happened.

Tahki peeked out one eye. Dyraien stood wide-eyed and panting. The room lay still. He opened both eyes and stared. Dyraien looked comical standing there, arms raised toward the placid black pool. It felt like a dream, or waking from a dream, realizing that the night's events had only occurred in your head. Tahki almost laughed at the absurdity of it all.

Dyraien waited another minute before lowering his arms. He stepped toward Gotem. "What is it? What did I do wrong?"

Gotem looked at him and, despite the blood covering his face, answered in a calm voice. "Clearly, the gods don't want you visiting."

Dyraien looked ready to punch Gotem, but before he could bring his arm across the monk's face, a burst of wind erupted from below the black pool. Tahki felt hot and cold air rush over his body, an acrid scent attached to it. The black water ascended, and Gotem's scream tore through the room. The monk's body flew upward to the ceiling like he weighed nothing at all. Tahki wanted to cry out, but everything inside his body locked up.

The waters wailed, a grief-stricken sound that devoured all others. A kind of electric current surged through the room. It pricked Tahki's skin. He could feel the discharge beneath his muscles. It jolted through his bones. He tasted the grit of iron across his teeth and heard a hundred voices cry out in agony. He smelled burnt flesh and felt the sting of bees across his eyelids. These weren't the same pleasant sensations he'd felt before when he'd seen the cat or spoken with Nii. These sensations were dark.

"Zinc," Dyraien's voice hissed over the wind and cries. "Why are you still here?"

Zinc didn't move. He stared at the reverse waterfall, at Gotem, at everything but Dyraien. It wasn't until Dyraien leaped across the room and brought his fist across Zinc's face that the man broke his fixation.

"Turn the machine on," Dyraien commanded.

Zinc fled the room without being told again. Both Tahki and Dyraien turned their attention back to the water as Gotem fell to the floor, landing directly in the middle of the obsidian X. The monk's eyes were wide and his chest rose and fell, but he didn't appear conscious. And then, over the monk's body, Tahki saw another surge of energy. It sparked, like a match trying to ignite. Once, twice, three times, and then the air tore like paper in front of Tahki's eyes. The tear started small, and then it grew.

Tahki was a man of logic. He'd accepted Pooka's existence, even his encounter with Nii, because there might have been explanations for those. He might have been able to reason with their existence. But as the tear expanded and he saw what looked like a world made of water and glass and stars on the other side, he could think of no explanation. He didn't know if the Dim existed, but this thing, this place that looked like no place at all and every place at once, was real.

Tahki felt his body lurch. The woman holding him cried out, and Tahki saw Rye elbow her in the face. He stood, fists clenched, eyes wild.

"The castle," Rye said. "Shut it down. I'll hold Dyraien here. We need to stop this thing from growing."

Tahki swallowed. It amazed him Rye could think so clearly when the world had broken apart in front of their eyes. Tahki wanted to say something romantic, like "I'm not leaving you" or "we'll make it out of this together."

"Go!" Rye yelled.

And Tahki bolted for the door without another word.

HE RAN and tried not to think about what he'd just seen. Instead, he concentrated on Zinc. In the entryway, he almost stopped when he saw the golden cylinder, skewering the castle like a hunter's spear. It ran from the third floor all the way down to the basement. This wasn't part of his design. The cylinder looked to be made of brass. Lines ran horizontally through it, like layers of a cake stacked on one another. The base appeared ten feet wide.

He sprinted up the stairway, his reflection elongating in the golden cylinder. It had to be a conduit of some kind, something Dyraien added to transfer power to the basement. He reached the circular room, the only room on the third floor, and when he walked inside, his breath caught in his throat. He'd only seen the room empty and only entered it to take measurements. Before, the room had been unremarkable, another unused, uninhabited space.

Now, it looked like a room you could control the world from.

The room had been converted to match his exact architectural designs. An intricate system of metal and glass and minerals covered nearly every inch of wall and floor. Twelve glass cylinders, each the size of his body, had been built into the walls. Pipes ran both inside and outside the obsidian. He could see them through the dark glasslike walls, as though they'd been frozen in black ice.

The glass cylinders, lined with a gold casing, boiled water to produce steam, which was then forced into the pipes. They had been made from lightning glass—Dyraien's idea—and could withstand extreme heat. The needles inside the temperature gages ticked upward. He'd been most proud of the piston valve. He'd modified his design from the steam locomotive he'd seen at the fair. It controlled the steam moving into the cylinders.

Tahki stepped forward and pressed his palm flat against one of the glass chambers. The thump of boiling water felt like a heartbeat. Water filled the pipes like blood filled veins. The firebox at the far end of the room inhaled coal and exhaled flames.

This wasn't a prototype or a schematic. It was real. A living thing. And it was his.

He'd spent years dreaming of the moment when his designs would come to life, but he'd never pictured it would be such a perfect blend of power and beauty. No one in the world had done something like this. His mother would have been proud of him.

But then he saw a series of smaller pipes that had been connected to circular outlets all along the wall, and a clear pipe that pumped water from below. He remembered the waterwheel outside. Dyraien had installed a siphon to bring water up from the river to convert to steam. Tahki had designed the machine to power multiple areas all over the castle. But instead of multiple points, Dyraien had all the steam funneled into the golden cylinder, which would carry all this power down into the basement.

That was how he planned to keep the Dim open. Not just by using the steam's power, but by converting the sacred waters into a searing, concentrated jet of steam. If sacred waters had been used to open the Dim in the first place, they could also be used to keep it open.

Tahki had to turn it off. He searched for the control levers. Two red levers should have been installed to release coal. As he searched the room, a hiss and a screech sounded from outside the door. He moved out into the hallway and followed the path around to the other side of the circular room. There he saw Zinc pulling the levers, a piece of paper in his hand—probably instructions on which levers to pull. He struggled with the last lever, a third lever that hadn't been part of Tahki's design.

Tahki didn't have any weapons. Just his mother's pencil, but the pencil wouldn't do much damage.

He bit his lip. The levers had been positioned near the railing. If he could sneak up and hit Zinc where Pooka had injured him, he might be able to knock him over the side. If the fall killed him, Tahki would be a murderer.

He'd reconcile with his conscience later.

He moved from the doorway. The hum of the machine blocked the sound of his boots. When Zinc's body was in reach, Tahki threw himself forward, aiming his elbow into Zinc's side. But Zinc turned at the last moment, and instead of shoving the man over the edge, Tahki only managed to make him stumble. Zinc didn't even cry out. He simply grabbed Tahki's neck and brought his knee hard into his stomach. Air left Tahki's body in a great heave, and he curled into a ball on the floor. He gasped and clawed at the marble. His own spit caught in his throat and he gagged.

"I swear," Zinc said. "When I'm done here, I'm going to burn your fucking body alive." He turned back to the levers and grasped the third one again. This time, he threw his body into it. His face twisted in pain as the lever jabbed into his wound, but he didn't stop. Again and again he heaved his body into it, until the lever finally gave way.

Tahki heard thunder inside the castle. He managed to pull himself into a sitting position. The giant golden cylinder moaned and whistled and shook. The hinges rattled, and for a moment he thought the entire thing might explode. Inside the circular room, the conduits bubbled and metal tapped against metal.

And then the golden cylinder roared, filling with steam that would be sent into the basement with deadly pressure. Tahki stared in wonder at this thing he had created. At this monster that shook the ground beneath them. It was frightening, and it was beautiful, and it would be used to slice the world open.

Zinc lifted Tahki off the ground by his hair. Even injured, Zinc was stronger than him.

"Time to burn," Zinc said between gritted teeth.

He dragged Tahki back into the circular room and dropped him in front of the firebox. Tahki tried to stand, but Zinc kicked him in the face. His head smashed against the wall. Zinc yanked open the iron door to the firebox, where coal burned in a massive flame. The chamber was a good six feet by six feet, and the heat rolling out of it was strong enough to singe his skin.

Terror flooded Tahki as Zinc pulled him up and positioned him in front of the firebox. Zinc grinned, yellow teeth glinting in the light of the fire, eyes moist and unblinking. Tahki's back burned. Sweat broke out all across his body. He could feel the flames licking the back of his head.

As Zinc heaved his body into the firebox, Tahki's right hand flew back and held the iron door. The metal burned so badly Tahki could only see white for a moment, but as his right hand prevented his body from falling into the chamber, his left hand reached into his pocket. He gripped his mother's pencil and swung it as hard as he could into Zinc.

This time, Zinc cried out and stumbled. The pencil dug a good inch into the tender part under his earlobe. Tahki tried to run, but Zinc reached out and snagged his shirt. Tahki tried to free himself, and they struggled and spun in a small circle for a moment, until Tahki's back was against the wall. He slammed his fist into the pencil by Zinc's jaw. Zinc released him and fumbled again.

Tahki didn't hesitate. He brought his legs up and kicked Zinc in the stomach. Zinc's legs hit the low rim of the firebox, and he fell back into the flames. His screams filled the room as the flames consumed him. Tahki watched Zinc twist and squeal, a sound he'd never forget. The cries finally ceased when Zinc's body collapsed into the fiery coals.

Tahki panted on the ground and kicked the door closed. His right hand pulsed bright red, and his face felt like he'd lain out in the summer sun for a week. Though the screams had stopped, Tahki still heard them in his mind. With great effort, he managed to drag himself up. He limped out to the levers. The golden cylinder shook and growled.

Tahki stood over the third lever. He needed to shut it off. But after he shut it off, what then? What would prevent someone from turning it back on? Zinc was dead, but Dyraien still had men on his side. Nothing would prevent Dyraien from doing this same thing again. The only way to be sure the Dim stayed closed would be to destroy the castle. Destroy his greatest achievement.

Tahki swallowed. He reached out and touched one of the levers. They felt smooth and cool beneath his burned hand. He remembered designing them so no one would have to manually load coal into the chamber. Dyraien had beamed at this idea and called him brilliant. His conduit system was a part of the castle now, which made the castle a part of him. His creation. His masterpiece. His dream.

He remembered then the words his mother had spoken to him the evening she died, before the fire had started.

"Why do you like inventing so much?" Tahki had asked her. "Wouldn't you rather be off playing games or swimming in the oasis with the empress?"

His mother had smiled that patient smile she always seemed to have and replied, "The greatest life one can live is the life of a creator. Whether you're creating a life, a song, or a machine, you are bringing something new into existence. You are helping the world grow."

With her words in mind, Tahki pulled the lever.

He used his left hand to yank the first lever all the way down, and then he moved the second, and then the third. From inside the circular room, he heard the conduits shake harder and harder, like someone was in there beating them with a hammer. He had pushed the levers all to their maximum output levels. None of them were supposed to be pushed that far, not all together. It would overheat the water chambers and flood the system. The entire thing would cave in on itself and destroy the inner support structure.

The castle would be destroyed the same way he'd accidentally destroyed the temple.

As the strain on the conduits increased, he heard glass crack, metal clank, water and fire collide with each other. He sprinted from the room, through the hallway, down the stairway. One of the bolts on the golden cylinder blew out like a bullet and almost hit him. Steam whistled out the hole. More bolts trembled and blew.

Tahki tried to reach the basement to warn Rye, but the golden cylinder screeched, and a powerful wave of steam knocked him on his back. He scrambled to his feet and watched as the top floor fell, crumbling in front of the door to the basement. He turned and ran from the entryway, dodging falling obsidian and copper pipes and marble, until he was out the front door.

The cold air struck him hard as he loped outside. His head throbbed, and sour bile rose in his throat. He didn't stop until he heard a tremendous roar, and he turned to watch the black spires of the castle collapse. The obsidian didn't break apart like normal stone. It shattered, the way a tall vase hitting stone shatters. Each spire dropped one after the other.

Tahki watched, his eyes thick with tears, his heart racing as he prayed Rye would be safe in the basement, that the tunnels would hold against the weight of the castle. The remainder of the castle fell not in a fiery, explosive heap but in a snuffed-out manner, slow and sinking.

And then it caved in. The obsidian, the marble, the golden cylinder, the dining table and stove and other furniture, all sunk. It fell below the dirt, into the basement. Onto the black gates.

Tahki gasped, trembling. The castle buried everything. Rye and Gotem and Dyraien. Steam and dust rose from the pile, and the world fell into a terrible silence.

For a moment, Tahki heard only the sound of the river. The castle had dammed it, and water started to flood in all directions. He ran to the destruction, waded into the water, into the black gunk that covered everything. He didn't care about drowning, about how the mud sucked at his feet. When the water touched his chin, he turned away and climbed onto a pile of sharp obsidian. It cut his hands, his leg, his chest. He stared into the darkness.

"Rye?" he said. "Rye? Rye!" He screamed until his voice was nothing more than a pitiful wail. He turned left and right. He dug deep through the debris. Sweat and blood and snot fell from his face. "Oh gods," Tahki whispered. "Please… please… oh gods."

The pile he sat on started to slide into the water. He scrambled away and used one of the wooden doors to steady himself. There was nothing he could do. The muck was too dense to even begin to sort through. He waded back onto land and collapsed in the dirt. Tears fell down his cheeks. He grabbed his head, dug his fingers into his grimy hair.

He should have stayed with Rye. They should have destroyed the castle together. Or maybe he should have gone home after his encounter with Nii, or he should have told Rye sooner, or he should have written to his father, or… or… or….

Something burst from beneath the water. A massive black shape dragged its body from the wreckage. Tahki tried to stand, fell, tried again, and found his balance. Pooka limped toward him. Her right side looked torn open, like something had taken a huge bite out of her. She panted and shook water from her coat. Something attached itself to her back and side. Not something, somebody. Three bodies clung to her, black grunge covering them. For a second, Tahki pictured Zinc, charred black from the fire, clawing his way out of the chamber.

He shook away the feeling and ran to the cat. "Rye." He put his arms around Rye and eased him to the ground. There was no word in the Dhaulenian language nor in the Vatolok dialect that could describe the tremendous feelings of relief and elation Tahki felt then. Rye's breath was unsteady, but he had strength to open his eyes and smile.

Tahki faced the other person, who was covered in black mud from head to toe and holding a third body.

"Sornjia," Tahki said. "How did you.... What are you doing here?" The bullet wound on his shoulder bled.

"Pooka said you needed help," Sornjia replied in a hoarse voice. He set the limp body down. A bit of blond hair popped through the gunk, and an immediate rage rose inside Tahki. He swiped up a shard of obsidian and raised it over Dyraien's unconscious body.

Rye coughed. "Tahki, no."

"He almost killed us!"

"We need him alive, to answer for his crimes." Rye's voice sounded so weak, like he barely hung on to consciousness himself.

Tahki had never wanted to take someone's life so badly, not even Zinc's.

"Tahki," Rye whispered. "If we don't take him alive, we might be blamed for the queen's death. We need to turn him over to the council."

Tahki sighed. He tossed the shard away and slumped beside Rye.

Rye shut his eyes.

Tahki wondered if Rye had other reasons for saving Dyraien, but he let the thought slide away. They were safe, and for now, that was enough.

Chapter 16

THEY SAT in the dirt, the three of them too tired to stand. Sornjia had rinsed his shoulder with river water upstream. He bled slowly now, but Rye said it wasn't life-threatening. Rye had broken his index finger on his left hand and found a piece of wood to brace it. All his other bruising appeared superficial. Tahki pressed his palm gently into the cool dirt. The cold grains soothed the tender skin from his burn, but not enough to take the pain away. Dyraien, least battered of them all, breathed slow, shallow breaths, and Tahki hoped he'd never wake up.

Out of all of them, Pooka looked most damaged, but she tended to herself, licking her wounds. Occasionally, a small bundle of oily eels would slither to the surface of her fur to suck on the bloody parts. Tahki didn't even flinch at the sight of them.

He glanced to Sornjia. His brother looked gaunt, like he'd been drained. He hadn't looked this bad when Zinc shot him. His eyes appeared a dull gray-green. Something was wrong with him, beyond the exhaustion he must be feeling from the fight. When Tahki tried to ask, Sornjia said he was fine. No smile, just a blank stare, his body tense, his nails digging into his arms.

When Rye finally spoke again, his words were slow, jagged. "After you left, your brother showed up with the cat. The cat, I mean Pooka, fought Zinc's men while Sornjia and I stopped Dyraien from entering that... that place." Rye stared down at the dirt as he spoke. "The pathway started to close. Dyraien panicked. He tried to climb inside, but Sornjia grabbed him. They both touched it. They touched the other world."

Tahki looked at his brother. "You mean you saw it? You saw the Dim?"

Sornjia didn't say anything.

"I'm not sure what happened." Rye gave Sornjia a wary glance. "It was like something out of a dream. Dyraien started to enter, and Sornjia stopped him. But when he did, when Sornjia touched the path, it was like… it was like… all the stars in the sky opened themselves up inside him. I thought he was going to die with all that energy passing through. It was like the energy shifted from Gotem to Sornjia, and he just—"

"I pulled Dyraien back," Sornjia said with unusual harshness. "I pulled him back into the room, away from the pathway. And then we fought. That's all there is to say on the matter."

Tahki stared at his brother, and Sornjia stared back at him. Rye hadn't seemed to understand, but Tahki did.

His brother was a mystic.

Somehow, this didn't surprise him. In fact, out of everything that had happened, it made the most sense. Sornjia's odd way of speaking, his ability to know things no one could know, his connection with Pooka. Tahki would have been more surprised if he hadn't been a mystic.

Tahki wanted to kill Dyraien now more than ever. Dyraien would have seen Sornjia; he would know what he was. Would that make Sornjia a target for others like Dyraien?

"After that," Rye went on, not seeming to sense the tension. "The pathway started to close again. Then there was a burst of steam from the ceiling. I assume Zinc turned the machine on. At first, it held the pathway open. The power of that thing." Rye released a shaky breath. "Tahki, the force of that thing was unbelievable. It could have torn open the world."

Tahki swallowed.

"The steam forced the pathway open," Rye continued. "But something was on the other side. Something angry."

"Something angry?"

Rye gripped his stomach and shut his eyes. "I don't know. I don't want to sound impertinent or disrespectful, but Tahki, whatever that thing was on the other side, it wasn't a god."

Tahki inched closer. "What makes you say that?"

"The cat—Pooka—she went crazy. She started attacking it, but the steam was everywhere. I couldn't see. I think the thing hurt her."

Beside them, Pooka growled. Rye reached out and set his hand on her head like she was one of his gingoats.

"The thing tried to go after Dyraien," Rye said. "It was chaos down there. And then the entire floor shook, and the ceiling started to cave in."

Tahki scooted closer. "What happened to the pathway?"

"When the roof started to fall, the steam stopped, and the pathway closed. Gotem, he...."

"He's dead," Sornjia said in a flat tone.

Tahki bowed his head. "I'm sorry, Gotem." It was all he could think to say. Gotem had saved his life, and Tahki had gotten him killed. But retribution would come later. For now, he needed to concentrate on what had happened. "What about that creature that escaped the Dim?"

Rye shrugged and then winced at the pain. "I don't know what happened to it. It knocked Dyraien out cold, and then I guess it got sucked back inside when the world closed." He didn't sound too sure. "Sornjia and I grabbed Dyraien and made it to the river, but everything was falling around us. If it wasn't for Pooka's help, we would have been crushed."

"So, I killed Gotem, and I almost killed you two." Tears welled in his eyes.

Rye locked his arm around Tahki's neck and drew him close. "Dyraien killed Gotem. And you did the right thing. We might all be dead had the pathway stayed open."

Sornjia didn't offer any sort of consolation. No cheery optimistic speeches, no comforting words of selflessness.

"Will your finger heal?"

"It should." Rye pressed on the makeshift brace. "Anyway, you're not exactly in great shape yourself. What happened to Zinc?"

Tahki heard the man's screams in his mind, smelled his burning flesh. "Dead."

"Good."

Tahki rubbed his wrist. "What do we do now?"

Rye coughed. "We'll turn Dyraien in, tell the council what happened."

"What if they don't believe us?"

Rye reached out and touched Tahki's hand lightly. "We'll convince them, somehow."

They sat in silence for a time and watched as bits of castle fell over the waterfall. The clouds drifted high and the sun warmed them. Tahki shut his eyes but then felt Rye stand with greater speed than he thought capable with his wounds.

"What is it? What's wrong?" Tahki grabbed Rye and pulled himself up.

Two people walked toward them. As they neared, he recognized Gale and Hona. Rye tensed. Gale walked past them—ignoring even Pooka—to the fallen castle. She folded her arms and shook her head. "What a damn fool."

Hona stopped beside Tahki and glanced at Pooka. "That's something you don't see everyday."

"She won't hurt you," Sornjia said.

Hona looked at Sornjia. "So, we have a monster cat and two Tahkis. Got to hand it to you, kid. You're one surprise after another."

Sornjia rose and extended his hand. "I'm Sornjia."

Hona shook. "That's a mouthful of a name. I'm going to call you S."

A little of Sornjia's old self seemed to creep back, but he still didn't smile.

"You knew about all this," Rye said to Hona. "You knew what Dyraien planned to do."

"It's more complicated than that," Hona said. "Dyraien blackmailed me." She glanced down at the prince's body, gave him a small kick.

"You helped him," Rye said between clenched teeth.

"To keep you safe." Hona set her jaw in the same stubborn manner Tahki had seen Rye do. She glanced at Pooka again. The cat licked her wounds and ignored them all. "I left Mom and you to find work, and when I returned, Dyraien had you. He said so long as I worked for him and never told you the truth, he'd keep you well looked after."

Rye folded his arms. "I don't believe that."

"Believe what you want," Hona said. "But you need me now. I'm the only one who knows the full extent of Dyraien's plans. I'm the only one who has evidence of his crimes."

Gale marched back to them. "She's right. If she wasn't, I would have thrown her in the river myself. We can't show up with news of the queen's death and a beaten prince without proof."

"What will you do?" Tahki asked.

"Hona and I will go to the capital," Gale said. "We'll tell them what happened." She eyed Pooka. "Maybe leave out a few details. As for you, I think it's best you leave Vatolokít."

Tahki felt on the verge of collapsing. He never thought he'd crave his home as badly as he did then.

THEY FOUND three gingoats in the stables. The animals pranced restlessly, agitated from the commotion. Tahki shared one with Rye, Sornjia doubled with Hona, and Gale took one for herself. Rye fashioned a makeshift cart out of a wheel barrel to haul Dyraien's body behind them, after properly tying the prince's arms and legs in case he woke.

Tahki sat behind Rye, leaned his head against him, and shut his eyes.

They rode together for a time. Hona explained Dyraien had planned to open the Dim, that he'd been obsessed since he was a child. She confirmed what Nii had told Tahki about the Királye history. She knew Dyraien sent people to Dhaulen'aii to find a mystic, that they'd been searching for years. Tahki shuddered to think he might have seen some of Dyraien's spies back home. He might have spoken to them. Might have bought curry from one of them.

Hona said Dyraien had planned to frame Gale for the queen's death in a careful setup. She was supposed to be scammed by Zinc, and, having a history of alcoholism, Dyraien would see to it that she relapsed after he blamed her for losing their money and materials. He planned on getting her drunk one night and killing the queen. He would place a blacked-out Gale in the room with the queen's corpse. Not only was he going to frame Gale, he planned to convince her she'd done it. The council would have no trouble believing it, either, since Gale's reputation as an honorable judge had been soiled already. Tahki saw Gale strangle her reins at that part.

But, Hona said, Tahki had interfered with Dyraien's plans, and when the opportunity presented itself, Dyraien decided to frame Tahki, a foreigner, instead. And then it would have played out like Dyraien wanted: his people, shocked and disgusted by the queen's death, would rally behind him for justice.

"He said after his people saw what he'd brought from the Dim, they would never question his leadership again," Hona said.

"But he never said what that thing was?" Rye asked, more to everyone than to Hona.

"He never told me, but whatever it was, he was convinced it would advance his country years ahead of its time. He only referred to it as his age of enlightenment."

Tahki glanced back at Dyraien's body rattling around in the cart. Dyraien had been willing to risk everything, even his own life, to achieve his goal. There had been a time not so long ago Tahki might have been able to empathize with him, but now, he couldn't imagine giving up his friends and family for his own conquest.

When they reached a fork in the road, Hona told Rye they needed to talk privately, but Rye said he wasn't ready. Hona said she would find them one day, and that she would make things right between them.

"You two have caused me a hell of a lot of trouble," Gale said. "I guess you expect me to say thank you for all you did."

"We'll meet again, won't we?" Sornjia asked. He hadn't said anything since the castle.

Gale clicked her tongue. "I doubt I'd like to see any of your faces again."

Tahki smiled and thought he might miss Gale.

And then they parted ways. Hona walked, giving Sornjia the goat, while Gale dragged Dyraien's body toward the capital. Tahki, Rye, and Sornjia headed east.

Rye glanced over his shoulder a few times, and Tahki knew he was saying his goodbyes to Dyraien. Despite everything, Rye still loved the prince, and Tahki wasn't sure how to feel about that. He supposed there was no crime Sornjia could commit that would totally alienate Tahki from him, but that was different, wasn't it?

Chapter 17

Tahki inhaled the sweet scent of rosewater in Rye's hair. Both their bodies dripped from the bath they'd taken. Rye only had a few coins left, the rest of his money had been in his room when the castle collapsed, but he had insisted they spend a little extra to properly clean themselves.

Tahki could hear Sornjia's snores in the bed next to them. They had reached Edgewater two hours ago, eaten fried fish, purchased a room in a tavern on the beach, bathed, and collapsed onto the bed. Sornjia had told Pooka to wait outside town. Tahki had no idea what they were going to do with a giant undead cat. He thought once the castle had been destroyed, she'd just dissolve like she had at the black pool.

But she hadn't. She continued to follow them, and that worried Tahki. The castle was gone, Dyraien had been detained, and Tahki's designs were lost in the rubble. He wondered if it had something to do with Sornjia being a mystic. He had no way to speak with Nii, now that the black pool had been destroyed. Maybe his father would have some insight. For a moment, he considered lying to his father but then thought better of it. He was done with the lies. Whatever havoc the truth might raise, he would accept the consequences.

Rye leaned in and kissed his neck. "What's wrong now?"

"Nothing."

Rye yawned. "Stop worrying about tomorrow."

"I still can't believe I let you talk me into sailing to Dhaulen'aii," Tahki muttered.

"It's the fastest way. Plus, it will give you time to forge us new documents."

"The ship will probably crash into a rock or something and we'll all drown."

Rye smiled against his shoulder. "There's the cynical Tahki I know and love."

Tahki's breath caught in his throat. It was the first time Rye had said he loved him. It was casual, maybe even a mistake, but it had been said aloud, which meant it was real.

"You'll be all right," Rye whispered in his ear. "Because I'll be there to distract you."

"And you're sure you don't mind leaving your home?"

Rye moved an inch away. "There's nothing left for me here."

"There's the sullen Rye I know and love." Tahki kissed him hard, despite the throbbing in his head and jaw.

"I want to see your home," Rye said once they pulled away. "I want to know everything about you, the truth, this time."

"Only the truth," Tahki said.

Tahki tucked himself close to Rye's chest, and all other worries drifted out the window to where the sea broke over the rocky shore. Tomorrow they would sail for home, and whatever awaited them on the open ocean, Tahki knew he wouldn't have to face it alone.

JADE MERE is a writer and illustrator who resides in the rainy Pacific Northwest. She has a passion for writing fantasy, science fiction, and paranormal stories. When Jade isn't tapping away at her computer or yelling at her drawing tablet, she enjoys hiking with her dogs, kayaking, and traveling.

Website: www.jademere.com
Instagram: www.instagram.com/jademere
Facebook: www.facebook.com/JadeMere

Also from Dreamspinner Press

TJ Klune

THE Consumption of MAGIC

www.dreamspinnerpress.com

Also from Dreamspinner Press

DRAGON'S HOARD
M.A. Church

DREAMSPUN BEYOND

To be loved by a dragon is to be treasured.

www.dreamspinnerpress.com

Also from Dreamspinner Press

Some lovers are as familiar as the family pet.

FAMILIAR ANGEL
Amy Lane

"Fantastic...a transcendent love story that will sweep you off your feet."
CINDY DEES,
NYT and *USA Today* Bestselling Author

www.dreamspinnerpress.com

Also from Dreamspinner Press

DREAMSPUN BEYOND
THE GRYPHON KING'S CONSORT
Jenn Burke

Love takes flight.

www.dreamspinnerpress.com

Also from Dreamspinner Press

His Mossy Boy
R. Cooper

www.dreamspinnerpress.com

Also from Dreamspinner Press

KIERNAN KELLY

THE KEEPER

www.dreamspinnerpress.com

FOR MORE OF THE BEST GAY ROMANCE

Dreamspinner Press
dreamspinnerpress.com